CRUSHING
THE
RED
FLOWERS

CRUSHING THE RED FLOWERS

JENNIFER
VOIGT KAPLAN

PUBLISHING

NEW YORK, NY

12/19

Printed in the United States of America.
Hardcover edition
10 9 8 7 6 5 4 3 2 1

Please direct inquiries to:
Ig Publishing, Inc
PO Box 2547
New York, NY 10163
www.igpub.com

ISBN: 978-1-632460-94-3 (Hardcover edition)
ISBN: 978-1-632460-95-0 (Paperback edition)

CONTENTS

For My Family

I

1. Pawns

Friedrich Weber hated this part.

"Today Germany hears us, and tomorrow the whole world!" He screamed the words until veins popped from his neck and his face was a convincing shade of red. He thought thrusting his boney twelve-year-old arm in the air would make him look tougher, so he did that too.

Shrieks and cries shot every which way from the energized mob of boys, but when Friedrich screamed, he felt like a shell. Hollow inside, jagged outside. Maybe it was the thick air in the meeting room. The stench of sweat soaked uniforms couldn't escape the crusty windows. Or maybe it was his new Jungvolk leader, Günter Beck, and his watchdog eyes. Only a couple minutes of service hours were left, but Günter still scanned the room, scribbling names of unfaithful boys into his red notebook.

Friedrich roared the words louder, hoping they would give him the feelings he was supposed to have. It didn't work. The words detached and drifted away, leaving him emptier. His mind fumbled for something else to shout. He would say any words, just to escape a beating afterward.

2. Another Pocket-Sized Mishap

Emil Rosen was certain he did not have a talent for trouble like Mama said. He only had one real talent, shooting marbles, and one secret talent, vomiting anytime and anywhere he pleased. It didn't matter that neither were all that useful. It mattered that a talent was something a boy could control and that wasn't what trouble was. Trouble snagged a person when he wasn't looking. Besides, trouble was big. What he got into were more like pocket-sized mishaps.

Emil tossed this thought around as he snatched as many poppies as he could from the meadow along the river. He needed an extra big bunch this time. He was late and knew the bright wildflowers would melt Mama's voice like butter on warm bread. As he wrapped his thick fingers around the stems, the wind made their bodies bend and petals flutter. Emil thought they looked like thousands of little people in red hats performing a show just for him.

When he was late last week, a big bunch of poppies had gotten him out of trouble. It was as good as magic. He had lost track of time because of the river minnows. They refused to be caught. Every time he trapped a little fish into lingering over his palm in the water, it wiggled out before he could lift it. When he had held the poppies up to Mama that day, the angry lines above her eyes vanished. She cradled them in her fleshy arms and said, "You are lucky you're charming, my dear Emil." Emil was certain Mama was the only person in the world who thought he was charming. But the poppies worked and he figured he could use them again if he ever got into another mishap.

Today he was late because of a river rock. He had started to leave on time, right when the sun teetered over the tallest tree, but tripped over a rock with a most bewitching pattern. He sat back down, pondering how the rock had journeyed down river from a faraway place. Every stone, branch, or fish it bumped into left its mark, each etching just a dot. By the time he shoved the rock into the pocket alongside his marbles, he noticed the sun had moved well below the treetops.

That's when he started gathering as many poppies as he could hold. He plucked as he said, "I pick you and you and you," being careful not to squash the ones he didn't choose. The bouquet was lopsided and the stems uneven, but it looked perfect, in a wild way. Emil hopped onto his bicycle, squeezing the stems over the handlebar with one hand, and turned toward home.

Even though his legs should have been moving quickly, at least as quickly as his stout legs were made to go, they weren't moving at all. He didn't want to leave. Nowhere else in all of Hannover was this free. If he liked, he could pitch mud balls, or somersault, or roar nonsense, or take off his pants to swim . . . and he did. Even shooting marbles didn't give him abandon like this.

Another curious rock caught his attention. Metallic slivers twinkled over a matted blue-gray surface. He was about to pocket it when his stomach rumbled. The snacks Mama had packed were gone. He pulled in thoughts of dumplings and his feet finally started pedaling.

The flowers thrashed against the handlebar. He squeezed the stems tighter, flattening the parts where his fingers pressed. As he rode, Emil thought about what was waiting at home, and his pace slowed. His unease came from more than just being late. Home hadn't felt like home for a while. Mama now spent a good part of her day making Mama-fuss, and when she wasn't, she forced Emil to practice piano or study Hebrew for his Bar Mitzvah. Vati never stopped grumbling about how news in 1937 was so much better than in 1938. His sister Sarah told stories about Germany that gave him stomach aches. And from morning to night, Uncle Leo complained how after twenty years, he could no longer be an accountant. Home was prickly, like stale December grass. That's why Emil had been visiting the river every day since summer vacation began.

Emil entered his apartment building and tossed his bike in the basement. A few poppy petals stuck to his clothes. He peeled them off and balanced them on top of the drooping bouquet. The flowers lost some perk on the ride home, but Emil thought Mama would still like them.

Emil sneezed twice and the petals flew off. That musty basement smell always got him. He started for the stairs. As he thumped up to the third floor, Mrs. Schmidt swung open her door.

"Pickles," he mumbled. Trouble just snuck up. Mrs. Schmidt was more than a mishap.

"Good evening," Emil said, dropping petals on the floor as he waved the hand holding the bouquet. Mrs. Schmidt's mouth formed into a straight crease. He couldn't tell where her mouth wrinkle stopped and her face wrinkles started. The only skin on her face that wasn't crinkly was the stretched skin around her hairline yanked into a gray bun.

Mama said Mrs. Schmidt was just a person turned bitter. A long time ago, they used to be lady friends. Emil remembered she would bring all sorts of treats when she visited. Creamy nutcakes were his favorite. But once Mrs. Schmidt's son started wearing a Nazi uniform, Emil never saw another nutcake.

But Emil suspected Mrs. Schmidt was something more than bitter. She reminded him of an evil, magical hag from a Grimm folktale. She looked like she was a hundred, but moved like an ant rushing a sugar cube. She caused lots of grief, only wore gray, and heard every noise Emil made. Mama said it was because her door was close to the staircase, but Emil thought it was really because Mrs. Schmidt had magical hearing.

Emil hurried the rest of the way up, trying to deflect any wicked spell she shot his way. Magic or not, he felt her daggers burn his back until he reached his apartment on the fifth floor. Emil groped for the knob and looked up toward their mezuzah nailed to the doorframe for help. The parchment folded inside the etched silver case was supposed to ward off evil. But Emil only saw two small holes where the mezuzah should have hung. Uncle Leo had been talking about taking down the mezuzah because he wanted the family to be what he called *inconspicuous*. That made no sense since everyone already knew they were Jewish. Plus no one in the history of the world had ever used the word *inconspicuous* to describe his family.

He started to turn the knob, but stopped short in the hall when he heard arguing. Through the door, Emil eavesdropped on four people. Words blended as they all yelled at the same time. Voices shot across the room, crisscrossing and filling the space to the top.

Emil considered running back to the river, but almost fell over when he heard a CLANG that sounded like a train crashing in his living room. His hand swung open the door before his brain could stop it. He found Mama banging two cooking pots together above his father's head. She looked as if she had gone mad.

"WE" *clang!* "ARE" *clang!* "LEAVING" *clang!* Mama shouted down at Vati. His father just hunched over the table, shielding his ears. The ends of her polka-dot apron flew up every time the pots collided. His sister Sarah and Uncle Leo hovered around the table, trying to holler above the clangs. If he had a talent for trouble, this was where he learned it.

3. Cowards

Günter Beck scanned the room. "Who will win the next biking competition?" Friedrich and the other eighteen boys sat taller. Günter could make any question sound sinister. He was eighteen and had been their new Jungvolk leader for two months, but commanded like he had been in charge for ten years.

"Will it be Johannes or will someone new rise up?" Günter asked.

Even before Günter was announced leader, Friedrich felt it coming. His skin prickled the same way it did before a storm rushed in. Günter had stood in the shadows, observing the boys for months. He carried a red leather notebook and scribbled in it when someone did something wrong, like lose their bearings on a hike or slow in formation.

Friedrich checked the time. Twenty-three and a half more minutes before he could leave. Each second of every minute stretched and distorted into that peculiar kind of time that happened only when he wanted to be someplace else.

Friedrich couldn't believe how everything had changed in just two months. Service hour meetings had always been full of halfwits, but they had still been good for planning camping and hiking trips. And good for getting out of the house and away from Mother. Nothing ever pleased her. Friedrich never had a choice in joining the Jungvolk, but had never minded it either. He only started hating service hours when Günter blasted into his world. Günter said it was the boys' duty to serve, not have fun. Since he became leader, Friedrich had only gone on two hiking trips, but had to compete in more races, stomp in more marches, and listen to more muddy hell lectures than he could count.

"And who will be the losers?" Günter asked. He liked talking about losing. And about weakness. And cowards. Günter despised cowards.

"It won't be Otto," a sneering voice from the front said. Günter didn't usually tolerate outbursts, but this time he smirked and let the boys laugh. When Friedrich thought of what happened to Otto, listening to Mother's endless criticism didn't seem so bad.

Otto was a coward. At least that's what Günter said. Otto slouched his flabby body and never looked anyone in the eye. He couldn't catch a long ball or even do five pull-ups. Friedrich never thought much of it until Günter came along.

Even back when Günter kept busy quietly writing in his red notebook, he looked at Otto differently. He would scowl and turn, as if watching Otto fumble was revolting. One time, Friedrich overheard Günter speak to his old group leader, "Otto is useless. He's dreadful to watch and has no ambition to improve. He's offensive not because he's inferior, but because he's satisfied that way." Everyone in the room had heard. Friedrich got the feeling Günter talked loudly on purpose.

So when Günter spoke as leader for the first time last month, it didn't surprise Friedrich that he pounced on Otto like a lion on a rabbit.

"The superior race is," Günter had paused glaring at Otto, "strong, not weak." Then he looked at the other boys. "That is who you are. It is yours to honor. Claim it or it can be taken away from you." Günter's message was clear. Otto jumped up and cheered along with the others after Günter's speech, but no one believed his performance. His arms flailed, his eyes unfocused. He looked like ragdoll, not the way a Jungvolk boy should look.

Afterward, the boys cornered him. Johannes rushed in first with a crowd at his heels. He won nearly all of Günter's competitions and other boys followed him like puppies. Johannes was an idiot, but slightly less of an idiot, about thirty percent as Friedrich figured, than the others.

"There is a problem, Otto," he said, and advanced so close their noses almost touched. "And problems must be fixed."

Friedrich had always gotten the feeling he should keep Johannes more friend than enemy, so last month, Friedrich helped Johannes on a hiking trip. Günter never found out Johannes couldn't light his own fire.

When Friedrich watched Johannes taunt Otto, he was glad he did.

In seconds, the others joined in Otto's attack. Fritz, the shortest boy in the Jungvolk, screamed, "Go home coward!" Otto looked ridiculous stepping back to a boy half his size. "You don't deserve to wear this," he said pulling at Otto's uniform. An adult probably would have tried to calm everyone, but there were none. Adults weren't allowed in service hours.

"Weakling! Pathetic! Hopeless! Undeserving!" Friedrich couldn't tell who yelled what. Each word made the fire blaze stronger. They pushed Otto back and forth. Friedrich wanted Otto to fight. But when the circle of boys closed in on Otto, he didn't cry or struggle, he just wilted. That made the accusations true. Friedrich was disgusted.

"He is a coward!" Friedrich had screamed. Günter's new rules for right and wrong carried Friedrich away, just as easily as the others. "He should go over to the Reds!" Since Otto was such a loser, he should just go and join the damn Communists.

A fist rose, poised high in the air. It could have belonged to any boy in the room. It was medium-sized and fair-skinned. It jutted out from a brown-sleeved arm, clenched hard. When it crashed down, Otto crumbled. The boys separated.

Otto whimpered as he rolled around clutching his stomach. The boys had never turned on each other before. Günter watched, smiling like a proud father. It was awful. But the worst part was the way Günter glanced at Friedrich after. Like he was next.

Friedrich drew in quick breaths. *Muddy Hell! Does Günter think I'm a coward?*

He felt his right eyebrow spasm and pretended to scratch his forehead to cover the tremor. It's been trembling more and more. He first felt it last month, the day of Otto's beating. He thought how odd it must look and odd was not good.

"No, it won't be Otto," Günter said and nodded toward Otto's empty seat. "We'll see everyone's dedication at the competition." The mass of fidgety boys froze in their seats at the reminder that they too were being judged. For a moment, Friedrich felt as if he weren't alone.

"First," Günter said, "I will discuss the rules of tomorrow's race and then announce last week's winners." As he spoke about each competition rule, for what felt like hours, Friedrich ached to be outside. He wanted to fill his lungs with crisp air and feel the uneven earth beneath his shoes. When he hiked and camped, he felt like that was what he was meant to do. Günter's competitions were meaningless, but navigating the terrain or fishing had real purpose.

Günter continued, "You must cross the designated finish place within one hour or there will be no winner. All participants, regardless of skill, will begin at the same place. Your bicycle must be maintained according to competition standards." He went on and on.

Friedrich blinked away the fog that made his eyelids droop. He needed to think of something else or Günter's rules would lull him to sleep. Günter wouldn't like it, but he figured he had three reasons that gave him the right to daydream: First, he knew the rules. Günter used the same rules for every biking competition. Second, he knew the course. It was the same as last week, with the same spots to rest, pass, and piss. And third, he knew he would not win. He never won.

Friedrich daydreamed about what Günter thought of him. What was good and what bad? He decided to make a Jungvolk Good–Bad Criteria List in his head. *First*, Friedrich considered, *the Good Side. Appearance.* In his uniform, no one could see how his skin hugged his ribs. His thick, blond hair was healthy. His gray eyes made him look cold. That was good.

Second is orienteering, Friedrich thought. He was great at reading maps and conquering the terrain. He could make camp or set a fire faster than anyone. Even Fritz and Ernst looked to Friedrich after they saw him help Johannes. Everyone knew he was the best, even Günter.

Friedrich felt the urge to chart his secret list. Graphing papers and rulers beckoned him. He liked thinking about his hand drawing precise, vertical lines to make places for percentages and categories. If he weren't so worried about Günter, he would really enjoy charting his traits.

Rustling paper jolted Friedrich from his thoughts. Günter flipped through his red notebook. He must have finished with the rules and would start announcing last week's winners.

Günter announced, "First position in rope tug, Johannes. First position in obstacle course, Johannes. First position in rowing, Ernst." Friedrich didn't know why this was necessary. Everyone already knew who had won.

Friedrich focused back on his Jungvolk Good–Bad Criteria List since he knew his name wouldn't be called. *Next good one*, he thought. *I'm sensible*. Boys who tried to make others laugh were fools. Friedrich glanced at Werner. When Werner wasn't hiccupping, he made noises that sounded like farts from his armpit. He seemed especially proud when he made them from under his knee.

Next, I hate communists, he thought. *Maybe more than Günter*. Ever since a couple of reds chased Friedrich with rocks last year, he swore payback. They probably saw his uniform and never bothered to think he was just a boy like them. Günter thought hating reds was good.

And then there was Papa's work. Everyone knew Papa wasn't just a Nazi. He was part of the SS, Adolf Hitler's most elite police. Papa even had to prove he was a pure Aryan when he joined. Günter was surely impressed by that, but probably wouldn't be as much if he knew Papa's position. He was a just an SS photographer, taking pictures of industrial equipment. And Günter definitely wouldn't be impressed with the real reason Papa joined. Money. Papa said he could take only so many years of his failing electrical business.

Check, check, check, check, check. Five points on the Good Side.

He thought of one more, but couldn't add it. Friedrich was inventive. He even earned the Award for Innovative Design at school last year for redesigning a train car. Friedrich spent hours at the station. Researching, examining, graphing. When he won the award, Papa ran to the bakery and bought apple strudel with butter crust and told the baker to fill their largest bowl with whipped cream. They ate on a table set with Mother's fancy linens. But none of that mattered for his list. Günter wanted obedience, not creativity.

Now the Bad Side, Friedrich thought. First was *running*. Friedrich never came in last like Otto, but almost last. *Exactly how bad am I?* Friedrich wondered and started to compute. He felt his eyebrow tremor as he finished: bottom twenty percent every time.

Second, he did not have *friends*. Once he had a good one, the best one, but that ended and no one else was worth his time. Other boys made plans and never asked him to join. This didn't matter to Friedrich since he never liked watching idiots out-burp each other, but he wasn't sure if it mattered to Günter. It probably wasn't worth a full point on the Bad Side, just a third, but he rounded to a half, just in case.

And then there was Uncle Hilmar. Friedrich wasn't sure who knew the family secret. The police put Mother's brother in jail years ago for making flyers against the Führer. They didn't care that his uncle was a hero in the Great War, or that he had never broken a law in his life, or that he was the best uncle in the world. Friedrich had nothing do to with his uncle's crime, but Günter would think him just as much a traitor.

Friedrich stifled a gulp he felt creeping up his throat. He had to look like he was tough and loyal, so Friedrich did the only thing that really made him feel tough and loyal. He rubbed his brown Jungvolk shirt between his fingers. Touching the fibers rejuvenated him. He loved his uniform. People didn't treat him like a child when he wore it. He was an important person serving his country. He was part of something bigger than himself.

"Deutschland, Deutschland über alles . . ." Friedrich jerked when the boys began singing the German anthem. That meant speeches were over. He joined in. Obedience and sacrifice, he said to himself. He made himself feel it, believe it deep down, so others would too. And then the singing stopped.

It's over! Friedrich thought. *Service hours are finally over!* He stood to leave.

"And for the last item," Günter began, but stopped when he spotted Friedrich. Every eye in the room burned into him, the only one standing. His skin prickled. Dread and shame mashed up in his gut. The room swayed. His private demons had betrayed him after all.

Muddy Hell! Friedrich thought. *I am next!*

4. Disorder

Emil's legs picked the most unfortunate times to stop following his brain's commands. They cemented themselves in his doorway, forcing him to hear not-so-inconspicuous clangs and shouts. Each sound absorbed the others until the noise built itself into a raging tornado that would devour the room. He did not want to get sucked in.

CLANG!

"Dear wife," Vati said, cupping his hands around his ears as he leaned over the table.

CLANG!

"Come now, Henriette," Uncle Leo shouted.

"We are leaving!" Mama shrieked.

CLANG! CLANG! CLANG!

"Stop it Mama!" Sarah screamed.

CLANG!

Emil realized this was more than regular Mama-fuss. He hadn't seen his family this upset since his cat, Lebkuchen, went missing. He decided he would try to tiptoe past everyone to hide in his bedroom.

"No ID card!" Mama yelled.

CLANG!

Emil looked down at his uncooperative legs. They

always seemed to freeze whenever he wanted them to go fast, so maybe if he promised them he'd sneak away nice and slow, they'd listen. Emil ever so gently lifted a foot to take a first step. He tried to think of his toes as delicate flower petals fluttering to the ground.

"I will not carry it!" Mama yelled.

CLANG! CLANG! CLANG! CLANG! CLANG!

Vati jumped up and slammed his palms down on the table. His golden pocket watch flew out of his suit. It would have smacked into the table if it weren't for the chain that jerked it back. It had once belonged to Vati's father and Emil still wasn't allowed to touch it. Vati stared at the watch spinning wildly, dangling from the chain attached to his vest. His face turned from his usual rosy shade to one as fiery as a poppy.

"HENRIETTE!" Vati hurled his newspaper across the room. "ENOUGH!"

The room silenced and Emil forgot about his foot in midair coming down fast. THUMP! was the sound it made when it landed. Everyone turned toward him.

Mama said "Hello Emil" like it was any ordinary day, but still kept her pots perched high above, ready to strike again. Vati, Uncle Leo, and Sarah stumbled into chairs as if they had just stepped off a carousel.

Once the room settled, Emil realized he still had the problem of being late. He wanted to get past apologies and closer to supper as quickly as he could, so he marched up to Mama, raised the drooping flower bouquet, and smiled the way he thought mothers liked to see sons smile.

Mama glanced at the flowers, then winked at Emil and clanged her pots once more. She sat down, smirking, and Emil realized she was just making regular, old Mama-fuss after all. Sarah and Vati looked as if they wanted to throw Mama's pots out the window.

Mama said, "Thank you for the flowers, but you are late." She glanced down. "Schmutzig! Look at the mud that followed you in!" She waved a pot handle toward the floor.

"What's going on?" he asked, trying to distract her from the dirt. He got sucked in after all, so maybe he could use it to get out of this mishap.

"Absurdity is going on," Vati said. "Our country and your mother have gone mad!"

"Mad!" Mama said. "I'll show you mad!"

Sarah dove and snatched Mama's pots from the table. Mama grabbed for them, but Sarah was too quick. Emil regretted asking. Mama's scolding would have been faster.

Vati said, "When the Nazis told us to register our antiques, we did, even though your mother's rings were none of their business!"

Then he muttered something Emil didn't understand, which Emil figured was Italian. Vati cursed in Italian because he thought it was more polite than cursing in German. Since Vati used to sell oil to companies in foreign countries, he knew how to speak French, Italian, Polish, as well as German and some Hebrew.

"Then they took my career!" Uncle Leo said.

Emil didn't want to hear these things. He got the sense no one would be eating anytime soon, so he took a step toward his room.

"And then my career," Vati said, slumping in his chair. His etched face looked heavy, like he'd been in battle. It looked like that ever since businessmen decided to stop buying his oil. That never made sense to Emil, since they were happy to buy from him for so many years. Back when Vati still took business trips, he used to come home and go straight to Emil's room to tell him all the best traveler's tales. Emil learned that riding on fast trains made sunflowers in Polish fields blur into golden streaks. And that the sound of ladies' shoes on Italian streets made old men feel like young men. And that gazing up from the foot of French cathedrals made the tallest tip look as if it touched the heavens. Some of Vati's stories were better than folktales. Now, Vati had no new adventures to share, so he just sat in his chair and spoke about things Emil didn't care about with that heavy face.

"We are fortunate you still have a few Jewish customers in Hannover," Mama said, and put her hand on Vati's shoulder.

Vati said more words Emil didn't understand and Emil snuck another couple steps. He figured they wouldn't notice him leaving if he walked really slowly.

"Not in front of the children, Josef," Mama said.

Vati grabbed the pot from Sarah and held it up high. "My dear, we disagree about what is and is not appropriate in front of the children."

Vati put the pot down and said, "What's happening in Germany? Is this the same country that held Rosh Hashana services for Jewish soldiers during the Great War?"

"That was twenty years ago," Uncle Leo said.

"I still wear my war scar with honor today!" Vati said, pointing toward the faint, raised line on his cheek.

"Josef, you can spare us the story of how you were wounded," Uncle Leo said. "I've heard it eighty-seven times."

"Four hundred and eighty-seven," Sarah said.

"THAT is my Germany," Vati said. "This is not," and pointed to a newspaper.

Emil slinked three more steps sideways toward his room. No one noticed.

"The Treaty of Versailles took that Germany," Uncle Leo said. "How could Germany heal when we had to pay other countries?"

"No, unemployment took it." Sarah wasn't even sixteen, but she acted like she knew everything.

"No!" Mama said, waving her finger. "The Treaty and unemployment just made Germany ready for the taking. The Nazis stole our Germany."

Mama snatched the pot from the table. "And now we need to leave," she said.

"No one disagrees, Henriette," Vati said, swatting at the pot in Mama's hand. "At least not anymore. So put your pots away!"

Vati stopped arguing with Mama about whether they should leave Germany after Uncle Leo lost his job. Before, Vati used to say that he was a German and would never leave, that his family had been in Germany for as long as anyone knew, and that he almost died in the Great War for his beloved Germany. He'd smile and say, "Just wait! the tough times will pass!" He didn't say that anymore.

"We want to go, but no country will take us," Sarah said in that know-it-all way. "Germany wants us out and no one wants us in."

Emil stole two more steps. Four more and he'd be out of sight.

"That's not completely true, Liebchen," Mama said and glanced toward Vati.

"What do you mean?" Sarah asked. "What's happened?"

Vati nodded and said, "Tell them." He moved next to Mama and put his arm around her shoulder. Emil stopped. He couldn't imagine what would make Mama's smile explode like a thousand butterflies bursting from a cage. His escape could wait a minute.

"Well, you know I began applying for visas and writing to financial sponsors from other countries a year ago." Mama rushed over to the writing table overflowing ith papers as if Emil and Sarah needed to see envelopes to understand what she was saying.

"Of course!" Sarah said.

"To everyone I knew and anyone they knew," Mama said.

"She's probably written a hundred," Vati said.

"Well, something has happened." Mama folded and unfolded her hands. "Very good news."

"What happened?" Sarah asked.

"I just found out two days ago," Mama said.

"What's the news?" Sarah asked.

"I've been trying to find the best time to tell you," Mama said.

"MAMA, WHAT IS IT?" Sarah shouted.

Mama breathed in and said, "We found a sponsor for you and Emil." Her words came quickly. "He's a distant relative. An architect from New York, but you never met him. Oma Hally's mother had a sister. Her daughter Gerda married an American. The architect is her son and he's very wealthy. He agreed to financially guarantee you!"

"Oh!" Emil yelped. He would have believed Mama had sprouted wings before believing they found a sponsor. No one had wanted to sponsor them for a whole year and Emil thought no one ever would. He figured he would live here, right in this house, which was the same house where Mama had always lived, which was the same house where Mama's Mama had always lived.

Emil hoped he would like it in America. He was German, after all. What if no one played marbles there? Or made sausages or rode bicycles like in Germany?

"But what about the other sponsor?" Sarah asked. "It's better to have two Affidavits of Support, not just one."

"Ugh," Emil mumbled. Sarah was trying to show off how much she knew.

"Now that we have this one, I'll write back to the people who said no," Mama said. "They'll feel better with one sponsor already secured. Did I mention he is very wealthy?"

Sarah slouched. "And what about the visa, Mama? Even if we get another sponsor, we still need visas. Everyone says getting visas from America is harder than getting sponsors."

"You are moving higher on the wait-list," Mama said. Her eyes sparkled. "I can feel it!"

Sarah's eyebrows creased. She asked, "Why did you say Emil and I got a sponsor?"

"Because you did."

"Why didn't you say that you and Vati got one? And Uncle Leo?"

Mama glanced at Vati and said, "Because we didn't."

"MAMA!" Sarah screamed.

Emil grabbed the wall to catch himself from falling. He had never thought about leaving Germany without his parents. Maybe things weren't so bad here after all. Maybe Vati was right and tough times would pass. Maybe it would all work itself out. Mama turned blurry as tears pooled in his eyes.

"You are old enough to care for your brother," Mama said.

"I'm fifteen!" Sarah yelled, and then tempered her voice. "Mama, Emil and I aren't going anywhere without you." For once, Emil wanted to hear his sister talk. She would convince Mama it was a bad idea.

"My children will live someplace where they are not required to carry ID cards because they are Jewish." Mama matched Sarah. "If you didn't understand my opinion about the ID cards before, I will bring back my pots to show you again."

"Cards?" Emil choked out.

Uncle Leo poked his head out from behind his newspaper. Emil squinted at the glare reflecting off his glasses. Uncle Leo said, "Haven't you heard the latest plan to better Germany? The Nazis are making us carry ID cards. This will help them keep track of all our Jewish comings and goings, because of course we are so fascinating."

"Just another way to marginalize us," Sarah said. Emil wasn't sure what *marginalize* meant, but he knew it was not good.

"And guess what else?" Uncle Leo shook his newspaper. "Only Jews can patronize Jewish-owned stores. It's putting everyone out of business!"

Four people looked up at Emil, waiting for a response.

They wanted him to care about the card, about the stores, about Mama registering jewelry, but he didn't. He cared about staying with Mama and what he would eat for supper. The world sped by wildly and all he could do was get splattered with muck as it roared past.

Emil considered stomping around and shouting words like *marginalize*, but that wouldn't change anything, so he left the room without a word.

Sarah called out, "You can turn from the wind, Emil, but it's still going to blow."

It will blow, he thought, *but not in my face.* The screechy noise of four frustrated people followed him to his bedroom. He kicked a few things out of the way to close his door, flopped on his bed with muddy clothes, and stared at the wallpaper. For some reason, Mama had thought it important to wallpaper his bedroom with fancy paper, but the repeating design made him dizzy. It reminded him of floating vases with hairy tails. Emil traced the pattern with his finger. He must have disturbed a sleeping layer of dust, because he sneezed three times.

Emil laid a pillow over his head to block out the world. His stomach ached the same way when he couldn't find his cat and when Sarah told him Uncle Leo lost his job because he was Jewish. He flicked at a marble in his pocket. It crashed into the others, making that clicking sound he liked. Letting bad thoughts grow wouldn't change Germany back, so there was no point thinking them. Emil clicked and clicked until he pushed all the bad thoughts out of his brain and pulled in ones of Mama's dumplings.

5. Lost and Found

Stupid! Friedrich scolded himself. Every head turned toward him. He didn't know what to do. Why would anyone stand in the middle of service hours? He couldn't look like he wanted to leave. That would be disloyal. He couldn't let them know he was embarrassed by the mistake. That would make him seem weak.

"Heil Hitler," Friedrich choked out and dropped back in his seat.

"A boy should exercise self-discipline," Günter said, staring into Friedrich. The room was so quiet Friedrich could hear his heart pound. The seconds wouldn't end. Günter smirked, which told Friedrich that Günter knew exactly what he was doing. It was punishment.

Everyone gawked as if they could see his crumbling insides. The disgrace was too much. Friedrich could no longer control how he looked. He felt his face blaze. His eyebrow twitched uncontrollably. His mouth fell open and jaw wouldn't work to tighten itself. Friedrich never loathed himself more than at that moment.

Finally, Günter took a breath and ended the chastising silence. "As I was saying before I was interrupted." Günter lowered his voice, like he was about to make an important announcement. "For the last item, I have information about a new Jungvolk competition."

Everyone turned back to the front. Friedrich had to compose himself fast. The ordinary sight of everyone's backs helped distance him from the mistake. No one watched him. He was in his own personal space with his own thoughts. Friedrich focused on Günter's words and felt the blotchy red spots reluctantly fade from his face. He added another check to the Bad Side of his Jungvolk Good–Bad Criteria List and prayed his list wasn't as long as Otto's.

By the time Günter got to the point of the new competition, only the tips of Friedrich's ears still tingled. "There may be a time you find yourself in the wilderness," Günter said. "You may have some supplies, but not many. How would you survive this situation?"

The words *wilderness* and *survive* echoed in Friedrich's head.

"This is your project," Günter continued. "Invent a clever way to live from the land. Test it. You have the rest of the summer, so get it right. The best wins. You are dismissed."

Friedrich couldn't believe it. A competition that rewarded resourcefulness. His heart beat faster. He could win. Dozens of ideas swirled in his head, but one already stood out. If he came in first place, the Good Side of his list would outweigh the Bad Side. The other boys would respect him. Günter would think he was loyal.

He waited until every person stood and then raced out of the building, eager to feel the walkway under his feet. The fresh air cleansed him. Foot over foot, each step freed him from what had happened a little more.

One block in, he turned in front of some shops and heard, "Yip! Yip!" The stray dog Friedrich saw after every meeting bounced next to him. It was feisty little mutt, but friendly in a mangy sort of way. Friedrich liked the way the dog's one white leg contrasted its brown bristly body. And how the scrawny animal looked strong and proud, as if it had already learned two lifetimes of wisdom.

Friedrich stopped and reached in his pocket. The stray locked eyes with him and crept closer than it ever had before, nearly touching Friedrich's leg.

"Easy, dog," Friedrich spoke aloud to the animal for the first time and realized calling it "dog" would not do. He tossed the yelpy creature the scraps he'd been saving. "I'm naming you Brutus."

The mutt chomped them down and scurried off, without a wag of gratitude. Friedrich hurried on as well, eager to begin the plan that could save him.

6. The Trespasser

Emil woke and wiped his nose on his pajama sleeve. Sunny rays poked through his window shades and flickered good morning. The brightness revealed dust floaters journeying around his room. He watched scores of them crisscross through the air. Emil couldn't guess their destination because when they floated out of the light, they vanished and were replaced with new ones. The steady rhythm and predictable unpredictability soothed him. He watched and thought of last night. Once Mama served dinner, conversation shifted away from ID cards and back to the usual. What book Sarah was reading. Why no one noticed the new way Mama arranged the dinner flowers. And why Emil preferred to use his shirt as a napkin rather than use a napkin.

Emil considered what to do with his day. He listened to the world's hum outside and was glad he didn't have to jump in. He loved many parts of summer break, but most of all, the freedom to do what he wanted. Mama would urge him to practice Hebrew for his Bar Mitzvah next year, but he had plenty of time for that. Mrs. Müller, the piano teacher, wouldn't come until tomorrow, so no need to practice. Emil thought of shooting marbles at the Bund, but Mama's been upset that the police have been checking in on the Jewish clubs. Emil gazed at the persistent sunbeams outside. They glowed with promise. He craved adventure and decided on a trip to his spot at the river. Like the dust floaters, he wanted to journey to a place no one could find.

"I'm getting some fresh air," Emil hollered as he made his way toward the door. Mama thought getting fresh air was even healthier than her cure-all tonic: radishes soaked in honey.

Mama popped out of the kitchen and handed him a neatly tied sack. "Take these sandwiches just in case you get hungry." Mama always planned for just-in-case.

"And don't be late!" She waved a spatula every time she said the word *don't*. It made a SWOOSH sound.

Emil accepted the bundle.

"And don't (SWOOSH) get yourself noticed outdoors," Mama said. "Don't (SWOOSH) go near those boys in uniform. Don't (SWOOSH) forget your ID. And don't (SWOOSH) use your talent for finding trouble."

"I don't find trouble on purpose," he said.

Mama crossed one hearty arm over the other and peered into Emil's eyes. "The police will start asking people who look Jewish to show ID cards. My dark-haired, disheveled Schatzi stands out from those blond ones and their crisp uniforms." She laughed. "No clothes iron can hold up against Emil Rosen."

Then her smile left and she forgot to blink. "I worry the day the police ask for your ID will be the day the marbles in your pocket make a hole big enough for an ID to slip out."

He reached in his pockets, pushed his marbles aside and felt around the bottom. He said, "The stitches are all fine, Mama." He drew out as much of the pocket that would budge against the weight. "See."

Her smile returned and with a final SWOOSH, she said, "Tie your shoes. You can practice piano and study Hebrew later. Mrs. Müller will be here after supper."

Emil groaned inside his head. Mrs. Müller would be here today after all. Now he really did need to get fresh air to be able to handle her old lady chicken stench. Emil could never figure why Mama loved smelly Mrs. Müller so much.

Emil tied them and gave Mama a kiss. He was too old, so he only did it when no one was watching. He clomped down the stairway to the basement to fetch his bicycle and thumped it back up to the front door. Emil rode and soaked in the hopeful warmth. It felt like it would be a good day. He forgot everything and let the world's beauty consume him.

As he pedaled, his mind wandered. He thought about how it was more than luck when he first found his spot along the river. Emil figured the spot wanted him to find it. Like it knew how much he would need it and love it.

It all happened last year, when Jews stopped being allowed to work as accountants. Uncle Leo started spending all day in Emil's living room. And right after that, when businessmen stopped buying Vati's oil, his father joined. Home got crowded really fast. Day after day, month after month, Uncle Leo, Mama, and Vati spent the day chitchatting and squabbling. Mama called it Finding New Purpose, but Emil called it boring.

That was also when Mama started making Mama-fuss. "Don't go near *the boys*" was her first rule. *The boys* lived in Emil's neighborhood and, except for one unfortunate day a long time ago, had always ignored him. But a few years ago, on a sweltering summer afternoon, *the boys* let him play marbles with them. It was so hot, the whole town smelled like rotten cabbage. Emil figured they only let him play since it was too warm for anything else.

Emil had never played a proper game before, but always carried a marble with crimson swirls that Opa had given him for luck. He was excited to finally use his grandfather's gift. So, he fished the marble out of his pocket, squatted over a roasting stoop, and knuckled down. Emil assumed the game would be quick and he'd lose, since that was the way games always ended. It was quick, but not the way he expected. Somehow, the pretty little balls glided just the way he wanted around the circle. Emil crushed his first opponent, and then four more. It was the first time Emil had ever won anything. And since Emil had no experience, he was a terrible winner.

"I win!" Emil had shrieked. "I am the champion!"

"Cheater!" they shouted.

He had jumped around in a sort of dance-skip-strut until a shoe bounced off his head. He got a lump on his forehead the size of a lemon, but Emil thought tasting victory for the first time was worth it. *The boys* never played with him after that, but Emil still thought it was worth it. It was only after the boys joined the Jungvolk and stomped around in their uniforms did he wonder if maybe it wasn't worth it.

So when Mama first told him to stay away from *the boys* last year, Emil listened. Instead of taking the quick way home that passed where *the boys* met for Jungvolk service hours, Emil rode his bicycle way around. That first day, since he was already discovering new routes, he decided to explore the quiet country road by the river. The sun nudged him along and he journeyed until his legs cramped. He stopped and noticed a large, flat rock. It was the perfect rock to find out what would happen if he smashed a marble as hard as he could. He had wondered many times, but never tried since there were always too many breakable things around. He picked his worst marble and was happy to find the clouded ball, as Mama would say, a new purpose.

"So long, ugly," he had said to the unlucky marble.

He kissed it and hurled it toward the rock. But instead of shattering, it ricocheted through an opening in the shrubs. He scurried off his bike to retrieve it. The overgrown bush swung shut behind him after he pushed through. He found his marble resting in the middle of what looked like a forgotten pathway. Branches poked out from both sides, trying to reclaim the carved space. The path was about twenty meters long and slanted up until it disappeared at the peak of a small hill. He couldn't see beyond the hill, but if someone had taken the time to slice through heaps of foliage, Emil wanted to know why. He kicked the marble aside and crept upward toward the peak.

He gasped at what he had found. Grand, old trees shaded a river bend packed with glistening rocks that begged to be overturned. Soft breezes held specks of dried flora aloft. Bright red poppies burst from surrounding green fields. The place was magic, somewhere between a fairytale and his imagination. It was alive and beautiful and all his. No one could see or hear him from the road. The world had gifted him his own personal hideaway.

Emil felt like he got a new purpose. He charged into the water fully clothed. His fingers raked through the sediment as lively patches of minnows swarmed around him. The feeling of being wet outside after so long of not being allowed in public pools was intoxicating. The spot claimed him as much as he claimed it.

Emil rode on, smiling at the memory from last year, until a pigeon flapped too close to his ear. Pickles! City birds flew close, not river birds. He must have forgotten to take the longer route. That sun, so full of promises, was sneaky. It relaxed him. He was in the middle of town, right where Mama didn't want him.

He sped up, eager to make it through the next few blocks, until shouting echoed in the street. He couldn't see where it came from, but when it became louder, he hopped off his bicycle. Emil wasn't involved in whatever was going on and he aimed to keep it that way. Walking a bicycle on a crowded sidewalk was less risky than riding.

He turned the corner and stopped when he saw that the commotion was coming from outside the Klein Stationary Shop across the street. Mr. Klein, an older Jewish man who owned the store, was the one shouting. Two Brownshirts stood on either side of the entrance. The bright red badges on their rigid arms popped from their drab uniforms. Vati called Brownshirts Hitler's thugs and the most brutal of all police, so Emil didn't understand why they needed to guard a quiet writing shop. A sign with neat lettering was pasted on the window that read: JEWISH STORE. NO ENTRANCE. Emil backed closer to the building behind him.

"I barely earn enough for bread!" Mr. Klein was now yelling right at the Brownshirts. A few pedestrians stopped to stare. "I cannot make do with fewer customers!"

This went on until the face on one of the Brownshirts knotted into a hard ball of wrinkles. Emil recognized the expression. It was rage. He knew because he had seen it once directed at him. When he won at marbles over the boys long ago, every boy had looked angry, but an older boy named Günter acted differently. Günter's face smoldered. It looked like the Brownshirt's face.

"Quiet, Jew!" the Brownshirt snarled. Then, before Emil knew what was happening, the Brownshirt reached out and slapped the old man's cheek. Mr. Klein stopped moving, his head frozen in the direction where the smack positioned it. The world became just as still. The man's silvery hair fluttering in the breeze was the only movement in the distorted picture. Emil stared at the gentle silver-gray waves and thought of his own grandfather. When Opa was alive, he had silvery hair just like that.

Finally, Mr. Klein turned toward the man who struck him. He said something Emil couldn't hear and then went inside his store. The Brownshirts remained. Emil looked around and felt his stomach churn. Why had no one done anything?

The sun burnt into the back of Emil's neck. The incident was over, but the world was different, twisted. He backed up around the corner he had come from, dragging his bike by the handlebar. Mama always said, "One disaster rarely comes alone." He touched the pocket with his ID card to make sure it hadn't fallen out.

His hands shook as he mounted his bike. *Pedal. Don't cry*, he told himself. He needed distance. Pedestrians blocked his way. He heard Mama's voice in his head, "Don't get yourself noticed because you never know where it will lead." He steered onto the street, where he was supposed to be riding. Dodging cars was better than the police catching him on the sidewalk.

He rode and rode, trying to think of something else, but the image of that young, strong hand striking the wrinkled, wise cheek wouldn't leave. Weren't the old supposed to guide and the young supposed to protect? Emil wondered if Opa's hair would have looked like that if someone had struck him. For the first time, he was glad Opa was dead. Emil didn't want him to live in a world where Opas were slapped.

The bumpy road jostled the marbles in his pocket. *Click, click, click*, he heard as they smashed together. Emil tried to think happy thoughts, but couldn't. Terrible ones rang through his brain. Then the Brownshirt's knotted face plowed across his mind and forced Emil's most awful memory to the surface. The one of Günter after Emil had beaten *the boys*, the one Emil struggled to keep buried. That next day after that game of marbles, Emil had passed Günter in the street. Günter crashed into Emil's shoulder and sneered, "Learn your place." Then he leaned in and whispered, "Your cat is quite the explorer, isn't he?"

Emil remembered every detail about the next three days: Searching his cat Lebkuchen's favorite basement spots, leaving food by the front door, and on the third afternoon, finding the little bell Lebkuchen wore around his neck on his front step. Emil never told his family about Günter. He didn't know where Günter had taken his cat and all he could do was pray Lebkuchen found another family.

Emotions pierced through him. The memory churned at Emil's stomach so badly, he almost stopped pedaling. He could not think about it anymore. Not Lebkuchen and not the store owner. *Click, click, click.* He focused on that happy sound. *Click, click, click,* keeping to the rhythm of pedaling. *Click, click, click.* His breathing steadied. *Click, click, click.* He rode on.

Emil arrived at his spot. Thick bush slapped his legs as he entered. Emil threw his bike behind a shrub and scurried up the path. He needed the purifying river and crisp air.

The sounds of trickling water and rustling grasses welcomed him. Emil threw off his shirt and kneeled in a shallow pool. Cool water rushed past his submerged fingers. Swaying poppies comforted him. He pried up half-buried stones, tilling the sediment with his fingers, until he could once again hear the birds. Then he closed his eyes, sat very still, and did nothing but breathe in the world's earthy sweetness.

Snap! A breaking twig caught his attention. Emil figured it must be one of the round, furry critters he liked to watch. It was strange that his skin prickled. Emil turned to look and nearly fell over. A boy with golden hair squatted behind the tree at the other end of the river bank. The boy wore a Jungvolk uniform. Emil was alone with one of *the boys.*

Emil dove behind a bush. After a minute, nothing happened, so Emil reasoned he hadn't spotted him. The boy started to undress. He took off his shirt. The boy folded it, then unfolded it and, more slowly, folded it again. He laid it on a high rock, far from water splatter. Then he removed his socks and shoes and rolled his pants. He squatted over the water, making the pointy parts of his spine jut out. Emil stared at his ribs through the fair skin. They boy just looked like a skinny kid playing in the river, not like a Jungvolk boy.

Emil strained to see more. The boy was building something out of two glass jars, a small one with a narrow neck and a larger one with a wide neck. The boy struggled to fit the smaller one inside the other and seal off the seams. He placed the contraption into the river. When water poured inside, the boy swore and snatched it up. Emil watched as he reconfigured the jars, dropped them in water, lifted them when they flooded, and cursed, over and over. The curious device reminded Emil of a simpler version of a trap he once saw fishermen use.

Emil's leg tingled from bending so long. He stretched it and startled a round, furry critter. It darted and Emil jumped. The boy shot up and swung in Emil's direction. His eyes found Emil. Red hot panic ripped through him.

"Oh! Oh!" Emil exclaimed. He dashed toward his bicycle. Fear made his body move so fast, he didn't even notice the boy had snatched Emil's shirt and run in the opposite direction.

7. Friedrich's Right

He was spying on me! So many thoughts slammed around Friedrich's mind, he ran half the meadow before he realized no one was chasing him. When he finally stopped, his breath came so quick, he nearly fell over. He should not have fled. Friedrich didn't even know why he had. He glanced down at his bare chest and realized how strange he must look practically naked, clutching his clothes, racing through a field of wildflowers like a scared baby rabbit. He groaned at the humiliating image.

He looked around and found no one. Only millions of red flowers stared back. He felt the slightest bit better that nobody saw him, like a crowded pincushion must feel when a single, pearly-headed pin fell out.

He ground his teeth as he imagined that chubby spy scanning the hollow indentations around his ribs. He must have looked weak, like he didn't exercise or his family was too poor to feed him. That awful, empty sensation Friedrich worked so hard to shut out slinked through him, making him feel worthless, defective. Friedrich ran his hand along his chest. Just skin on top of bone and nothing in between. He cursed the spy for making him feel this way.

"Muddy Hell!" Friedrich screamed. Birds shot up

from the field, their black silhouettes popping against the quiet blue sky. Squawks cut through the low breezy hum.

Then Friedrich had a really awful thought. One that made his eyebrow twitch like never before. What if Günter found out? Friedrich knew the spy. He was that muddy-hell Jew always playing marbles. Jews were tricky. His teachers said it, Günter said it, everyone said it. The spy could tell his friends. All of Hannover would call him pathetic. If only he hadn't run.

"I wasn't scared! Just surprised!" he yelled, as if the words would somehow implant themselves in the spy's head.

Friedrich had always assumed he would act bravely in this kind of situation; now he knew the truth. Everywhere he looked, he saw those awful red flowers gawking back, mocking him. He felt an urge to punch each dreadful one. To damn them all for watching his misery. Maybe that would make the hurt stop. Friedrich grabbed up a handful of poppies and threw them as hard as he could. It felt good. He grabbed and threw sloppy handfuls over and over, until he jerked too hard. Pain seared through his shoulder. The flowers punched back.

He slumped down, squeezing the fiery spot in his muscle. Aggression drained from his body. The tingling in his limbs dwindled. He heard millions of insects sing a layered song and smelled the floral scent mashed on his fingers.

Friedrich glanced at the trees. Their long shadows reminded him it was time to leave. He walked back through the meadow under the late afternoon sun, searching for something to get his mind off what happened. He started on the pathway to the road and thought of that wonderful day long ago when Papa cut the passage. As he dragged his hand along the pointed branches, he liked to think how they were the same as the ones he touched when he was young.

The path was Papa's gift. Back when Papa owned an electrical business, there were lots of lazy days. Spending so much time together made Friedrich feel like there was nothing Papa loved more. It filled him to the brim. Friedrich was grateful for it, because now, when Papa's work took him every day, Friedrich could just reach inside and hold on to that feeling.

A small round object caught Friedrich's eye and he stopped to pick it up. A cloudy, lopsided marble wobbled in his palm. It was cracked on one side. The ugly, misshaped ball had to belong to someone ugly. Friedrich was certain it belonged to the spy. And that meant the spy used Papa's pathway.

A new kind of fury rose within Friedrich. "This place is mine!" He screamed so loud, it tore at his voice. Tears squeezed out.

Papa had shown Friedrich this place on the Leine river long ago. It was their special place, their secret. They first came to collect rocks. Papa knew so much about nature. After a full day of collecting, Friedrich loved spending the evening organizing his specimens into boxes, with all the tidy rows of little squares.

On hot days, Friedrich leapt into the river as Papa lay on the bank watching. His soft smile made his bristly mustache spring up at the sides. Friedrich had sat on the moist bank and smeared handfuls of oozing sediment over his legs. He wasn't sure which he liked more, the way his calf muscles felt under the cool weight or the thought of Mother's face if she could see him covered in mud. Then he would scoot toward the water and let the current wash the muck away in seconds. Friedrich loved creating a muddy chaos and having the river correct it, righting his wrong. Chaos, swoosh, order. Chaos, swoosh, order. It reassured him that the way of the world was right.

Friedrich remembered the day Papa finished the pathway. Papa had placed a hand on Friedrich's shoulder and said, "In the spiderweb of facts, many truths are strangled. I love you, Friedrich. Nothing can choke that truth." Friedrich wasn't sure why Papa talked that way, but he soaked it right in like a dry sponge.

Soon after, Papa started his new job. The job gave them all enough to eat, but stole Papa's time. Friedrich never wanted to come back to his special place without Papa, so years slipped by, until now, when Günter's project gave him a reason to return.

Friedrich dropped the ugly marble. "I belong here,"

he said aloud. Friedrich promised himself he would finish his project. He'd return to the river, his rightful place, and never, ever run again.

Friedrich looked at the position of the sun to gauge the time. He stood to leave, thinking about all the plans he had made for the day at breakfast. If he rode quickly, he still had time to drop off a bag at Johannes' house, exchange a gift at a store, eat supper, and arrive at Jungvolk service hours on time.

Friedrich dressed, smoothing each garment for wrinkles. He finished, but found one extra piece of clothing. He held it out with both hands. It was a shirt, too large for him.

It must be the spy's! He crumpled it and laughed aloud at the thought of the spy waddling shirtless around Hannover. A person who spied should be punished. Ten more pins fell out of the pincushion. A smile stayed on Friedrich's face even as he rode off.

Friedrich pedaled and angled his puffy eyelids toward the sun to dry any evidence of tears. Soon city noise filled the air. By the time the streets were saturated with the smells of cigar smoke, car fumes, and bakery yeast, he felt like himself again.

First, he had to leave a bag at Johannes's house. Günter had called out Johannes for not tying knots properly, so Friedrich made samples and wrote out diagrams. He had tucked it all in a bag marked with Johannes's name.

Friedrich made good time and dropped the bag at

Johannes's door. He then rode off in a pattern one block south, two blocks east to his next stop, the stationary store. Friedrich had received two of the same mechanical pencils for his last birthday. Two were unnecessary, so he figured he could use return the extra and use the money for special graphing paper for Günter's project.

Friedrich arrived at the shops and to his surprise, found Brutus, the straggly stray dog. Friedrich wondered how his one white leg managed to stay white when the rest of his brown body grew dirtier every time he saw him.

"Hello Brutus," Friedrich said.

"Yip, yip, yip," Brutus barked. He bounced straight up as if he had springs on his paws.

Friedrich reached in his pocket for breakfast scraps, but found nothing. They must have fallen out when he had run through the meadow. Now Brutus had reason to hate the spy too.

"I'll bring some tomorrow," he said.

Brutus barked, spraying Friedrich's shoes with slobber, and dashed away.

Friedrich shook his shoe and pulled the mechanical pencil out of his leather sack. He approached the stationary store and found two Brownshirts standing guard. A new sign that read: JEWISH STORE. NO ENTRANCE, was posted in the window. Friedrich had shopped here many times when no one cared who owned it.

The scowling Brownshirt said, "No entrance, you

little fart." Friedrich hated dealing with Brownshirts. They weren't known for cleverness.

"I need graphing paper," Friedrich said, and wished he had returned the pencil sooner. Regular paper would not do. The Brownshirt wasn't there last week.

The man's eyes narrowed. Friedrich glanced past his looming figure and spotted an old man slumped on a chair behind the counter. He recognized him as the knowledgeable shop owner who had always been helpful.

Friedrich had no money, so he couldn't buy the paper at another store. He pleaded, "I must make a return," but as soon as the words left his mouth, he wished he could shove them back in. He just begged a Brownshirt to shop in a Jewish store.

"Are you suited to wear that uniform?" The Brownshirt looked as if he would rip Friedrich's shirt right off.

"Yes, of course!" Friedrich cried and glanced around to see if anyone else heard.

Friedrich didn't know why his judgment was so clouded today. Normally, he would have used Uncle Hilmar's Would–Could–Should technique before he spoke. He always used it for making difficult decisions. Uncle Hilmar had taught it to him when he was little. It was simple. Just ask three questions and proceed ONLY if the answer to all three was yes. *Would* Friedrich have the guts to speak to the Brownshirt? *Could* he physically do it? *Should* he do it? Yes, yes, no. One no, so he would have known to keep his mouth shut.

Friedrich hurried away with tears dried onto his cheeks, dog drool stuck to his shoe, and an expensive pencil he did not need in his hand. He felt like curling up in a gutter.

Muddy Hell! Friedrich thought. *This day can't get worse.*

8. Clouds Were Forming

Emil pedaled so hard, he couldn't feel his feet. After too many zigzags to count, he was finally convinced that Jungvolk boy was not following him. He never actually saw anyone behind him, but after what happened to his cat Lebkuchen, he knew well enough how *the boys* worked. His neck ached from looking back every few seconds.

He made it. Emil eased up pedaling and took one of those long, deep breaths that made his lungs ache. Relief swept over him like the river current. Mama would never have to know. If she found out, she'd never let him outside again. He told himself not telling was different than lying.

Around the time the streets became busy with cafés and trolleys, he noticed his back felt oddly warm. At the same moment, an old lady wearing a fancy green hat overflowing with droopy flowers put down her coffee cup and pointed a witch-like crooked finger at him. The group of ancient ladies she sat with squawked in Emil's direction. Emil's bike wobbled as he slowed down and stared at them, wondering what the pickles they were saying.

He followed the direction of her pointed finger. It ended at his stomach, his naked stomach. Sweat on his bare middle glistened. The fleshy parts oozed over his pants and jiggled at every bump. He wasn't wearing a shirt.

He zipped past another group of ladies and heard them shriek, "Indecent! Lewd! Vulgar!" but they were drowned out by laughs from men standing next to them. Emil's face burned. He tried to cover his belly with one arm, but that hid nothing and almost made him topple.

As he glanced back at the grimacing ladies, the direness of his situation sank into his brain. This was more than an embarrassing situation. It was more than a mishap. This was terrible, awful trouble. Screaming ladies in fancy hats brought police. And the police, as Mama told him every day, itched to hassle Jewish-looking boys. A muddy, half-naked Jewish-looking boy would really get it. Emil's heart raced and his body turned blotchy. His blemished naked belly made him look even worse and he became even more upset.

He swerved his bike into a small alley, and tried to stop, but his sweaty palms slipped off the handles. The bike fell over and he tumbled off like a big, flesh-colored sack of potatoes. He scampered up to his knees, grabbed a handlebar, and dragged his bike into the alley with him.

Emil swayed back and forth, hugging himself, trying to calm down. The only way out was to cover his top parts. His thoughts raced. Maybe he could pull his shorts up to his armpits. Maybe he could steal a shirt from a store. Maybe one of the ladies had an extra shirt.

He grabbed at the ridiculous solutions like dust floaters, unable to catch any.

Emil's eyes scanned the alley floor for something, anything that could conceal him. Through the clutter, he spotted a long strip of beige fabric. It may have once been a cloth bag. It looked mostly clean, except for a few brown spots, but had a putrid sewer smell. He tried not to think what had caused the brown spots. Emil snatched it and tried twisting it around his body like a cape. It was long enough to tie around his neck, but too narrow to cover his back.

As he fiddled with the cloth, Emil heard the hollow sound of shoes hitting the stone sidewalk. The police! Emil flattened himself along the clammy stone wall. The alley felt as if it was closing in. His heart was about to burst right out of his chest. He held his breath as the sound grew louder. The shoes were right on top of him and then . . . continued on. It was just the men who had laughed. They didn't see him.

Emil's feet had sunk in the muck from standing still so long. If he didn't leave soon, the rank alley would swallow him up and turn him into another smelly clump on the ground. He seized the cloth, rolled it, fastened it as a necktie and hopped on his bike. It was the only plan he could think of. He heard and felt nothing as he rode, as fast as he could, street after street. His fog lifted only when he saw his hand pushing open the front door of his apartment building.

He threw his bike down in the basement and leaped up the stairs, climbing two or three steps in a stride. He rounded the banister on the first floor. The police hadn't caught him, the embarrassment hadn't killed him and he could even smell Mama's stuffed cabbage. He thumped past the second floor. *Almost there, almost there*, he told himself. *Just two more flights and . . .*

"My God!" shrieked a voice so shrill, it made him freeze midstep. The voice lassoed and spun him slowly around until he faced Mrs. Schmidt. Her eyes shot from his bare belly to his muddied shorts to the filthy rag around his neck. She looked as if someone had just vomited in her apartment. She opened her mouth, but something must have gotten clogged because only "Agck! Agck!" came out. Emil wasn't sure how to respond to "agck, agck" so he said, "Good afternoon, Mrs. Schmidt." His thumb tangled in his neck rag as he raised his hand to wave hello.

Emil had never seen a person turn so many colors. Blue veins popped out from both sides of her neck and her face must have turned ten shades of red. Her knuckles whitened as she clung hard onto the door frame with one hand. She flung the other hand around as if she was swatting flies and placing an evil curse on him at the same time.

His nose tickled, so he stopped watching for a moment and used his neck rag to wipe it. That unclogged her words.

"Outrageous!" Mrs. Schmidt grabbed Emil by the ear and marched up the stairs, dragging him along behind her.

"Do you think we live in an animal house?" She screamed higher than Emil had ever heard.

A few doors clicked open from downstairs. As they rounded the platform between the third and fourth floors, Emil saw a flash of Mrs. Heller before her door slammed shut.

"Unthinkable!" Mrs. Schmidt said, still holding tight to his ear. As they ascended the last couple steps, Mama swung open their apartment door. She wore her apron and held the same spatula from earlier.

"This is an absolute disgrace!" Mrs. Schmidt shrieked at Mama.

Mama raised one eyebrow higher than the other. She looked Emil up and down. As she put her unspatulaed hand on her hip, something fiery bubbled up from behind her eyes. Emil had only seen Mama like this a few times before. He hung his head, thinking how much he was disappointing her. Out of the whole day, this was the worst. Mama sucked in her breath. Emil braced himself.

"Unhand the child," she ordered in such a firm voice, Emil envisioned hundreds of red-faced ladies all over Hannover letting go of children's ears. Mrs. Schmidt released her claw-like grip and Emil cupped his ear to make sure all the bits were still there.

Mama grabbed Emil from the hall and pulled him inside. She didn't let go of his wrist even after he slid in behind her. He poked his head past Mama to look at Mrs. Schmidt. Her eyes grew wide, as if she couldn't make sense of the world around her.

Tucked behind Mama, he realized that one way or another, he made it back to his home. Emil opened his mouth for a big breath of fresh air, but felt his throat tighten. Before he could stop it, he hiccupped.

The hiccup made Mrs. Schmidt's face turn colors again. "Doch!" she said, "Mrs. Rosen, your son is naked."

Mama looked at Emil. Her eyes lingered over his muddied shoes and neck rag.

Mama turned back and said, "He is wearing pants."

"And I suppose we should be grateful, but it is unacceptable for that child to run in our beloved streets draped in rags with that . . . that belly flopping about." Mrs. Schmidt lowered her voice, "Mrs. Rosen, I have no choice but to call the authorities."

Emil felt Mama's grip tighten. "There is no need for that." Mama tilted her head and changed to her sugary-sweet way of speaking. "Emil has never been in this condition, so I'm sure there is an explanation."

Mrs. Schmidt grunted.

"Now, your son plays piano beautifully, does he not?" Mama asked. Mama was working her magic. She was as good at schmoozing as she was at making a fuss.

"Well . . . Yes." Mrs. Schmidt held her head so high,

Emil could see a nose hair curl from underneath. "One needs discipline," she scowled at Emil, "which my son has acquired serving Germany in the Hitler Youth. But that has nothing do to with . . ."

"Such natural piano talent," Mama interrupted. "I've been meaning to give you something special. One moment." Mama shoved Emil further inside and walked into her bedroom, leaving Mrs. Schmidt in the hallway.

"Mrs. Rosen!" Mrs. Schmidt hollered.

Sarah, who sat at the dining table, darted to the doorway and said, "Mrs. Schmidt, would you like coffee and a fresh piece of apple cake? It's right from the bakery."

"No, I would not like your apple cake," she said. "And see here . . ."

"Mrs. Schmidt," Mama said in a sing-song way emerging from her bedroom. She held a small black velvet case.

Sarah said softly, "Oh no, Mama."

"I remember you remarked on this brooch some time ago," Mama said. "Some time ago" meant when Mama and Mrs. Schmidt ate apple cake together.

Emil caught a glimpse of shiny black stones in Mama's hand. It was Mama's special piano brooch, with little black onyx and white opal keys. Mama had it for as long as Emil could remember. It looked so perfect, Emil used to think it could really play music.

"When you wear it," Mama said, extending the gift, "you will honor the beautiful music your son plays."

The women stared at each other from opposite sides of the door. Mama was paying for Emil's mistake. He glanced at the pitiful rag around his neck. Mama was so wise and he was so stupid.

Mrs. Schmidt said, "When I wear it, I will honor the German music my son plays." Emil stretched his neck to steal one last glimpse of the brooch. He caught just a twinkle before Mrs. Schmidt snatched the bribe and stomped downstairs.

Mama shut the door. She walked over to Emil and took his hand in hers. It was warm. When Emil saw Mama's eyes all mixed up with love and sadness, he looked down to the floor.

"Are you hurt, Schatzi?" Mama stroked Emil's hair. Her love wrapped around him like a life preserver.

"No, Mama." He didn't mean for his voice to come out so shaky.

"What happened?" she whispered.

He couldn't tell her. Instead, memories of Mama wearing the brooch to elegant parties swirled in his head. Back then, ladies like Mrs. Schmidt used to cut across the room to talk to her. Now, they all ran the other way.

He croaked, "Mrs. Schmidt was our friend."

Mama sighed. "When it starts to rain, a tree is a good shelter. But then the leaves become waterlogged and that same tree drips on everything below even when the sun starts shining. The tree is now a bad shelter." Mama looked tired. "Things change, Emil, and Mrs. Schmidt is no longer our friend. She doesn't like any Jewish person anymore."

"I'm sorry, Mama. I, I . . ." Emil couldn't put the words together to tell her how sorry he was she had to give away something special and how sorry he was for embarrassing her and how sorry he was that Mrs. Schmidt didn't want to be her friend.

Mama let go of his hand and kissed his forehead. "I'll rest for later." She stepped into her bedroom before Emil could answer. The moment her bedroom door clicked closed, Sarah rushed at Emil.

"That was Mama's favorite brooch!" Sarah hushed-yelled at him. "You're lucky Vati and Uncle Leo are at the market."

That was all he needed for everything in the miserable day to percolate over. Tears streamed down, landing on his pale stomach. He sobbed quietly so Mama wouldn't hear.

Sarah stood next to him. "At least losing a shirt is cheaper than losing a shoe." She put a hand on his shoulder until Emil used his neck rag to wipe his nose.

"Give me that disgusting thing," she said.

Emil unraveled the dirty cloth from his neck and handed it over.

"What is this?" She pinched it between two fingers and held it far from her.

"Why do people hate us?" Emil asked, ignoring Sarah. "Why is this happening now?"

"Happening now? *This* has been with us for a long time. It's been like a fog all around us, but you couldn't see it. Think about your old school friends. The ones you used to play with. They started ignoring you years ago, right? Then they gossiped about you. Now who knows what they'll do. The fog has clumped into clouds. Now you can see it."

Emil nodded.

"What happened to you, Emil?"

Maybe talking to Sarah about the dreadful day would get the awfulness inside him out, but he knew it would get back to Mama and then the awfulness would go into her. So, he looked straight at his sister and said, "I can't remember where I left my shirt." The Brownshirts, the Jungvolk boy, and the cruel ladies with fancy hats would have to stay bottled.

"You need to grow up." She put her hands on her hips. "Can you at least set the table for Shabbat? I'll finish for Mama in the Kitchen." She started walking away, but called back, "And don't bother Mama."

Emil walked to the heavy cabinet where all sorts of expensive, breakable things were kept. He took out two candles and the silver candlesticks his family used every Friday night. They were the same that Mama had used for Shabbat since he could remember. Tarnished spots in the etched crevices had darkened since last week. He grabbed the polishing cloth and scrubbed. It was hard to keep them shiny. Mama polished them every month and they still weren't perfect. He thought about how much easier it would be if he were Christian and there wasn't so much work on Fridays. Actually, he realized, everything would be easier if he weren't Jewish. There would be no clouds following him around. The sky would always be blue.

As soon as he thought it, he hated that he did. Not being Jewish meant not lighting candles, not being part of something ancient, not eating special foods on holidays, and not being part of his family. Being Jewish was who he was. Maybe it would be easier, but he didn't want to be anything else.

He looked around, as if someone caught him with that thought. Richly framed pictures of people in outdated clothes clung to the walls. Thick mouldings crept along the ceilings. Vases decorated with tiny paint brushes crowded every surface. Emil could almost hear the ornately carved server say, "tsk-tsk," like an old Oma. The room seemed like it was warning him to stay inside and study for his Bar Mitzvah, practice the piano, and listen to Vati's stories all day long. But he knew he couldn't.

As much as he never wanted to see that Jungvolk boy again, he needed his spot. His apartment was suffocating. He needed space. He clicked the marbles in his pocket. Maybe the Jungvolk boy wouldn't return. Maybe the wind would blow all the clouds away. Or maybe, just because he wanted it so much, everything would be fine.

9. Ghosts and Monsters

A car edged so close to Friedrich, he felt its heat bake his legs as he rode his bicycle home. It reminded him of the old wives' tale that bad things happen in threes. Friedrich didn't believe in superstitions, but he counted anyway. The spy was number one and the screaming Brownshirt was number two. Getting stuck with a pencil didn't count, so according to the wives' tale, the third was still coming. He rode his bike up on the sidewalk between pedestrians. Bicycles weren't allowed, but he'd take his chances with the police. It was just a senseless superstition, but he didn't want getting splattered by a trolley to be number three. The bumpy cobblestones made his bike jerk. He stood up to pedal so his teeth wouldn't clatter.

"Friedrich!" A voice screamed from behind. "You dropped something!" The voice was familiar, in a sentimental way, like walking into a bakery and breathing in a wonderful scent you remember from when you were young, but not knowing what it was.

Friedrich stopped and turned to see who called him. A boy with dark wavy hair brushed over to one side picked something off the ground. He straightened and smiled at Friedrich.

The grinning boy walked toward him, limping. "You dropped something when you swerved back there." Friedrich knew that limp, that smile and those friendly eyes.

"Albert?" Friedrich asked. Albert lived just a few buildings over and Friedrich sometimes saw him around the neighborhood, but he couldn't remember the last time he had spoken to his Jewish friend. Technically his Jewish ex-friend. Albert was taller and thinner than he used to be, but his walk hadn't changed. Albert was born with one leg longer than the other.

Albert looked happy to see him. He handed the pencil to Friedrich and said, "Here you go." Everyone Friedrich had seen that day had been cruel. But here was Albert. It was as different as east and west.

Friedrich choked out, "Thank you," and realized how awkward he sounded.

He wished he could have his best friend back more than anything. Albert was clever and fun and knew him like no one else. But because of Mother, it was impossible.

"Stay well." Albert turned and took his smile.

Long ago, when boys were allowed to play with anyone they wanted, Albert and Friedrich had been friends. They ran through the streets, not caring if their voices echoed into apartments above. They played hopscotch and tag, collected scraps, and swapped riddles. And best of all, they spent hours playing their favorite game, basement explorer. Nothing was more fun than hunting for metal scraps and forgotten treasures. Intertwining passages led them to sooty coal rooms, laundry washing spaces, and storage rooms where richer people kept heaps of potatoes. They weren't allowed down there, so they invented twenty-two hand signals so they could silently communicate. They were never caught.

Friedrich hadn't thought about Albert being Jewish until the day Mother told him to.

She had said, "Papa has important work now. You can't have Jewish friends," like it was nothing more than telling him he couldn't have a new ball.

"But I like him," he protested. It was the first time he had said no to Mother.

Her eyes iced.

"Papa can get a different job."

Mother squeezed Friedrich's arm. "Cooperation is a requirement, not an option."

Friedrich had always liked to follow rules. It kept his world logical and easy. But as Mother pressed into his arm, rebellion felt right.

Friedrich pulled his arm back and shouted, "Albert is my best friend!"

Mother's face contorted. "You will not defy me!" Friedrich was fighting for his friend, but Mother sounded like she was fighting for power.

"There must be no association with Jews by any member of this family. People say Jews are why there is not enough work. If you play with a Jew, how will that look?" Her voice screeched higher. "People will think we are disloyal!"

Friedrich stared at Mother and said, "We play hopscotch."

She arched her back as if she would slap him, but then Papa ran in.

"Friedrich and I should speak," he had said.

Finally! Friedrich thought. *Papa will talk sense into Mother.*

Mother left. Papa sat on his bed and took Friedrich's hand. "Times have changed. Our family business did not prosper as I had hoped and I am lucky to have a new occupation."

It was not what Friedrich expected. Why didn't Papa say Mother was being ridiculous?

"Albert is my best friend." Maybe Papa didn't understand how important Albert was.

Papa moved his body to face Friedrich. "This is important. In more ways than you know."

"You're on her side!" Friedrich couldn't believe it. "I hate your new job! I never see you and now you're taking away my friend!" Ugly words spewed out. "Albert wants to be with me and you don't." Tears had streamed down Friedrich's face.

When the words ran out, Friedrich curled up and wrapped his arms around his legs. He felt as if he floated in an endless sea of his parents' bad decisions. The weight of his own helplessness was making him sink.

"Friedrich," Papa said. The word was gentle, but Friedrich refused it. He blinked back more tears.

"Albert is a nice boy," Papa said. "But times are hard and we need to think about our family. This has to be."

One more tear ran down Friedrich's cheek, taking a bit of anger, just enough that Friedrich could peek at Papa. His eyes landed on Papa's arm. It surprised to see that it was thinner than he remembered. Friedrich wiped his eyes and took a longer look. The bones of Papa's wrist jutted sharply. His wedding ring angled loosely around his finger. Friedrich scanned Papa all over, as if he was just seeing him after a long time away.

Fragments of memories clicked together like puzzle pieces. He remembered Papa eating smaller portions at supper, but never thought much of it, since the food on his own plate hadn't changed. Friedrich looked at Papa's middle. Instead of a round belly, folds of material bunched together. How could Friedrich have not seen something so obvious? His anger dissolved. Papa had been making sacrifices. Friedrich felt childish for not recognizing it.

Family business, tough times, lucky new job. Friedrich understood. Papa had been starving himself to shield him. Friedrich looked into Papa's kind eyes. He had to take care of Papa like Papa had been taking care of him.

The next day Friedrich walked to Albert's house. When Albert opened the door, Friedrich caught a whiff of sizzling onions from inside and realized he would never again fill his belly with Albert's grandmother's fried potatoes.

Friedrich blurted, "My mother won't let me be your friend anymore because you're Jewish," before Albert could say hello. Friedrich felt tears swell and blinked like a flickering lightbulb to keep them from spilling over.

Albert didn't look as surprised as Friedrich expected, which made Friedrich wonder if this had happened to him before. Part of him wished Albert would have yelled or cried or slammed the door. That would have made it easier.

Friedrich added, "This isn't my choice," and the tears burst through.

"One moment." Albert left Friedrich crying in the hall. He returned with a map of Friedrich's apartment building basement. Albert smiled as he handed it over. Friedrich stared at the painstaking sketch charting their secret spots, coal piles, and even mouse holes. It was marvelous.

"I was going to surprise you, but . . ." Albert's voice shook. He reached toward Friedrich and pulled him into a hug. If Friedrich could freeze himself into one moment of his entire life, that would be it. He would never find a friend like Albert again.

Now standing next to his bicycle holding a pencil he didn't want, Friedrich savored the memories. He watched his friend walk away. A door closed between them once again. Albert was gone and Friedrich was alone on the bustling sidewalk.

Friedrich secured the pencil in his sack and started pedaling north. When he arrived home, he situated his bicycle in the park place.

"Muddy hell," he said aloud when he nearly tripped over another bike not positioned correctly. He couldn't understand how anyone could leave their bicycle in a heap with limbs sticking out every which way.

He walked up stairs and entered his home. As soon as he stepped in, he smelled pickles, mustard, and roasting beef. It was Rouladen, his favorite dish. His family now had enough money to buy meat every week, almost every day, but Rouladen was saved for special occasions. He inhaled the aroma and wondered if Papa was coming home for supper for once.

The scratchy sound of Mother's scrub brush echoed in the hall. She was in the living room cleaning. Her thin figure zipped from here to there. If someone didn't know Mother, they would have thought she expected the Führer to walk in. But this was just how she cleaned every day. She hung handwritten signs that read CLEANLINESS IS NEXT TO GODLINESS with capital letters curling around and around in every room. Friedrich agreed with being orderly, but Mother went too far.

Friedrich knew the time without looking at the clock. Mother's routine never changed. She made to-do lists in the mornings with those curly letters. Then she cleaned the apartment, ran errands, and prepared supper. Once food was in the oven, she cleaned the whole apartment again. She crossed out each task on her list as she finished, but the big letter curls always poked out from the top and bottom, so the task never looked completely crossed out. Maybe that's why Mother never stopped.

Friedrich crept to his room without calling hello. He wanted a few moments for himself to write down his thoughts after a confusing day. Arranging notes and charts helped control the world's chaos. He sat at his desk and thought about the minnow trap he was building for the Jungvolk project. Before the spy had interrupted him, Friedrich discovered the trap wasn't collecting the correct level of water. He figured a different sized container could fix it, but didn't know what proportions would work best.

He was about to make a list of standard bottles when a realization as cruel as his day made him drop his pencil: he had left all his project supplies at the river. There it was, number three, the third bad thing. Hungry creatures could gnaw the supplies. The wind could ram them into rocks. Or worse, the river could carry them away.

"Muddy Hell!"

Mother ran in. "Watch your tongue!" She pursed her mouth like she didn't want to breathe in the air Friedrich dirtied. She didn't ask why he was upset.

"Sorry, Mother."

She didn't answer. Instead, she tilted her head and stared at Friedrich's waist.

"Your shirt," she said slowly, "is filthy!"

Friedrich scanned the garment. He spotted two mud dots, each the size of a freckle. To Mother, they were probably a muddy hell. Mother always gossiped that other wives couldn't keep their families tidy, so now here was evidence of her own poor housekeeping. Maybe she thought they would gossip about her.

"Give it to me," she barked, pointing. Her fingers shook like they would rip the shirt off his back. "Quickly!"

Friedrich fumbled with the buttons. He wrestled it off and handed it over. The skin on his naked back prickled. She folded the offensive flecks out of sight and asked, "What time do service hours begin?" He wished she would ask, *How was your day?*

"One hour," he said quickly. Friedrich hated that Mother growled at him when he hesitated for more than two seconds.

"I will clean it before your meeting," she said. "Impressions are important."

Friedrich thought even Günter wouldn't care about a fleck of dirt.

"I'm hungry," Friedrich said, trying to change the subject.

"I've put out bread and cheese."

"But what's that smell?" The meaty cabbage roll would make his day better.

"Rouladen for the ladies club."

"They won't miss one." Friedrich tried to grin, but his face wasn't used to stretching that way and he felt like a wolf exposing his teeth.

"Yes they will." She ignored the wolf grin. "The dish won't look right."

Friedrich hung his head. There was no point in asking again. Mother's decisions were final. That empty feeling he always got after talking to her weighed in. If only he had a Mother who loved him as a Mother should. He was half hollow, flimsy in the parts where she didn't build him. It would be easier to stop expecting anything, since she never gave even a little.

Mother sniffed at the air and wrinkled her nose. "The air is not fresh," she said, cranking the window wide open, and dashed out with his shirt.

Friedrich glanced at his bureau. His Innovative Award certificate, Papa's old toy trains, and Albert's basement map were lined in their places. He picked up a train and spun the little wheels. They glided perfectly. He liked to think about Papa playing with his cherished toys when he was a boy.

Friedrich spun the wheels a few more times and put down the train. *Enough about Mother*, he thought, and refocused on the project. He grabbed his birthday pencil and started jotting notes. Friedrich needed to win this contest. He was tired of being afraid of Günter.

Friedrich mapped out a solution that looked like one

straight, simple line. Every step was easy except for the first: rescuing his supplies. Since service hours started in an hour, he didn't have time to fetch the supplies today. He could get them tomorrow, but what if the spy was there? The spy would get a better look at him. News that he was a coward would travel faster than Mother running to buy soap. If he stayed away for a week, maybe the spy wouldn't remember him. But the animals would claw at them if he left the supplies for too long.

Friedrich checked the calendar. Summer ended in a few weeks. He scanned his project notes and calculated the time he needed to finish building and testing.

"Muddy Hell," he whispered. He needed every day to finish by Günter's deadline. He'd have to go back tomorrow. The spy could recognize him, but the project was too important.

"Stupid, stupid Friedrich." He spotted his reflection in the mirror and placed a hand over his eyebrow. It twitched so much, it looked as if it would fly away. He wished he could fly away with it instead of facing what would come.

10. Emil's Claim

Emil squatted in the quiet graveyard. He traced the carved letters on a tombstone with a long, crooked stick. Today was the second anniversary of Opa's death. His family didn't have to visit the grave since Vati said reciting the Mourner's Kaddish prayer would be enough, but Mama insisted. She wanted to check up on Opa's grave to do what she called *remembering*. It seemed silly she came all this way to do her remembering; Emil could remember Opa anytime. His stories, his smell, his laugh, his hands. It was all as fresh as if Emil saw him yesterday. Sometimes Emil stretched his mind for a little detail, like on which Hanukah night Opa gave him his favorite marble with crimson swirls, but most times Opa just jumped into his head. That kind of remembering made Opa still seem alive. Like he was in another room, but could pop in any minute. The cemetery kind of remembering made Opa feel far away.

"Exactly how many Americans wrote they wouldn't sponsor you?" He heard Uncle Leo ask Mama. Uncle Leo had been grumpy for a week. Vati said it was because of that synagogue that burnt down in Nuremberg. Uncle Leo lived there when he was young and used to go inside that very temple all the time. Emil couldn't blame him for being grouchy. Even Emil's stomach hurt when he saw the picture of thick black smoke pouring out of its windows in the newspaper.

"There are some who haven't written," Mama said. "It takes time for this kind of consideration." Her voice came sharp and high, like it did when Emil got into mishaps.

"And I suppose you still haven't heard anything about the visas," Uncle Leo snapped.

Emil sidestepped a few tombstones away from his family. He didn't want to hear the rest. He knew how quickly Mama's high-pitched voice turned into her enough-is-enough voice. Emil turned his back on Vati, Mama, Uncle Leo, and Sarah hovering over the hefty tombstone they called Opa and slipped to the next row of stones. Emil wished he could take Opa with him. He was sure Opa didn't want to hear their squabbling either.

Emil inhaled the sweet, earthy smell. It was piney and natural, not rotten, which was good since he didn't want to think about being surrounded by dead people. The fresh scent made him long for the river. For nearly two weeks, he had been determined to go back to his spot. Every day he promised himself he would do it tomorrow. But when tomorrow came, he was too scared to face the Jungvolk boy.

"It's time, Emil," Vati called, interrupting his thoughts.

Emil turned toward his family. As part of remembering,

everyone was supposed to place a small stone on top of Opa's tombstone when they visited. His hand searched for the small stone he had put in his pocket earlier. He felt every part of his pocket, even in the folds and corners where his marbles sometimes hid, but there was no stone.

"You lost it, didn't you?" Sarah said.

Since everybody who visited someone in the grave-yard was supposed to do this, finding an unclaimed stone in a Jewish cemetery was harder than finding a marble in a river. That's why his family always collected stones near home to bring along.

Emil walked back to Opa and saw four little stones on top of his tombstone. A space was left for Emil's.

"What happened to your stone?" Sarah asked.

Emil looked around. Plenty of stones sat on top of other tombstones.

"I'll just take one from Mrs. Reichstein," Emil said eyeing Opa's neighbor. "She won't miss it."

"Doch!" Uncle Leo said.

"You can't do that," Sarah said.

"Absolutely not," Vati said.

"Everyone calm down," Mama said opening her purse. Her hand moved around inside and came out holding a stone. "I just happen to have a just-in-case stone."

"Mama," Sarah said. "The things you do for him!"

Vati smiled and kissed Mama on the cheek and said, "As sweet as a Spanish honey cake."

Emil took the stone.

"Mama, you can't carry around stones in your purse. It will hurt your back," Sarah said.

"I carried you around for nine months and my back was fine. It will take more than one little stone to hurt me."

Sarah grunted.

Mama reached for her children. She held Emil with one hand and Sarah with the other. "To remember your Opa," she said.

Emil turned the gray stone over his palm to make sure it was a good one. He felt four sets of eyes coax him on, so he placed it on top of Opa's tombstone, figuring it was okay even if it wasn't perfect because Opa liked anything Emil gave him. When he stepped back, he was surprised to feel a connection, like Opa knew he was there. Giving Opa something real was nice.

There was nothing else to do so Emil asked, "Can we go?"

"In a few minutes," Mama said.

"You can explore," Vati said.

Emil leapt off. The graveyard was disorderly and wild. Overgrown grasses wrapped around tombstones, which made it seem like nature was trying to swallow up civilization. Tombstones of all different sizes and ages were packed together side by side. Older ones covered in light green moss leaned in different directions, while straight, new ones were crammed in between. The really ancient ones were so worn, all the letters had rubbed off.

Emil made it past six tombstones before Uncle Leo called, "Don't disturb anything!"

"What's there to disturb?" Emil called back at the same time he stepped on wild ivy growing in front of Lina Katz's tombstone. It was a newer-looking tombstone and had a single Jewish star in a circle carved in the center.

"Oopsie Doopsie," Emil said to himself and glanced back to see if Uncle Leo saw. He was speaking to Mama, so Emil knew he didn't.

The ivy spread all over Mrs. Katz's tombstone like a blanket, so Emil figured she wouldn't mind a few little trampled leaves. But just in case, he whispered, "Sorry Mrs. Katz," and bent down to fluff up the squashed leaves.

He was about to stand when he noticed a small stone on the ground. An empty spot in between other stones stood out on top of her tombstone. Emil wondered if the fallen stone broke the connection between Mrs. Katz and whomever gave it to her. Emil would hate for that to happen to the stone he gave Opa. He picked up Mrs. Katz's stone and carefully placed it where it belonged. He never knew Mrs. Katz, and probably didn't know the person who visited her, but he wanted to help. He walked to the next tombstone, Mr. Josef Gruenstein. Two little stones lay on the ground in front. Emil picked them up and placed them where they belonged. He scanned the ground all around and spotted fallen stones everywhere. So many lost connections between people who loved each other! He scurried from one tombstone to the next, picking up stones.

"Come Emil," Mama called. "It's time to go home and light candles for Opa."

"I'm not finished!" Emil shouted. He couldn't stop putting stones in their rightful place.

He thought he heard Mama say, "Let him be. We have a few minutes to spare." He sensed his family watching him, but didn't care. He needed to finish.

The click of Vati's pocket watch opening and closing echoed through the peaceful graveyard. A short while later, Vati called out, "Emil Abraham Rosen! It is time to go home!" When Emil didn't answer, Vati added, "and time for lunch!"

When Emil still didn't answer he heard Vati say, "Get your brother."

Sarah stumbled through the uneven ground to reach him. "Come on, Vati is hungry. He said he'll tell his war scar story if he doesn't get food soon."

Without stopping, Emil said, "I have to pick up the stones. People came all this way to visit and their stones fell off."

Sarah watched Emil as he increased his speed.

"Emil, it happens when it's windy. They just slide off." Sarah looked at the sky. "The next time it's windy, the stones will fall again."

Emil turned to look at his stone on top of Opa's tombstone.

"It's okay," she said. "It happens to everyone."

"But . . ." Emil started to protest, but couldn't organize his thoughts. Emil knew helping was the right thing to do. He knew it like he knew the difference between pickles and pie. The right thing had never been clear to him, so now that it was, he couldn't ignore it. But Sarah's words also made sense. If it rains tomorrow, should he come back and fix everything all over? And then after that? How could two opposite ideas both make sense?

Sarah took his hand and pulled him toward their parents. "We'll miss the trolley."

Emil felt like he had a duty to all the people who were buried in the graveyard, but he was already exhausted. The endless task would have him fighting forever against the will of the world. He glanced at his family. He had a duty to them too.

"Come." Sarah gently tugged on his arm. "It's okay."

Emil surrendered. It did not feel okay, but his head was too full and too confused. He followed her to their family and then onto the trolley for home. He followed her through Hannover's streets to their apartment building. And up the stairs and to the table. And as he ate potato salad and dark bread, the feeling of it not being okay stayed with him. The stones had a specific place in the world and it didn't seem right they were pushed out.

After lunch, he lay on his bed thinking about it for an hour until Sarah pushed his door open and said, "Mama and Vati are talking about you, you know."

Emil hated when his family talked about him. It made him feel like a baby. They would blow up a small thing and then fuss about his health all day. It started with everyone agreeing he looked pale and end with a noisy debate about his poop.

"Snap out of it! You'll get Mama worried!" Sarah clomped off and called back, "Sometimes forces just push things out of their place, that's all."

He sat straight up bed and repeated, "Forces push things out of their place." That was it!

His thoughts unclouded like an evil spell had been broken. He was a fallen stone! He was the one who had been pushed out of his place in the world. His world hadn't been right all this time he wasn't at the river. He had to return to where he belonged. Right now.

Mama always said courage was fleeting, so seize it when it came. If he could help strangers in the graveyard, he should be able to help himself. He tore off his fancy clothes and threw on his outside clothes.

He raced to the living room and said, "I'm going for a bike ride!"

"You look pale, Liebchen," Mama said. "Did you have a bowel movement today?"

"Was it normal? You know, not too loose?" Vati asked.

"It should look like a brown, stubby snake," Uncle Leo said.

"Yes, Emil, was it shaped like a stubby snake?" Sarah looked like she would burst with laughter.

The house felt smaller than ever. Four people waited for his response like it would determine life or death. Not knowing any of the answers, he hollered, "Sure!" and stretched his smile as far as it would go. He waved his hands around like a person with lots of energy, thinking that would show them he felt fine.

Emil added, "Outside has lots of fresh air!"

"Why, yes." Mama fixed her eyes on Emil's wildly waving hand. He slowed it down so they wouldn't have anything else to talk about.

"Did you study your Hebrew?" Mama asked.

"Of course," Emil said, figuring that thinking of studying just about counted as studying.

"What about piano? Mrs. Müller will be here tomorrow."

"I'll do it after supper!" Emil said as he rushed toward the door.

Sarah said, "See Mama. He's um, fine," as the door clicked shut behind him.

Emil dragged his bike out of the basement so quickly the musty cellar air didn't make him sneeze. He jumped on it like a knight riding into battle and raced through the streets. "It's my place in the world," he said to himself over and over to seal every bit of bravery inside him.

He made it to his spot and ran through the path. He couldn't slow down. If he did, he would back out like every other day. At the end of the path, he charged toward the river, threw off his shirt, and plopped himself on the bank. Emil gulped mouthfuls of air, twisting his head to look around, expecting to see three, or five, or ten Jungvolk boys staring back.

"Ha!" he shouted. He was alone, wonderfully alone at his rightful place.

Emil dug holes in the moist sediment and felt as contented as a cat in the sun. He was finally free. It had only been a couple weeks, but felt like a year. The sounds, the breeze, the gritty earth transported him into that safe, magical place in his head.

That's probably why his brain didn't sense that the rustling behind him was not from one of those little round furry critters. Then a few twigs snapped at once, which was much more damage than a little paw could manage.

Emil's head swung around as if a train barreled toward him. A boy, wearing a Jungvolk uniform, stood watching him. This was no mishap, this was sneaky, awful trouble of the worst kind.

Emil had been lounging on his rear and was in no position to sprint away. In a second, the boy could hurl a rock and that would be the end of him. His body would melt into the earth, never to be seen again.

Emil studied the Jungvolk boy. His eyebrow twitched and his mouth twisted into an angry scowl, but he wasn't holding a rock. The boy wasn't even looking for a rock. And then, as if Emil weren't there, the boy dropped his sack and took off his uniform. He folded and stacked the garments into neat piles. Emil had no doubt this boy was the same as the one he saw last time. Then the boy unpacked bottles and tools and turned his boney back toward Emil.

After some time of the sun dropping, Emil realized the boy wanted nothing to do with him. He never spoke, only cursed every few minutes, and hunched over his work with such focus, Emil didn't think he'd notice if a bomb exploded. Maybe the boy was building something important. Maybe the boy was important. It appeared that if Emil didn't bother the boy, the boy wouldn't bother him. But as the boy fussed over his strange contraption, curiosity took over. Emil stilled himself and watched through the corner of his eye.

Long shadows reminded Emil it was time to leave. It would be best if the boy left first, but it was late, so Emil had no choice. Emil slowly stood. Keeping an eye on the boy, Emil grabbed his shirt and tried to take a step. But when he lifted his leg, a mischievous branch clung to his pants like it didn't want him to leave. Emil yelped and tumbled. Mud sprayed everywhere as he landed belly down in a puddle.

Emil groaned at the thought of Mrs. Schmidt catching him all muddied up in the hall. He stood and took a few steps to leave, but froze when he caught sight of the boy. The boy's eyes were locked onto Emil's. His smirk so spiteful, it felt as if he had tripped Emil himself. The boy may not be harmless after all.

11. Sounds of Silence

Friedrich strode past the boy who looked like he ate too much pudding to get to his work place along the river. Today Pudding Boy played the *PLSPLAT* game. He sat, extending his legs, and used his arms to prop himself up so his bottom floated centimeters from the ground. He held this position for a few seconds and then dropped his rear down, splattering mud everywhere. When he landed on the ground, he made a plop-splat sound, like *PLSPLAT*, which made him snicker worse than when Werner made fart sounds from his armpit.

Friedrich hadn't seen the boy play this senseless game before, but it didn't surprise him. Yesterday Pudding Boy projectile-spat river water from his mouth. He did it over and over, measuring each spray's distance. And last week he smeared mud all over his hair, shook like a wet dog and then inspected the brown patterns on the rocks. A cool September breeze made Friedrich wonder what idiotic activities the boy would think up when cold weather set in.

Pudding Boy was allowed to waste his own time with whatever nonsense he chose, as long as it did not involve Friedrich. That was the rule. When Pudding Boy tumbled on a branch a few weeks ago, Friedrich saw fear flood his eyes. Right then he knew the idiot wouldn't make trouble. Friedrich had more power than he first thought.

But to keep control, he needed to establish terms. He outlined three pages of what he called Shared River Space: Guidelines for Association. He must have created twenty rules covering communication, acceptable actions, and visiting times, but then realized it could all be reduced to two simple rules to keep order:

1. Friedrich would pretend Pudding Boy did not exist.

2. Pudding Boy was not permitted to speak to Friedrich.

Enforcing rule #1 was easy. For the past seventeen days, Friedrich had not acknowledged Pudding Boy. Not once. When he worked, he kept his head down and ignored all of Pudding Boy's burps, snaps, and PLSPLATs. But Friedrich still used that unfocused sliver of sight on the farthest side of his eye to keep watch, just in case the boy wasn't as dumb as he seemed.

It took a whole day for Pudding Boy to catch on to rule #2. The first full day, Pudding Boy was like runny rice pudding, creeping all over the plate. He waddled over the river bank and stared at Friedrich's work. Friedrich ignored him. After some time, Pudding Boy began fiddling with twigs and rocks, tinkering more loudly than needed. Friedrich ignored him. Then the boy lay down, straightened his body stiff as a plank, and rolled back and forth. He spun over and yelped, "Ow! That's sharp!"

in Friedrich's direction. He rubbed his back in dramatic circles with one hand and held up a crooked stick with the other. Pudding Boy was not a good actor.

Friedrich raised a jagged stone high above and smashed it down on the flat boulder where he worked. The violent sound cut between them. Birds squawked and animals scurried. Then Friedrich continued his work as if nothing happened. He had to smash the stone twenty minutes later when the boy said, "It sure is getting hot, isn't it?" After that, Pudding Boy seemed to figure out rule #2. He still glanced at Friedrich every now and then, but hadn't spoken aloud.

PLSPLAT!

Pudding Boy wasn't tiring of slamming his butt into the ground. Friedrich ignored the *plspats* and spread out his minnow trap supplies.

PLSPLAT!

Out of the corner of his eye, Friedrich caught the boy's belly jiggle like pudding.

PLSPLAT!

Friedrich now found it hard to believe this boy set out to spy on him that first time. Maybe he was eating wild berries. Or burying worms or pissing in a bush.

PLSPLAT!

Or maybe he was hiding. Friedrich glanced at his Jungvolk shirt set far from the water. Friedrich knew how important he looked when he wore it. Perhaps to Pudding Boy he looked as important as Günter.

PLSPLAT!

Friedrich's Racial Science teacher taught him he was superior, so perhaps Pudding Boy was taught that he was inferior. It made sense he'd hide.

PLSPLAT! pppffffrrr.

Pudding Boy giggled. Was that a muddy hell fart?

PLSPLAT!

Friedrich gazed at his minnow trap and smiled a wide, true grin. After reconfiguring the trap sixty-eight times, it worked perfectly. Last week, he had found a jumble of odd bottles on the roadside a few minutes ride from the path. The glass caught the sun's rays and projected shafts of light, like a beacon. It was impossible to miss the sparkling pile in the dull September grass. He grabbed them all.

Why anyone would leave behind perfectly good containers was their business. His business was building the best minnow trap. His trap had been working just okay, not great. A smaller bottle with an open bottom and a skinny neck needed to be secured into a larger one. Then bait could be placed inside so minnows would stream in, but not be able to get out. The minnows could then be used to catch a proper meal. He had tied the trap in place every night and checked for minnows every morning. Results were mixed. Sometimes he caught a handful of minnows and sometimes none. He had planted the trap at different spots along the river and switched around the angle, but saw no consistent improvement until he experimented with the new bottles.

It had turned out to be a water-flow issue and the bottleneck size made the difference. He discovered the skinnier the bottlenecks were, the more minnows he caught.

PLSPLAT!

The project presentation was tonight, so tomorrow, Friedrich's life would be better. Günter had said, "The best will win." How could he not win? Friedrich had drawn up colored charts of bottle dimensions and minnow yields. He could explain how to chip and shape bottles with common tools. And he even knew of other materials that could be used instead of glass containers. Friedrich's project had to be the best. Tonight he wouldn't care if Günter whipped out his red notebook because Friedrich knew Günter wouldn't find anything to write about him.

Friedrich heard a *CLICK* pierce the soft river sounds. Without turning, he knew Pudding Boy must have gotten bored of the plop-splat game and pulled out marbles. Last week, Friedrich saw him play marbles on a flat stretch of ground. Side vision wasn't great for details, but he could tell by the pace of clicks that Pudding Boy played well. It reminded him of an old story he heard about a Jew beating German boys in a marble game. Günter was supposed to have been there, and had gotten so angry, he stole the Jew's cat. Friedrich never believed someone would steal a pet, but now that he knew Günter, he just might. Jungvolk boys had swapped the tale around campfires, but Friedrich hadn't heard it in a while. Probably because no one dared tell a story about a Jew beating Günter anymore.

Friedrich listened to the marble clicks echo above the streaming water. The unfailing click-clacks sounded steady enough to be a clock's tick-tocks. The marbles never seemed to miss. Could Pudding Boy have actually beaten Günter? Friedrich stifled a laugh. How could a boy who gurgled river water be the greatest marble player in Hannover?

The clicks stopped. Pudding Boy walked back to the riverbank. He sat and dug his fingers deep in the mud, raking sediment toward himself. Friedrich cringed at the thought of all that dirt caked under his fingernails. He couldn't imagine how any mother would tolerate it.

Friedrich checked the sun and saw it was almost time to leave. It was Mother's birthday and there was still time to collect flowers. He had never given her flowers before, but had seen other boys offer them to their mothers. The other mothers always smiled and looked happy, so Friedrich figured giving Mother a bouquet on her birthday may make her more cheerful.

He walked to the endless meadow rippling with browning-green grasses. Mother was forty-one today, so Friedrich considered giving her 4.1 flowers, but wasn't sure how to handle a tenth of a flower. He decided four flowers would be fine, since forty-one could be rounded to forty. Red poppies had blanketed the field a few weeks earlier, but were now dwindling. He walked past patches of half-wilted flowers until he found a lively bunch.

He bent to inspect. No flower was perfect. All the petals had spots. But they were still the best in the meadow, so would have to do. Friedrich pulled out his pocketknife. The rubbery stems easily relented against the sharp blade. After cutting the best four, he trimmed the ends, and tied them into a neat bundle with a wild grass knot.

He walked back to his supplies to clean up. As he packed, Friedrich inhaled the crisp air. His lungs tingled when they couldn't hold any more. Now that he completed the project, he may not return to the river for a while. He'd miss the views. The scene looked like it could be painted and hung in a museum. But even more, he'd miss the air that felt like it blew in from heaven.

Friedrich dressed and walked past Pudding Boy toward the path. The boy lay on his back splashing his hands and feet in shallow puddles. The hungry sun had turned his large belly pink. That was a view he wouldn't miss.

In just a few hours, he would unpack his supplies in front of Günter. As he grabbed his bike, his stomach suddenly felt like a minnow was trapped inside. Was his project really the best? Fritz could be clever and Günter did have a way of twisting apples into oil. Tomorrow Friedrich could wake up and his life could be the same, or be better, or be muddy hell worse. The only thing Friedrich knew for certain was that with Günter, anything was possible.

12. The Flagbearer

Emil waited for Sarah to return from the bakery with his midmorning snack. He tapped out a melody with all ten fingers on the table to take his mind off waiting. He wasn't hungry, but his mouth watered when he thought of sinking his teeth into a dark bread's chewy outside to get to its warm, fluffy insides. He loved slowly peeling apart the crust and sticking his nose in yeasty steam.

Sarah was taking longer than usual. Emil figured it must be busy outside because of the start-of-school parade. It was the first year he wasn't marching alongside his classmates to celebrate the beginning of school. Last spring a bunch of his Jewish friends were expelled from his public school. Only a few were left and he knew others mumbled that was still too many, so Emil figured he wouldn't be missed if he didn't march.

But the mumblings didn't stop Mr. Gruen from picking Ari Goldberg, one of the few Jews, to lead the class as school flagbearer in the parade. Mr. Gruen was the only teacher who said hello to Emil in the hallway. Jews weren't allowed to hold the German flag, but Mr. Gruen seemed to think carrying the school flag would be fine. No one but Mr. Gruen thought it was a good idea.

Even with the Jewish kids ousted and all the flagbearer

grumblings, Emil still would have gone to the parade, just to watch, if it weren't for his uncle. Uncle Leo hated parades. Mama called it a phobia. Uncle Leo once saw Adolf Hitler march past and now thought watching a parade was as dangerous as waking a sleeping dragon. He told the story as if he had almost died. It happened when a bunch of German officials were in town for *Stahlhelm Tag*.[*] According to his uncle, he was walking to the movies, minding his own business, when a bunch of Brownshirts jumped out. They ran down the street, blocking off cheering mobs. Uncle Leo was trapped until Adolf Hitler made his way by. Sarah rolled her eyes whenever she heard him tell it. Once she whispered, "Nothing happened. The man who hates surprises got surprised."

Emil cranked open the window and a faint thumping filtered in. The parade would start just a few blocks away. The children were probably rushing to their places. He bet some drummers were pretending to practice, but really just couldn't wait to start. The air smelled sweet. Emil thought of all the bakery doors opening and closing as people hurried to buy treats.

Emil's foot tapped. Maybe if he promised not to march and stayed way, way, way back, he could talk his parents into letting him watch. If Sarah came soon, he'd still have time for a quick snack.

---

[*] Veterans Day.

"What's keeping Sarah?" He asked absently.

No one answered. Emil glanced at Mama. Deep lines crisscrossed her forehead. She sat in the velvet red chair dripping with golden swirls, sewing Emil's torn pants. The chair sat on an oriental rug and was surrounded by fancy things Emil was not allowed to touch: portraits of dead relatives, a bust perched on a pedestal, and porcelain vases along the mantle. Mama called it the royalty chair, but Emil called it the cuddle chair since he felt like it hugged him whenever he curled up in it. He wished the chair would start hugging Mama because if her forehead lines got any deeper, they would all be in for a big Mama-fuss.

"I should have gone out into that crowd, not her," Uncle Leo said.

"That crowd of school children?" Vati said.

That was as heroic as Uncle Leo got. Emil swallowed back a laugh.

"The streets are crowded," Vati said, watching Mama. "She'll be back any minute. I could tell the story of how I got my war scar to pass the time."

"My God, no, Josef!" Uncle Leo said.

"Anyway . . . ," Vati said, grinning. "What was in that letter from Paraguay, Henriette?"

Mama looked up and opened her mouth, but right at that moment, the door opened. Sarah walked in clutching a round bundle. She stepped slowly, cautiously. Sarah set the loaf on the table, said, "Still warm," and turned toward her room without looking at anyone.

"What's wrong, Liebchen?" Mama put down her sewing and walked toward Sarah.

Everyone looked at Sarah, so Emil reached over and ripped off a chunk of bread. He shoved it in his mouth before Mama could stop him.

"Oh those crowds!" Sarah cried. "I'm exhausted from walking two blocks!" Her voice sounded like it did when she tried to get Mama out of the house for a surprise birthday dinner.

"Is that all?" Uncle Leo asked, peering over his newspaper. Light reflected from his bald spot and his glasses.

Sarah put her hands on her hips. "Really, Uncle Leo. Do you think the big important Führer would come to a parade for children? I've heard he keeps quite busy." She spun on her heels and walked out. She did not seem right. As she left, Emil noticed something in her hair.

"Such a fresh mouth, Henriette." Uncle Leo shook out his newspaper.

Emil wanted to find out what happened, but didn't want to worry Mama. He reached over to grab another chunk of bread. Mama slapped the back of his hand and said, "Wash your hands and I will serve you a proper plate with Würstchen." That was his chance.

Emil headed right to Sarah's room. He pried open the door without knocking and found her sitting on the bed, staring at the floor.

"Out," she said without looking up.

He slid in and shut the door behind him.

"What happened?" he asked.

"I told you. The crowds."

"Come on, Sarah. Are you eighty years old?" He stepped closer to see what was in her hair. Little bits of balled white paper popped out from her black waves.

"What happened?"

"It's nothing. I ran into some girls from school."

"Which girls?"

Sarah snorted and looked up. "Ursula and Gerda, okay?"

"You mean the girls who try to get you in trouble?"

Emil had heard how these girls raised their hands in class and told lies about Sarah to the teacher. Mama talked to their mothers, but Emil didn't think that did much good.

"Don't tell Mama," she said. "I don't care what they do to me, but Mama does."

"Did they spit white things in your hair?"

Sarah's hand shot up. Her fingers trembled as she plucked out the foul bits.

"There's more on the other side."

"Leave," she said.

Email watched as she picked out the last bits in front of the mirror. She picked up a brush and slowly ran it through her dark hair from top to bottom. Emil wasn't sure what to do. He didn't like seeing Sarah like this.

"Let's watch the parade," Emil suggested, spewing out the first idea that popped in his head.

"Not interested." Sarah put down the brush. "Besides, Mama won't let us go."

"She will if we promise to stay together."

Sarah didn't answer.

"And watch from far off," he added.

Emil stepped closer, but Sarah still didn't say a word.

"Come on, Mama knows Uncle Leo is just being dramatic."

Emil flailed his arms around like Uncle Leo did when he told the parade story, but she didn't smile.

"Ari is the flagbearer," Emil said, about to give up.

"Oh, right." Sarah looked up. Emil had forgotten Sarah liked Ari. Her face turned red when she met Ari during a party at the Bund last year.

"Sure, Ari," Emil said. "And, um, he'd probably really like it if you were there."

"Why? Did he say anything?" Sarah's face reddened.

"Well, no. I get an impression. Sort of a feeling." Emil had no idea what he was saying.

Sarah ran her fingers through her hair.

"Come on," Emil said. "It'll be fun."

"Okay," she said and checked herself in the mirror.

The name *Ari* seemed to have magical powers on his sister. He had to remember that.

"Let's go," he said.

Emil and Sarah walked back in the living room. Mama and Uncle Leo were in their same spots. A neat plate of bread and meat waited for him. Emil nudged

Sarah and whispered, "You ask. They listen to you." He shot over to the table and gulped down his snack.

"Mama, Emil and I would like to watch the parade. Together. I've scouted the crowd and promise you Adolf Hitler is not there."

"Doch," Uncle Leo muttered from behind his newspaper. Emil chocked back a laugh.

"The same crowd that made you tired five minutes ago is still there," Mama said.

"Oh, um, my tiredness passed. I'm fine," Sarah puttered out. Sarah was a terrible liar.

Mama stared at her the way she stared at Emil when he came home without socks. "All right then," she said. "Take sweaters just in case, remember your ID cards, and stay together."

"Henriette!" Uncle Leo exclaimed.

"They can't stay indoors all day," Mama said.

"And I thought you loved your children," Uncle Leo said.

"It's a children's parade, Leo," Vati said.

Emil mouthed *Ari* to Sarah with a full mouth of bread to hurry her before Mama changed her mind.

Sarah cringed, but said, "Okay, See you lat . . ."

"Oh, Emil," Vati said. "Before you go, I've been meaning to ask. Have you seen my special 4711?"

"Whaa . . . ?" Emil replied. He hoped his stuffed mouth made it sound like he didn't know what Vati was talking about.

"I think the parade's starting." Sarah moved toward the door and Emil followed.

"My empty Glockengasse No. 4711 cologne bottle," Vati said, "The one I've kept on the shelf by my bed since before you were born. That's what I wore when I met your mother. I've told you, haven't I?"

"We've heard that story," Uncle Leo groaned.

"The most beautiful woman in the world thought I was the most handsome man in room," Vati winked in Mama's direction. "Isn't that right? It was like all the colors leapt right off Spanish tiles and painted the world. Surely I've told you about Spanish tiles, haven't I?"

Sarah checked the clock. "Can we talk about this later?"

Mama looked up from her mending to smile at Vati.

"Why do you keep that old thing?" Uncle Leo asked. "We don't need useless items."

"Useless!" Vati said. "Whenever Henriette is angry with me, I show her the bottle and she falls madly in love with me all over. That bottle is my most functional possession."

"Actually . . ." Mama looked up. "I can't find my condiment bottles. The green ones with long necks."

Pickles, Emil thought. He needed to leave fast.

"And come to think of it, where's my hair tonic?" Uncle Leo asked. "Bottles are vanishing around here like slices of apple strudel."

They stopped talking and all turned toward Emil.

He sucked in his breath. Emil could not tell his family why he took the bottles.

"Emil?" Vati asked.

He wished he hadn't taken the 4711.

"I've got to keep the few hairs I have left nice and spiffy," Uncle Leo said.

Maybe that Jungvolk River Boy didn't use the 4711, so he could get it back.

"Emil, what do you know about this?" Mama asked.

Pickles! Pickles! Pickles! he thought. Another mishap. Four sets of eyes burned into him. He needed a distraction. Emil could make himself vomit whenever he wanted, but his family knew that old trick and Mama would be angry about the mess. His mind raced. Emil came up with nothing good, so he did the only thing that popped in his head. He raised his pointer finger, stuck it up his nose, gave it a twirl, and pulled out a blob of yellow mucus.

"Emil Rosen!" Mama screamed.

"This is not a barn!" Uncle Leo said.

"Give the boy a handkerchief!" Vati hollered, fumbling through his pockets.

"That is really disgusting," Sarah said.

"These are manners?" Uncle Leo said.

"Someone get him a handkerchief!" Vati screamed.

"Henriette, what have you taught this boy?" Uncle Leo asked.

"What a talent for trouble this one has," Mama said.

"Emil!" screamed Vati, pockets inside out. "GET YOURSELF A HANDKERCHIEF!"

Emil ran to his room and pulled a crisp, folded handkerchief out of his drawer. He wiped the slime off and ran out back to his family, thinking how well his plan worked. He'd ride the commotion right out the door.

"Okay, got the handkerchief!" Emil said as he raced through the living room. "And I grabbed an extra one just in case, Mama. Let's go! The parade already started!"

Emil grabbed a just-in-case sweater, shoved the ID card down his pocket next to his marbles, and ran out the door. He wasn't sure if the conversation had ended, but figured it would end if he pretended it did.

Emil hopped side-to-side down the stairs. He balanced on his right leg as he touched the wall and then sprung to his left leg on the next step. Every step came down with what Mrs. Schmidt would call a barnyard clomp, so he paused a few seconds before he took the next, figuring no one would mind the clomps if there was plenty of silence in between. But his fingertips must have scraped up a coating of dust on the walls because he started sneezing. He sneezed, then clomped, then sneezed, and then clomped until he was at the bottom.

Emil swung open the front door and plopped down on the front steps to wait for Sarah. The sound of happy cackling children, bicycle bells, and instruments wafted to his ears from blocks away.

Sarah finally pushed the heavy front door open and Emil jumped up to avoid being struck.

"What took you so long?"

Sarah closed her eyes and let out a long, even exhale. She opened them and said, "First I reassured Mama you are feeling well after she asked whether you had a normal bowel movement. Second, I said good morning to a furious Mrs. Schmidt. And last, I walked as gently as I could down the stairs while Mrs. Schmidt watched every step. Emil, is it possible, just once, to not sound like an elephant in the hallway?"

Emil ignored Sarah's question as the festive energy and sounds around him swelled into something too big to ignore.

Emil decided to try the magic word. "We don't want to miss Ari."

"Right," she said, smoothing her hair. It worked like a spell. She whirled around, raced two steps and then stopped as quickly as she started. Emil crashed into her back. He looked past her and saw what she saw. A pack of boys wearing uniforms walked straight toward them. They bellowed "Rotten Bones Are Trembling," the song of the Hitler Youth.

13. Friedrich's Choice

After buying bread from the bakery, Friedrich hurried upstairs to his apartment. The warm loaf smelled yeasty, but he didn't care to eat. He had lost his appetite in the long line waiting behind plump ladies pecking around their purses for change. He almost ground his teeth to nubs as the last lady inspected both sides of every coin she handed over. There must be fifty bakeries in Hannover and he chose the slowest. It would have been quicker to bake the bread himself. Fortunately he was already dressed in his Jungvolk uniform and still had an hour before everyone lined up for the start-of-school parade.

Friedrich entered his home and placed the bakery bundle in the kitchen near the birthday poppies he had given Mother weeks ago. They sat on a sunny windowsill in a little crystal vase. He had given them to her the same day he won Günter's project. He was so happy, he even told her all about the minnow trap when he presented them. Friedrich had expected her to be proud or at least pleased with the flowers, but after he was done talking, she just wrinkled her nose and said, "If only my birthday was last month when flowers were bursting with beauty." Now many of the petals had wrinkled and fallen and Friedrich wondered why she kept them at all.

A breeze swept through the kitchen. The few remaining petals clung on. Friedrich reached over and cranked the window closed, slicing off shouts and rumbles from outside. Once it clicked shut, Friedrich heard a voice. A man was inside his home.

The muffled voice said, "Hitler was clever. He said, 'I'll get you out of this mess.' The unemployed were easy pickings. Of course, starving men would follow. But then he went after our children."

Of all rooms, the voice came from Friedrich's bedroom. He craned his neck to listen.

"Don't tell me to take it easy!" the voice snapped. "Hitler shut down youth groups and started his own with shiny badges and hero stories. He took over the schools. Now he has his claws deep in them."

Friedrich never heard anyone speak like this. He treaded lightly toward his room and paused by the closed door.

The man continued, "It's gone too far!" Friedrich recognized the voice as one he knew from long ago. "If the Jungvolk want Friedrich during his lessons, he must go. If they want him during church, you can't stop him!" The words were angry, but the voice was too familiar to scare him. "Just think, Ute, with Friedrich we could . . ."

"He knows nothing!" Mother's voice made Friedrich jump.

Friedrich couldn't believe Mother would speak about him as if he was some drippy-nosed kid. He knew all about politics. He lived it every day.

"We can pick up where we left off," the man said. "And with Friedrich close, we could get information and . . ."

"The Jungvolk is different now," Mother said. "For the sake of you both, Friedrich stays out, Hilmar."

It was Uncle Hilmar! He was out of jail! Friedrich swung open his bedroom door. Mother and Papa stood in different corners while his uncle sat on his bed like it was his own. His blue eyes sparkled just the way Friedrich remembered, but his round belly was gone and his mustache had turned gray.

His uncle's face lit up when he saw Friedrich.

"Friedrich, my wonderful nephew!" The two-meter-tall man sprang up and filled the room. He walked toward Friedrich with arms so wide, they almost touched the walls. "Oh, how I missed you."

Friedrich couldn't move. Was this strange-looking man the uncle who had played with him so many times in the park? Or was this the traitor who spent two years in jail for speaking against the Führer?

Before he could think, the man grabbed him into an embrace that made everything melt away. It was his uncle. Memories whirled through his mind. He remembered how they talked about trains for hours. And how they played Chinese checkers after supper. And how he used his large hands to toss bread scraps to baby birds. And how Friedrich used to love that his uncle wore two different-colored socks, as Mother said, just to be difficult.

Uncle Hilmar released him and stepped back. As Uncle Hilmar scanned him up and down, Friedrich smiled at his uncle's ankles. One black sock poked out from under his pants on the right and a blue on the left.

"It's been too long. How big and handsome you are, Friedrich!" Uncle Hilmar turned toward Mother. "Ute, you've done well."

Friedrich glanced at Mother. He figured she'd look different with her traitorous brother in her house, but she looked as she always did: lips pursed, arms crossed, her eyes squinting, judging everything.

"I've missed you too," Friedrich said and looked around. "But why are you all in my room?" His room was the smallest in their small home.

"Ah, yes! I brought you a present!" Uncle Hilmar reached for a sack and handed it to Friedrich. "I came in to make sure you didn't already have it."

Childish excitement fluttered through him. No one had given him a present for some time. As he took the sack, his arm sank from its unexpected weight. He reached in and pulled out two shiny model trains. They were beautiful. He turned them around, inspecting every angle.

"Thank you!" Friedrich said. "It's very generous."

"The train cars have hidden surprises, like me." His uncle winked. "Take a look at the construction." He reached over and flicked open a little door.

Friedrich wondered how his uncle paid for these.

He had little money; Friedrich knew he would not steal. Perhaps someone owed him a favor. Like his uncle said, he was full of surprises.

"So," Uncle Hilmar said taking a step back and scanning Friedrich up and down. "That is a very neat uniform, isn't it? Must you wear it every day?"

"The world has changed in the last two years," Mother said.

"No, Uncle. It's just that we have our school parade today."

"So why not wear your school clothes?" Uncle Hilmar asked.

"Hilmar," Mother said. "Don't take risks."

Friedrich's eyes shot between Mother and her brother. "Because my Jungvolk leader told us to wear our uniforms in the parade," Friedrich said, but thought, *What risk?*

"So, you have no choice!" Uncle Hilmar clapped his hands. The sharp slap stung Friedrich's ears. "You see," he said turning toward Mother as he waved his finger. "Hitler has them all."

"Hilmar!" Mother said in a half-whispering, half-yelling voice. "Quiet!"

Jail had not seemed to change his uncle.

"Hitler's promises make them follow him like the pied piper." Uncle Hilmar wagged his finger toward the window. "He's leading our children down a road to war."

"Come, come," Papa said. "Let's not speak of war. I want to forget what we went through twenty years ago."

Papa ran his fingers through his hair, which he only did when he was tense.

Friedrich looked at his uncle and had the peculiar feeling he had been here before. In this room, with his family, having this conversation. But he was certain he hadn't. He listened to his uncle go on and on criticizing the Führer until he realized he had this strange feeling because Günter had gone over, step by step, what to do if he ever encountered a traitor. The Jungvolk would want him to exit the building. March to Günter and tell everything. Friedrich held the new train cars close and felt his eyebrow twitch.

His uncle smiled. "So tell me. Do you like the Jungvolk?"

Mother stepped closer. There was something Friedrich didn't understand going on between them.

"Naturally," Friedrich said. What else could he say? The Jungvolk had been a little better since he won Günter's project. Günter still eyed him, but had hardly been scribbling about him in the red notebook.

"The Jungvolk has not been so bad for Friedrich," Papa said in an odd tone. "They've instilled a desire to achieve excellence and a sense of purpose."

Mother snorted.

"Purpose?" his uncle said. "The children think they are helping Germany, but they are destroying it." Uncle Hilmar poured out words like a broken faucet. Friedrich could see why he got caught two years ago.

"Hilmar," Mother said. "The walls have ears." Friedrich realized if someone heard Uncle Hilmar, Papa would get into trouble with his work. Maybe that's why Mother was acting strange. He looked around his room and realized no wall was directly adjacent to a neighbor's. His parents' room was to the south, the living area north, the hall east, and outside west. Maybe that's why they were in Friedrich's room. Friedrich looked down. Neighbors were still above and below.

"Of course," Uncle Hilmar said softly, and turned back to Friedrich. "But do tell me. Wouldn't you at least like to have a choice? A choice to participate?"

Mother didn't hush his uncle this time, so Friedrich considered the question. He heard of a boy who was dismissed from the Jungvolk for not following orders. That would always be on the boy's record. And another boy had sticks thrown at him when he refused to join. Friedrich never thought about it before, because no one had a choice. But now that he mulled it over, he realized he did want one.

Friedrich's eyebrow twitched. He wasn't ready to share the dangerous idea. He needed time to understand it. He said, "I must be a member of the Jungvolk. It's required."

Uncle Hilmar put a hand on Friedrich's shoulder. The touch made his anger bloat. His uncle was gone for two years and, after being back for two minutes, dragged Friedrich down an awful path.

Friedrich pulled away. "My choice is to wear the uniform." His voice quivered.

"Then I am happy for you to wear your uniform," Uncle Hilmar said. "Friedrich, I've shared some ideas you may not be used to hearing, yes? Some people have them, but unfortunately few say them."

"Too far," Mother said barely over a whisper.

"I've heard of children becoming so intoxicated with power they harass teachers who don't agree with Hitler and even report their parents." Uncle Hilmar leaned in and whispered, "Are you planning to report me?"

Mother sucked in her breath. Friedrich thought she had been protecting him from his uncle. Perhaps it was the other way around. Friedrich looked from Papa to Mother and then toward his uncle.

"I am not like other children," Friedrich said.

As he heard himself say it, he realized how true it was. He stammered backward. The words exposed him like an old, dusty chest of secrets pried open. He was different. When children played, he organized. When they laughed, he analyzed. He saw inefficiencies and possibilities where others did not. He rarely connected with someone. How could he? He had an uncle in jail, a father who was rarely home, and a Mother who preferred housework over him. Albert had been his only friend. Years of feeling like an outsider flooded him. Why did his uncle have to dig up this buried muck?

Friedrich inhaled to steady himself, but couldn't get

enough oxygen. Opening the chest poisoned the air. He had to leave.

"I have to go to the parade now," Friedrich lied.

"Okay," Papa said. "And now, Hilmar, it's time to show off my new camera."

"Camera?" Uncle Hilmar perked up.

"Still can't resist a new gadget?" Papa teased.

Mother rushed out. The heavy mood vanished, but Friedrich's dizziness did not. He stumbled out of the shrinking room.

"Friedrich, I look forward to the rest of our conversation when you return," Uncle Hilmar called just as Friedrich reached the front door.

The rest? thought Friedrich. He didn't want the rest.

As Friedrich grabbed the doorknob, Mother's arm flung out. She grabbed his wrist and stared at him, as if trying to read his thoughts. He stared back until he felt like he would vomit.

"Yes?" Friedrich asked.

"I want to make sure your uniform is tidy," she said, not looking at his uniform.

"It always is." Friedrich wasn't sure what he saw in her eyes.

Mother stared for a few moments before she released his hand. She whipped out a cleaning brush. Friedrich closed the front door behind him to the steady sound of Mother's scrubbing. He imagined she was scouring Uncle Hilmar's words away.

Friedrich clutched the banister with both hands all the way to the bottom to keep from falling. He shoved open the front door, wobbled down the stoop, and fell back into the building.

Friedrich pressed his back up against the uneven bricks. Pre-parade clatter overwhelmed his senses, smothering him. It reminded him he was different. He covered his ears as he staggered a few steps down the sidewalk, but stopped when a low hanging branch swiped his face. He needed fresh air to fight through his feelings, but there wasn't enough oxygen. He grabbed at the blurry leaves, crumpled them near his mouth, and breathed through them until he could walk.

Friedrich set off toward the river, syncing his quick, short breaths to his footsteps. For three blocks, step by step, he tuned out the painful world. The suffocating blanket lifted just enough so that the noise no longer crushed him. He felt the bumpy cobblestones beneath his feet and heard bird songs floating above. But as his senses returned, so did his judgment. He realized if he didn't join in the parade, it would be noticed.

His loud uncle would also be noticed. He was noisy and as Mother said, the walls had ears. Friedrich stopped midstep at the thought of the Gestapo marching up the staircase toward his apartment. They would call him a traitor. They would call Papa a traitor. Papa would lose his job. Maybe Papa would go to jail.

Friedrich's brain couldn't keep up with the raging

thoughts. There were too many emotions, too many ideas to work through. Logic shut down. At the corner, instead of turning left toward the river, his body turned right. Instinct took over. Jungvolk training guided his legs. Friedrich was walking toward Günter's house. He would report his Uncle to save Papa. If he did, he would be a hero. If he didn't, an enemy. He was acting like an ordinary Jungvolk boy. This time, he would not be different.

It was easy. Friedrich knew what it would look like in the end and knew how to snap each step together. Friedrich would watch Günter grin as he absorbed the news. The police would come for Uncle Hilmar. Friedrich would be commended. The men at Papa's work would call him courageous. Uncle Hilmar would go back to jail and this time change his ways. He would come back home in a year with his hearty laugh and kind eyes and play cards with Friedrich until midnight.

Friedrich charged on, but another image popped into his mind. Even older and grayer, his uncle sat alone in jail. What if Uncle Hilmar didn't change? Friedrich's eyebrow spasmed. What if Papa thought Friedrich was making the wrong decision?

"Muddy hell!" he said.

The right choice now felt like the wrong one. His heart beat fast. He focused on the sidewalk ahead, meter by meter. Friedrich didn't know what to do. Why had his uncle put him in this situation? Any outcome would make Friedrich hate himself.

Friedrich turned east and saw Günter's apartment building at the end of the street. He had to make a choice. Step over step, he walked his steadfast pace. If he slowed, he would faint.

Uncle Hilmar's Would–Could–Should method! The idea exploded in Friedrich's mind. The technique his uncle taught him long ago for making tough choices would tell him what to do. He had used it when he thought about swiping sweets from a store and hiding Mother's scrub brushes. Now he would use it to decide his uncle's life. All he needed was a "yes" to each of the three questions.

Foot over foot. Two more buildings until Günter's.

Would I have the guts to turn in my uncle to save Papa? He felt queasy as he thought yes. Two more questions to go.

Could I physically make it to Günter's house and knock on his door without obstacles? Friedrich walked up the front steps and pulled open the main entrance door. He didn't know which apartment was Günter's, but found a directory in the vestibule. A second yes.

If he answered yes to the third question, he would report his uncle. If he answered no, he wouldn't. *Should I report my uncle for traitorous words?* His breath quickened and he felt his eyebrow spasm, but an answer did not come. He scanned the directory names and asked again.

Should I report my uncle for being a traitor?

No answer. Apartment #2, first floor.

Should I report him?

Friedrich swung open the door and stepped in the darkened hallway. He stormed toward the second door.

Should I report him? If he didn't, someone else would.

Friedrich stood at Günter's front door. He raised his hand to knock.

SHOULD I REPORT MY UNCLE?

As his hand trembled above the large, black number two, the answer finally exploded in his head: No.

Maybe it was because his uncle loved him. Or because he loved his uncle. Or maybe it was because Friedrich thought a person should have a choice to say what he believed. Friedrich couldn't make sense of it, but he knew for certain that he would not report his uncle.

He now stood at Günter's door with two yeses and one no and realized he needed to get out of there. Fast.

Friedrich took one gentle step backward.

"Idiot!" An angry voice swept through the dark hallway. Friedrich froze. He wasn't alone. The voice came from just around the staircase bend, but Friedrich couldn't see who it belonged to.

"You do nothing right!" Smack! Friedrich flinched at the unmistakable snappy sound of a face being slapped. Luckily, the voice wasn't directed at him. Maybe he could still slip out.

"I'm sorry, Papa." Friedrich heard a younger voice plead.

Friedrich took a silent, slow step. He didn't want whoever was around that bend to know he had heard.

"Never touch my belongings!" A balding, scowling man swung around the bend. The stringent scent of alcohol and cologne filled the hall. Friedrich flattened himself against the wall as the man staggered by, paying as much attention to Friedrich as he would to a fly. He watched the man shove open the front door mumbling, "Worthless son."

Friedrich heard the floor creak and spun back toward the staircase bend.

Muddy hell! Friedrich thought. There, standing in the middle of the hall was Günter. A drop of blood bulged on his upper lip.

Günter charged toward Friedrich. He grabbed Friedrich's shirt and threw him up against the hard plaster.

"Were you spying on me?" Spit flew out of Günter's mouth, splattering Friedrich's cheek.

"I–I am ready for the parade," Friedrich's voice crackled.

"I told you to meet me at the parade site." Günter slammed Friedrich against the wall. "You are not one to misunderstand instructions."

Friedrich turned to escape Günter's hot breath and braced for more pain.

"WHY ARE YOU HERE?"

Friedrich's mind raced as Günter tightened his grip around his shirt. He said, "I wanted to thank you for giving me the award."

Friedrich watched the blood droplet on Günter's lip

bubble and then drip onto his collar. Finally, Günter released him. Friedrich doubled over, catching his breath.

"One should be awarded for serving the Führer." Günter punched his fist into his palm. "Are you ready to do it again?"

"Y–Yes, always," Friedrich said, still hunched.

Günter whispered, "Good. Because we have an assignment. You won't march in the parade." Günter grabbed Friedrich's arm and dragged him outside to the sidewalk.

"The school selected a Jew as flagbearer." Günter grabbed Friedrich's hand and balled it into a fist. "We will show them this is unacceptable."

Friedrich felt the blood drain from this face as he realized what Günter wanted him to do. He never hit anyone in his life. Friedrich wished he could run and hide in those secret basement spots he found with Albert long ago. He wondered how long he could live on potatoes.

"Let's go," Günter barked.

Like in a dream, Friedrich watched Günter turn. His red leather notebook poked out of his back pocket as he walked. Everything moved in slow motion. Friedrich heard the birds sing and felt his skin prickle from the subtle breeze. Friedrich gazed above. Fluffy white clouds dotted an endless sea of light blue. The same perfect sky must be shining over his spot at the river, but it seemed far, so very far, it could have been from another world in another time.

Günter stopped and turned back to face Friedrich. "Is there a problem?"

Friedrich wanted to launch up and soar with the birds. But that was impossible, so he looked at Günter and said what a Jungvolk boy should say: "We are lucky to have Hitler weather on such a day."

Günter nodded and started off. Friedrich followed, wishing he had a choice.

14. The Burning Fire

The pack of Jungvolk boys advanced toward Emil and his sister. They snaked their arms around each other's shoulders and hijacked the sidewalk. An older lady stepped out of their path. Emil's stomach tightened when they started bellowing out that song.

"The rotten bones are trembling!" Each syllable fused like it was being sung by one person. "Of the world before the war!"

Emil willed himself to stay calm. Maybe these boys were like River Boy. That skinny Jungvolk boy wasn't bad. When he wasn't cursing, he sweated under the sun, blew his nose, and scratched itches, just like Emil.

"We have smashed this terror," they sang. More pedestrians jumped sideways as they passed. The mass of Jungvolk boys moved like a dog marking its territory. Emil's breath quickened. River Boy didn't move like that.

"For us a great victory!" They were a marble's throw away and closing in. There was no time to run. Emil and Sarah couldn't turn and dart back upstairs. It would look like they were fleeing. And Emil knew *the boys* liked a good chase.

Sarah gazed across the street, as if she weren't watching. Emil knew Sarah was hoping they wouldn't notice her. Mama always told them, "Don't look too long at a fire, or it will surely burn your eyes." He tried to do as his sister. But not staring at the approaching tangle of brown uniforms was like not looking at a dragon setting fire to a castle. Curious and horrified, Emil couldn't peel his eyes away. One by one each Jungvolk boy locked eyes with Emil.

A boy with neatly combed hair and sharp eyes was the first to stop. He stepped so close, Emil could see up the boy's nose. He looked like the leader boy.

"What are you staring at?"

The other boys formed a wide triangle, cornering Emil against the steps. Two boys behind the first and three behind the two. Emil wondered if they were taught this or if it just came naturally.

Emil didn't know what to say, but he couldn't ignore them. If he didn't say anything, Sarah would speak up and then they would turn on her. He would not let that happen.

"I, um, I," Emil shifted from one foot to another, looking at each boy. This was no mishap. Big, terrible trouble was here. They stepped closer and Emil almost bumped into Leader Boy.

"Well?" Spit flew out of the boy's mouth onto Emil's forehead.

The marbles in his pockets clacked as he stepped side to side. Emil groped around to quiet them.

Leader Boy reached over and shoved Emil's shoulder.

"I'm not going to ask again!" The push forced Emil's clenched fist, cupping a handful of marbles, to fly out of his pocket and stop midair near the boy's head. His favorite marble with crimson swirls was near his thumb. As the boy's eyes narrowed, glaring at Emil's awkwardly raised fist, Emil got an idea.

"I have marbles," Emil said holding them high. "Want to play with me?"

The rigid triangle collapsed like toppled bowling pins. Laughter burst out of them. They flung arms around each other's necks and fell over.

"He wants us to play with him!" Leader Boy yelped between hoots.

Sarah grabbed Emil's arm and dragged him closer to her.

A short, freckle-faced boy who stood right behind Leader Boy gasped for breath as he said, "Sure, we'll play with you. We just need to ask our Mamas." They crumpled lower, turning red from laughing so hard.

"Johannes, why don't you ask your Mama to join us?" squeaked out a boy with a large head and platinum blond hair to Leader Boy. Tears rolled down his huge cheeks.

Still chuckling, Leader Boy Johannes stood straight and wiped his moist eyes. He turned toward the others and said with an unsteady voice, "Come on. We can't keep Günter waiting."

The cackling and snorting bunch turned from Emil and Sarah. Emil didn't know he had been holding his breath until he heard himself exhale enough to fill a hot air balloon.

Emil watched them stagger off. But right before the corner, a tall, gangly boy who was standing at the rear of the triangle stopped. He whirled back toward them and yelled, "Hey! Maybe that's the Jewish marble kid? You know, the one they say beat Günter."

Through the corner of his eye, Emil eyed the distance to the front door. He had time to grab his sister and make it in.

"That story's not true," Big Head said and punched Gangly Boy in the arm. "That's just something the Jews made up."

"Come on," Johannes ordered without slowing. "We can't be late." There was no more laughter in his voice.

Gangly Boy held his arm where it was hit, but still watched Emil. Then he spun around to catch up with his group and they all vanished around the corner.

"Only . . . you . . . Emil," Sarah said, shaking her head. She grabbed both of Emil's arms. "Are you okay?"

"Dandy." And Emil did feel dandy. He just overcame six Jungvolk boys! A strange mix of relief and anxiety swirled up around him. He felt like a candy cane of emotion dipped in a coat of invincibility.

"I don't think Mama needs to hear about this, do you?" Sarah asked. She didn't look as frazzled as he expected. He wondered if this kind of thing had happened to her before.

"Nope." Emil looked up at his apartment's shut windows. Mama would never let them out again.

Emil puffed out his chest and looked toward the parade. Nothing could hold him back. He took a couple steps before realizing Sarah was not walking.

He turned back and said, "Well come on."

Sarah furrowed her brow and looked toward the direction of the parade, the same direction the Jungvolk boys had gone.

"Mama will know something happened if we go back," he said.

She didn't answer.

"Ari," Emil said, testing to see if the word still held a little magic.

Her lips curled into a shy smile.

"It's a big deal to be school flagbearer," he said. "We should support him."

"Alright." Sarah smoothed her hair. "It's the right thing to do."

They set off and before long Sarah slipped into her usual speedy pace. Emil had to hustle in a sort of slow-run, fast-walk to keep up. She led him past an old building where Jungvolk boys held service hours. The finely carved building loomed above them like a boot over ants. Emil felt a strange urge. He wanted to kick dirt on that building. Cover it with muck the way those boys wanted to cover him. Emil had never felt such an impulse.

He rotated his head to see if anyone was looking.

No one. Not even Sarah. He stepped once more and when he passed the front door, his foot took aim at a clump of dirt. But when his foot came down, he missed. It swished past and scraped up the top layer. A puff of dust ballooned to the size of an egg and disintegrated a second later. It never reached the building. Emil still smirked at his first ever rebellion.

As Emil and Sarah approached the parade, they found it had already started. Clatter filled the city. The ground vibrated. A wall of parents breaking from their day lined the street's edge.

"Let's stand there." Sarah pointed to an opening toward the front of the crowd.

Emil almost reminded her about their promise to Mama to watch from afar, but he wanted to be close too.

"So Ari can see you?"

Sarah ignored him and they slinked through the maze of people until they reached the front. Younger school children marching in unison were streaming by. Emil figured Ari must be coming soon in the older group. Emil waved his arms and cheered just like everyone else. The parade's beat pulsed through him. Belonging felt nice.

Emil looked past the marching children and gazed at the sea of smiling, clapping onlookers facing him from the opposite side of the street. He squinted in a way so it seemed like they applauded him. A snowy haired lady grinned and waved. He imagined it was Mrs. Schmidt and waved back. It probably looked like he was waving to the marchers.

Emil was so busy waving to spectators across the street, he hadn't noticed Ari drawing near. Suddenly, a shout sliced through the collective beat. Then more shouts. Cheering funneled down to a murmur. Everyone strained their necks to see what was happening. Right at the center, Emil saw Ari gripping the school-flag pole with both hands, standing nose-to-nose with a blond boy in a uniform. The boy blocked Ari's path. All the marchers behind Ari had to stop, so a big bunch of children clustered behind. The blond boy looked as if he wanted to snatch the flag. Ari looked as if he would crash the flag down on the boy's head before he would let that happen.

The uniformed boy was facing the opposite direction and screamed words Emil couldn't make out. A fiery red book poked out from his pocket and matched the color of his swastika armband. The uniformed boy circled Ari. The other children stepped back. Emil turned his right ear toward the scene. He heard fragments. J*ew. Flagbearer. Disgrace.* He didn't need to hear more to understand.

The silent crowd viewed the scene like it was a performance. No one did anything. The uniformed boy yelled, but Ari did not falter. Even from a distance, Emil could see Ari clenching his jaw and tightening his grip. The yelling boy kept circling. Emil could almost see his face. He wondered if it was one of the six Jungvolk boys from earlier. And then, with one more step, Emil saw him. It wasn't one of the six. This boy's eyes were much more vicious. They were the eyes of the older boy he had beaten at marbles. They were the eyes of the boy who stole his cat. They were the eyes of Günter Beck.

Just as Emil recognized those eyes, they locked onto Emil's and Günter's rage took on a perverse new life. Somehow, his fury targeted Emil and Ari. He looked right at Emil as he circled around, yelling at Ari. Emil was defenseless. It cut through him like butter. He wished he had listened to Mama and watched from afar.

Then Günter circled more and his hateful eyes turned with him. The chilling connection was broken.

A man who was shaped like Vati, but had a great round belly, took a step forward from the crowd. He called, "It's a children's parade! Let them march!"

Günter spun toward the man and screamed, "They cannot march! A Jew holding the school flag disgraces the Führer!"

"Children were never outspoken before Hitler!" the man said, throwing his arms up.

"Before the Führer, Germany was a mess," Günter said. "It's our hard work that's rebuilding this country."

A bunch of heads nodded.

"And how about the food the Führer put in your stomach?" Günter pointed at the man's middle. "Before, we didn't have enough food, clothes, work!"

Emil heard someone behind him whisper, "Before the Führer, children walked around with the tips of their shoes cut off in winter and begged for scraps like dogs." Emil wished that weren't true.

Günter took a step closer to the man. "Do you disagree?"

Mr. Weber, the music teacher, stepped behind Günter. Emil thought he would try to calm Günter, but he crossed his arms over his chest and glared at the man with the large belly. Everyone knew Mr. Weber supported Hitler. No Jewish student ever got a good mark on their report card in music.

The man with the large belly stepped back and disappeared into the crowd.

Emil felt Sarah's fingers wrap around his wrist. "Let's go," she whispered. Emil was about to leave, but heard Günter shout to the crowd. Six shorter boys in uniforms slivered out from behind. They were the Jungvolk boys from earlier! They stood like trained dogs.

The flag waved violently in the wind. "Ari . . . ," Emil whispered.

The boys stood side by side in a neat line with their fists clenched like little cannon balls. And there, not quite in the line, but not in the mob of onlookers either, stood a seventh boy. His uniform was the same and his eyes were just as cross, but his eyebrow jerked wildly. River Boy. Emil hadn't seen him since the day he packed all his supplies. At some point, Emil had stopped thinking

CRUSHING THE RED FLOWERS

of him as one of *the boys*, but here he was, standing right along with *the boys*.

Mr. Gruen, the teacher who chose Ari, rushed out from behind the other children. His steady, sharp claps echoed down the hushed street. "Thank you, thank you," he called loudly.

He faced the mass of onlookers and said, "The flag-bearer was successful. The school flag was held in the proper position! Now we will give another student a turn. It's a heavy pole and best to change hands."

Sarah tried to tug Emil back behind the crowd, but he wanted to see what Ari would do. Mr. Gruen reached for the flag, but Ari held on. The teacher got close to Ari and Emil saw his lips move quickly. Ari looked at the snarling Jungvolk boys and then at Mr. Weber. Mr. Gruen put one hand on the pole and another on Ari's shoulder. Ari didn't let go. Emil squinted to read Mr. Gruen's lips and thought he made out, "other ways." Finally, Mr. Gruen wiggled the pole out of Ari's grasp and handed it to the next, closest marching boy.

"Thank you! Thank you, again," Mr. Gruen said. A handful of onlookers applauded as the new flagbearer took his position, struggling to steady the pole.

Emil looked back toward the boys in uniform. They smirked and jostled one another like a pack of wolf puppies. All but two. River Boy stood frozen, staring at Günter. And Günter stood like leader of a wolf pack, staring at Emil.

Günter took a step in Emil's direction.

"Emil, now!" Sarah yanked at his arm, but his legs wouldn't budge. Günter was closing in. A monster was coming to snatch him up and swallow him whole and his feet felt like they were stuck in cement. The other boys jumped in to follow their leader. In just a second, they would reach him. Emil glanced at each of them down the line. At the end, he found River Boy. When he turned back to the front, he was face to face with Günter Beck.

Günter took one more step, almost passing him. For a moment, Emil thought he would keep walking and everything would be okay. But then Günter made a throaty sound. He opened his mouth and a yellow wad of mucus shot out. Emil heard Sarah scream "No!" at the same time he felt the slimy blob hit his cheek. He looked down and saw it drip onto his just-in-case sweater.

Günter walked on, not missing a beat, making Emil feel like he wasn't worth one second of his time. Günter said, "Still too many Jews in the schools, but not for long." Emil watched the Jungvolk boys pass one by one. They snickered and pointed as Emil wiped the dripping gob off with his shirt sleeve. Only the last boy did not laugh. Instead, his eyebrow flapped as if it was starting a fire.

15. When Words Came Like Falling Bricks

"Muddy hell," Friedrich cried, trudging toward home. He gagged at the thought of mucus oozing down Pudding's face. The skin on his own cheek crawled as if it had been slapped by Günter's slimy glob. Friedrich wanted to tear off his uniform and scrub the day away in a hot bath. His frenzied breathing told him how desperately he wanted home, the same home he had run from earlier.

His eyebrow convulsed and he didn't care who saw. Scenes of the parade flashed through his mind. Mr. Weber, Mr. Gruen, the crowds, and the flagbearer's eyes. Those fiery eyes. Ready to take on anyone. If only Friedrich could muster strength like that. And then there was Günter. He lectured and threatened grown-ups like he did the boys. And the grown-ups just nodded along, like they were the boys. Friedrich never imagined Günter's power could spread beyond their Jungvolk meeting room.

Pedestrians moved like crippled snails on the sidewalk. Friedrich wanted to thrash and shove them out of his way. He pushed through an opening and raced forward a few steps, but then had to dodge a tangle of small children attached to a mountainous woman. He was ready to start screaming, but then heard, "Yip! Yip!"

Out popped Brutus from a tiny space between buildings. The little brown-and-white stray seemed happy to see him. Friedrich stopped and moved close. Brutus bounced in circles, jumping to the same height each time, around and around. He looked like a windup toy. Friedrich almost smiled. He knew Brutus would run off as soon as he found out there was no food, so he let the animal spin some more. Friedrich finally bent down, feeling bad the dog might wear out. The dog sniffed Friedrich's pocket.

"Sorry Brutus. No snacks today." But instead of running away, Brutus tilted his head and squeaked, "Yip."

Friedrich tilted his head to match Brutus. The dog scooted closer and gave another yip. Friedrich felt an urge to pet the dirty animal. Friedrich had always longed for that connection he saw other boys have with dogs. He squatted, extended his hand and held it very still. Brutus could bite. The dog's cold, wet nose tickled his fingers.

Friedrich lowered his hand on Brutus' back. He braced himself for a bite, but as his fingers met the matted fur, Brutus wagged his tail. Friedrich stroked the dog. It must have taken years of neglect for Brutus's fur to twist into such smelly thick locks. Brutus looked unlovable, but by the way the stray put his paw on Friedrich's knee, he wondered if a person had once loved Brutus.

Friedrich patted Brutus, soothing the hyper dog and

CRUSHING THE RED FLOWERS

himself. Impressions of the day reshaped. As bad as it was, it could have been worse. No one got hurt. Günter didn't force him to hit anyone. And most importantly, Pudding didn't let on that he knew Friedrich. If Pudding had spoken to him in front of Günter, it would have been disastrous.

Another dog barked in the distance. Brutus spun toward it and stiffened as if he just remembered he needed to look like a tough dog.

"Go," Friedrich commanded. He knew all about needing to look tough. Brutus bolted down the street. Friedrich breathed calm, deep breaths as he watched Brutus' little body disappear into the city grit. Friedrich turned north toward home.

When he opened his front door, he smelled a rich, meaty aroma. It reminded him that Uncle Hilmar was home. Mother must have made what she called a proper German lunch with meat and vegetables.

"Hello," he called, heading to the kitchen. No one answered.

One perfect plate, crowded with sauerbraten and dumplings, waited for him on the table. It was the best welcome he could imagine. Uncle Hilmar must have arranged it. He stumbled into a chair and sliced through the meat drenched in tangy gravy. He couldn't remember ever being so happy to be home.

Friedrich mopped up every morsel and carried the empty plate to the sink. He placed it flat inside because

Mother would not want him to clean it. His dishwashing, she told him, was not good enough. He splashed water on top to prevent crusting and then the front door opened.

Uncle Hilmar entered the kitchen and bellowed, "Hello Friedrich, I'm glad to find you!"

"Hi Uncle," Friedrich glanced past him. "Where are Mother and Papa?"

"Well that's just it." Uncle Hilmar took a few steps closer and ran his fingers through his hair like Papa did when he was nervous. His mouth opened and then shut. He looked as if he wanted to say something. What now?

"Uncle?"

"After lunch we went out to purchase supplies for my journey."

"Journey?"

"You see, just as you left, I learned of an opportunity to continue my work." Uncle Hilmar paused and watched Friedrich. "I need to leave quickly."

"When?" Friedrich didn't want to hear about the work his uncle needed to continue.

"My train arrives in a few hours."

Friedrich hung his head. His stomach felt as if he fell down a well. He was losing his uncle as quickly as he got him back.

"Your parents are finishing shopping for me, so we can have time." Uncle Hilmar softened his voice. "It is best I don't stay."

"It is best for a person to be with his family," Friedrich said.

Uncle Hilmar placed his hand on Friedrich's shoulder. "Friedrich, I love you like a son. Nothing comes close to filling my heart more than our times together. But staying here will bring trouble."

His uncle's eyes dampened. "I must go," he whispered in a high, raspy pitch that made Friedrich feel like he was loved and betrayed at the same time. Friedrich watched a few tears roll down his uncle's face and disappear into his mustache. Each tear filled a tiny bit of Friedrich's emptiness.

Uncle Hilmar turned quickly and cleared his throat, "Eh-Cheh!" Friedrich jumped at the loud, old-man noise.

"So," Uncle Hilmar said, obviously trying to collect himself. "Before I go, I wanted to speak with you. To see who you have become since I last saw you."

Friedrich didn't know what he meant. Maybe he wanted to hear about his hobbies. He could tell him more about his train collection. Or his minnow trap. Or his mechanical pencils.

"Okay," Friedrich said.

Friedrich followed Uncle Hilmar to the living room. His uncle reclined in Papa's plush chair, folding his hands neatly on his belly, while Friedrich sat straight on the end of Mother's wooden chair.

"Friedrich, what is your purest truth?" Uncle Hilmar's eyes sparkled the way Friedrich remembered.

"My what?" Maybe Uncle didn't want to hear about trains and minnow traps. He seemed to love talking about things that were hard to talk about.

"A purest truth is an idea that defines you. If you change the people around you, or the time you live in, it would still be correct. It is a truth you think is right above all."

Was this a test? Friedrich thought. He had the feeling he was being watched.

"Germany," Friedrich sputtered out.

"No one is listening." His uncle seemed to read Friedrich's mind. "That is the Jungvolk's purest truth. What is yours?"

Uncle Hilmar was right. Friedrich did love Germany, but it wasn't his purest truth. Rebuilding his country had too many layers that made the world look right sometimes and wrong others. The Jungvolk, church, parents, and teachers spent years shoveling ideas into him that didn't fit together. Friedrich liked the idea of a purest truth and wanted to know if he had one.

"Take your time," Uncle Hilmar said.

"Maybe truth is a spectrum," Friedrich said. "Nothing ever seems completely right or wrong. It's always a mix. It just falls closer to one side or another."

Uncle Hilmar smiled and Friedrich felt like he said something right. "My clever boy, I think that applies to most things, but not a purest truth. That is different . . . Special."

Friedrich thought. His mind wandered to how frustrated he felt navigating the slow pedestrians earlier and then, like glimpsing a shiny coin in the sand, an answer flashed in his mind.

Friedrich said, "There is one true, best way for everything. A best way to walk, a best time of day to think, a best way to chew your food. And everyone should follow."

"This defines you?" Uncle Hilmar raised his eyebrows.

Two years ago, Friedrich would have changed his answer to please his uncle, but not today.

"Isn't it best to brush your teeth in order so you don't miss one? Or eat each food on your plate one at a time so you taste the real flavors? And for every person to walk the same pace on the sidewalk for efficiency?" Friedrich reclined in the stiff chair. This answer felt right and he was sticking with it. "There is one superior way for everything."

Uncle Hilmar rubbed the insides of his eyes with his thumb and forefinger and said, "I'm not sure I agree there is one best way for everything. And I'm not sure this is your purest truth. Friedrich, I think you may be following your mother's organized rhythm."

"No!" Friedrich was nothing like Mother. She was selfish and empty and understood nothing. Friedrich huffed and crossed his arms.

"Friedrich, I'm sorry if I angered you," Uncle Hilmar said. "But think about it. Did you always feel this natural beat?"

Friedrich couldn't believe his uncle was trying to prove he was like Mother. "Not when I was young," he said quickly, aiming to say something that would distance himself from Mother.

"That's right," his uncle said. "I remember a boy who rolled in the grass, kept an untidy room, and stomped in puddles. When did your orderliness start?"

"A few years ago." Friedrich would not look at his uncle.

"A few years ago," Uncle Hilmar repeated. "Perhaps around when I left?"

Friedrich turned toward his uncle. He wasn't sure where he was heading.

"And a few years ago was around when your mother started to be . . . let's say, very orderly."

"I don't know." Friedrich shrugged. Describing Mother as very orderly was like describing the sun as very warm.

Uncle Hilmar said, "She's always been an organized person, but never like she is now." Friedrich had never heard Mother's strange behavior put into words. He felt oddly relieved that someone else understood.

"You do remember a time when your mother played with you, don't you?"

Like seeing pieces of an old, torn photograph, his mind's eye flashed snippets of smiles and rosy cheeks. He did remember her laugh, but Mother had been Mother for so long, it hardly mattered. The past wasn't going to change his present.

"Friedrich I wish I had time to ease you into what I have to say, but I don't." Uncle Hilmar took a deep breath. "I believe you became orderly to earn back your mother's affections the way you used to have them."

"Ha!" It was such a crazy idea, he couldn't hold back his laugh. Friedrich was twelve years old, almost a man! Yearning for Mother's affection was ridiculous. He had never been a mama's boy and wouldn't start now. Prison must have knocked a few gears loose in his uncle's head.

Friedrich snapped, "How many minutes have you been home today before you discovered this?"

"I kept in touch with your mother and papa when I was in prison." Uncle Hilmar's face was serious.

"Uncle, it's not true."

"Friedrich, I will tell you what is true. Your mother doesn't think you are old enough, but I do. You need to know where you came from."

What did Mother think he was too young to hear? It felt as if Uncle Hilmar was about to open another old chest.

His uncle looked at the door and inched closer. He whispered, "Do you know what motivated me to take a stance against Hitler? To make me risk my life and everything I cared for?"

"No," Friedrich said, unnerved his uncle was whispering and surveying the room.

"My big sister."

"You're joking!" Friedrich couldn't believe Mother

had anything to do with Uncle Hilmar's crimes. "She would never have supported you."

Uncle Hilmar didn't look like he was joking. "She didn't support me, but she started it. Did you know she made flyers? Times weren't as grave as they are today, but there were still risks. She kept it secret from everyone. Friends, you, me. Everyone except your papa. Then one day I found them in her closet. Friedrich, it was like a spirit awoke inside me that wouldn't go back to sleep. I had to get involved. Hitler was getting more powerful, twisting Germany into something it wasn't. I begged to help her, but she refused. It was dangerous, even back then. She always tried to protect me."

Uncle Hilmar's words came quick, like falling bricks. They were too heavy to catch all of them.

"So I began making my own flyers. The more I made, the fewer she did. Then she stopped to try to get me to stop." His uncle jumped up. "But I wouldn't! Hitler was stealing our children. Thousands and thousands were falling under his spell. Flyers were no longer enough." His uncle's voice squeaked when he added, "What if he stole you?"

Friedrich's eyes moistened.

"So, I wrote on walls, went where I wasn't allowed, talked when I wasn't permitted. Your mother begged me to stop, but I believed that old saying, one does evil when one does nothing good. It was the right thing no matter how I looked at it."

"Your purest truth." Friedrich's voice croaked.

"When they caught me," his uncle said, "your mother crumbled. She thought my behavior was her fault. The guilt was too much for her. Your papa told me she cleaned the house from morning to night when I went to jail. I believe her mind twisted things around and she believed acting like the perfect German housewife would somehow keep you and Papa safe."

"That makes no sense!"

"Of course not. But think about it like this. When she was defiant, bad things happened to her family. So perhaps she reasoned if she behaved as our society expected a housewife to behave, good things would happen to her family. But now her behavior has ballooned to a scale beyond normal."

Uncle Hilmar crossed his legs and folded his hands. "Friedrich, this is why Papa joined the SS. Of course the money was better, but as your mother saw it, nothing looked better than a husband in the SS. Joining the enemy would throw off suspicion and keep the three of you safe."

"It sounds ridiculous." Words were flying everywhere. It was too much to take in.

Uncle Hilmar pulled out a folded paper, spotted with tiny brown dots, from his pocket. The edges were frayed. The faint scent of mold made Friedrich wonder where it had been.

"What is this?" Friedrich took the paper.

"Proof. It's one of her first flyers."

Friedrich's heart beat as if the paper was a live grenade. He heard about flyers like these. They were destroyed as fast as they were made.

"Open it," his uncle coaxed.

The paper trembled in his palm. Anyone caught reading and not reporting could be arrested. But he wanted the truth. He wanted to read the forbidden words. The paper crackled as he unfolded it.

"Anyone could have written it," Friedrich said.

"Just look."

Friedrich inhaled and glanced at the first word. It felt as if Uncle Hilmar had thrown him into an icy ocean. Uncle was right. It was proof. He didn't need to see the whole word, just the first letter, a "W." Each end curled around and around. Friedrich had never seen anyone other than Mother write a "W" that way.

As much as he wanted to read the message, he handed it back like a hot coal. It was all too much. It meant Mother used to take a stance, make chaos in order, care about other people. That was not Mother.

"Well, she doesn't think this way anymore," Friedrich said.

"I believe her heart is the same, but fear and pain crusted it shut." Uncle Hilmar stopped talking and checked the time.

Friedrich said nothing.

After some time, his uncle whispered, "Friedrich, I'm sorry. It's time for me to go. Your parents are waiting at the train station." He reached over and pulled Friedrich toward him. Friedrich felt his uncle's heart pound and tears wet the top of his hair. He didn't want the embrace to ever end.

Then Uncle Hilmar separated himself from him. He shook Friedrich's arms and yelled, "Don't forget how much I love you. Promise me you will never forget!"

"I promise."

Uncle Hilmar sucked in his breath and ran out of the apartment. As the front door clicked shut, Friedrich tried to inhale as much of his uncle's smoky sweater that lingered in the air as he could. After only a few breaths, the nutty odor was gone. Friedrich was alone.

Friedrich might never see his uncle again. His temples tightened and he felt his face flush. His whole body was uncomfortable, with parts numb and parts blazing at the same time. Maybe Uncle Hilmar thought Mother was a hero, but making those flyers was just another thing that made Friedrich's life harder. He was tired of dealing with the consequences of her selfishness. Friedrich didn't know what would happen to his uncle, but knew it was Mother's fault.

She took away Uncle Hilmar so now he would take something away from her. He puffed out his chest and headed for his parents' bedroom, balling his fists into tight knots to hold back tears. He kicked the hall chair along the way. Friedrich stopped in the doorway and looked around, trying to find the best way to hurt her.

Mother loved the nylon stockings Papa had given her. Friedrich could snip little holes in them. They would tear when she put them on and she would never know he did it.

He ran back to the kitchen for scissors. He opened the drawer, but the burst of red from the few poppy petals on the windowsill made him stop. They throbbed the color he was feeling. He inched closer. Why did Mother keep them? They were nearly bald. Maybe she loved them. If she did, he wanted to ruin them. He reached over and plucked off a petal. His fingers cracked as he crushed it between his forefinger and thumb. It didn't fall apart as he expected. He mashed it, squeezing it back and forth, trying to tear its resilient fibers. It just rolled into a crimson tube. The petal did not want to be destroyed, so he shoved it into his pocket. He would take all her petals. Mother didn't deserve them.

He grabbed a flower stem and yanked out four petals. Then Friedrich snatched a second flower, but before he could damage it, he noticed people stirring down the street through the window. Four figures and four large bags fussed around a car. Something about the scene made Friedrich put the flower down and watch. A man packed luggage into the trunk, but when it did not fit, he removed it and then repacked all over. A woman directed the man by waving a hand around. A little girl danced around her skirt. The man motioned to a boy. The boy picked up a suitcase and limped around to the trunk. It was Albert.

Friedrich wondered why Albert's family had so much luggage. It was more than what was needed for a holiday. Friedrich watched them struggle for a few minutes until Albert's father secured the last piece. He patted the closed trunk and signaled, "Let's go." He climbed into the car after the little girl. Albert's mother turned back toward their apartment and pulled out a handkerchief. That's when it struck Friedrich. They were leaving. Not for holiday, but forever.

Friedrich clawed the window. All this time, Friedrich secretly believed he and Albert would one day be friends again. The thought that they would never reconnect hadn't really entered Friedrich's heart.

Where were they going? There were almost 200 countries in the world. How would Friedrich find him? Friedrich pressed his forehead against the window and whispered, "Albert." He lost his uncle and he was losing Albert. It all happened too quickly.

Albert's mother stepped into the car. Only Albert was left. Friedrich watched. There was nothing to do but let him go. Maybe Albert would live in a place with no Günters. As much as he wished for Albert to stay, part of Friedrich wanted him to get in that car and race to some faraway land where he could have any friend he wanted.

An arm beckoned Albert out the car window. Albert nodded, but then turned toward Friedrich's building, and stared right toward Friedrich's window. Friedrich's heart pounded. Albert held his arms up over his head, spreading out ten fingers and crossing his thumbs, like a butterfly. It was the "I'm okay" signal they invented years ago when they explored basements together. Tears flooded Friedrich's eyes. Albert hadn't forgotten. Then Albert put down his hands and stepped into the car. As Friedrich watched it speed away, the last fragments of his childhood severed.

"Please God, watch over him," Friedrich pleaded with all his might. "Keep him safe. Give him everything good." Friedrich collapsed on the floor and cried loud, desperate sobs. He barely registered that the primal wails he heard were coming from him. Friedrich cried for all the day's losses. His friend, his uncle, his country, and himself. In one terrible day, his youth ended and something else, not as good, had begun.

16. The Certainty

"The boy is not progressing!" Mrs. Müller, Emil's piano teacher, hustled toward the door. Her legs took speedy little steps below a rounded body. A chicken smell trailed behind her. The farther she scurried, the fresher Emil's air became. Emil grabbed up music sheets and shoved them back in his portfolio. The papers creased as he pushed them in every which way.

"The summer distracted him," Mama said and shot Emil an *I am very annoyed* look.

Emil smiled, but thought, *Mrs. Müller's chicken smell distracted me.* He wondered how it was possible he could smell it over Mama's smoky Kielbasa lunch. Maybe she cooked chicken in the same suit she wore to teach lessons.

"It's October 16th!" Mrs. Müller squawked. "Mrs. Rosen, I will work with any child who possesses talent. Emil is not one of them. This arrangement will no longer work."

Emil perked up. That was the best thing he had heard all month. He would love for this arrangement to no longer work.

"He will try harder," Mama said in the same sugary tone she used with Mrs. Schmidt. "He will learn the importance of your lessons and how lucky he is to have you as his teacher."

Emil wasn't sure if Mama meant he was lucky because Mrs. Müller was a good teacher or lucky because Mrs. Müller would teach a Jew when everyone else had refused.

"Mrs. Rosen, he's shown no improvement and I've spent too much time researching simpler pieces. I'm sorry, but we are all wasting our time."

"Mrs. Müller, we could not imagine our family without your guidance. Your musical talents and reputation are among the best in Hannover." Sarah, Vati, and Uncle Leo smirked. Mama had said flattery got you everywhere with Mrs. Müller, but this was thick even for her.

"Other students his age are levels above," Mrs. Müller said, but her eyes twinkled. Mama's magic was working.

"I understand you put in extra work and we would like to compensate you fairly." Mama reached for her purse. "Grace and patience can only be expected from such a gifted professional like yourself."

"Why, yes." Mrs. Müller straightened. "Grace and patience is expected from a gifted professional such as myself." She was beaming.

When Mrs. Müller's arm reached for the money, Emil caught another whiff of chicken.

"He must practice every day for at least one hour!" Mrs. Müller wagged a finger at Emil. "No exceptions."

"Thank you!" Mama said, as the chicken lady made

her way out. "We look forward to seeing you next week." The door clicked shut and Emil grumbled. Mama always talked her way into getting what she wanted.

Mama spun toward Emil. "You must take this seriously!"

"Perhaps it's time to give it up," Vati said. "Clearly, Emil is not interested."

"Neither was I, but I had to do it!" Sarah snapped.

Mama glared at Vati.

"It costs money, Henriette." Vati waved a hand around. "Nowadays we've got plenty going out and not much coming in."

Mama spoke slowly, "As long as the piano isn't going out, my son will learn to play." She turned toward Sarah. "Just as my daughter did."

Mama walked over to the piano and wiped an already spotless surface with a cloth. The gentle motions reminded Emil of a mother grooming a beloved child. "We are still civilized, aren't we?" she said.

The room quieted and the silence reminded Emil of the old fairy tale, "The Emperor's New Clothes," where nobody spoke but everybody knew something was wrong. So much had changed the last few weeks, but his family never talked about it. Mama had hired a Hebrew tutor for Emil's Bar Mitzvah studies, since she thought it had become too dangerous to go to synagogue. His parents shopped for groceries together so Mama wouldn't need to venture out as much. Sarah read in her room more than she talked. And Uncle Leo now slept on the couch as many nights as in his own apartment.

Emil struck a key to stop the silence. Its richness filled the space, like a storyteller's first word. After a few moments, the vibration faded and quietness returned. He struck another key. It swelled from nothing to something glorious and then faded away like the other. Emil hated practicing and the chicken lady so much, he had stopped seeing the piano for the wonder it was.

"So, let's hear it," Mama said. "Practice an hour every day."

The word *practice* sucked the wonder right out.

"Every day starts tomorrow." Emil smiled. "And besides, I've already played for an hour with Mrs. Müller."

"You've played, not practiced."

Emil opened his mouth, but couldn't think of a good excuse. He squirmed and looked from Sarah to Vati to Uncle Leo. They grinned back at him as if they were enjoying a show. Emil looked at the keys and smelled chicken. There was no way out.

As his hand fumbled around for a music sheet in his portfolio, the telephone rang.

"Telephone! Better answer the telephone, Mama!" Emil said, trying not to sound too happy. He sent a silent thanks to whomever called. Everyone's eyes followed Mama as she rushed to answer it.

"Rosen Family," Mama said when she picked up. "Lina, dear! Oh, we are all wel . . ."

CRUSHING THE RED FLOWERS

Lina was Emil's Aunt. She talked so much, Mama never got to finish her sentences. Emil didn't know why, but Mama always tapped her fingers on the telephone table to the tune of Beethoven's 5th symphony when she spoke to people who talked too much.

"How's Herbert, Lina dea . . . ? *Tap-t-tap, t-tap, t-tap, t-tap*.

"Why, that's wonderful! It was yesterday? I had forgotten the date. When . . ."

Uncle Leo put down his newspaper. Everyone turned their ears in Mama's direction to hear about Herbert, Emil's older cousin.

"Real butter on the ship! How did it tas . . ." *Tap-t-tap, t-tap, t-tap, t-tap*.

Mama lowered her voice, but Emil made out, "No, I haven't told them yet, dear. I . . ."

The tapping stopped and Mama nodded.

"Alright then. Thank you for calling, dear. We'll talk soo . . ." *T-tap*.

"Yes. Bye dear."

Mama walked back and announced, "Wonderful news! Herbert left for America yesterday! He set sail on a boat called the *St. Louis* from Hamburg. Lina had a farewell lunch with him right on the boat and the food was delicious. They ate real butter from America!"

"Wonderful! He's grown into a fine young man," Vati said.

"How big was the boat?" Sarah asked.

"Is it safe?" Uncle Leo asked.

"How much butter?" Emil asked.

"Yes, it truly is wonderful," Mama said to Vati and then turned toward each person as she answered. "Sarah, the boat is quite large, I believe. Leo, of course it's safe. The *St. Louis* has sailed the ocean back and forth many times without issue and I'm certain that will continue long after this voyage. Emil, there was lots and lots of butter."

Emil slouched and looked down at his fingers hovering over the ivory keys. He was happy for Herbert, but at the same time something pulled at him, making him uncomfortable. Deep down, he wished it was him going to America on that big ship eating lots and lots of butter.

"Things are looking up," Mama said. Emil noticed Mama and Vati exchange sly glances.

"Looking up?" Uncle Leo said. "Henriette, you know their situation is different. Herbert was able to get that American visa because Lina married Rudolf." He snapped his newspaper open as curtly as he spoke and held it up so Emil couldn't see his face.

"What does that have to do with it?" Emil asked. He had heard the story months ago, but it seemed so boring then, he didn't bother to listen. Now it wasn't boring.

"Rudolf's father is from Poland," Sarah said. "So Herbert could claim Polish citizenship."

Uncle Leo threw his newspaper aside and barked toward Emil. "It's easier to get a visa from the Americans if you're Polish since the quota isn't filled up like it is for Germans." His face was red as a beet.

"But what about Aunt Lina and Uncle Rudolf?" Emil asked.

"Herbert will find work in America and then he can give his parents affidavits. It will be easier for Lina and Rudolf to get visas once Herbert is over there," Mama said in her calm-down voice. "This is wonderful news, Leo."

"Of course it is wonderful, but you can't say things are looking up." Uncle Leo pointed to his newspaper. "Look, they are still writing about that new law from October 5th that forces us to stamp a red *J* on our passports. The handwriting is on the wall, Henriette."

Emil didn't know if practicing piano or listening to his uncle grumble was worse. He glanced out the window at the rust-colored leaves dangling in the sun and then back to the lifeless black-and-white piano keys in front of him. He needed an escape plan.

Mama's forehead wrinkled like Uncle Leo's. "It will work out," she said softly and walked toward him.

Emil thought now was as good a time as any. Mama would never let him leave, but he had to try.

"It's sunny with fresh air outside." Emil pointed at the window. "I'm going to get some healthy, fresh air." He walked to the door, expecting Mama to fire out a round of objections, but no one said a word. Everyone was looking at Uncle Leo.

Emil was halfway to the door when his uncle said, "Herbert's my nephew and I'm happy for him. And you are set, but what about me, Henriette?" He wondered what Uncle Leo was talking about.

"Yes, Emil, go ahead," Mama finally said. Her eyes stayed fixed on Uncle Leo. "Remember your ID and stay away from trouble. And take a sweater, just in case."

Emil stopped. Why didn't she care about practicing? With all her new fears, why was she letting him out?

Then Mama looked up at him and said, "We'll have a discussion later." That usually meant Mama would speak in a tight voice as Emil sank in the red velvet chair trying to look like he was sorry.

"Go on, Emil." Did Mama want him to leave?

"Uh—okay." Something peculiar was happening, but Emil wasn't about to lose his chance. He grabbed a sweater, pocketed his ID, and shut the door behind him.

Emil tiptoed down the stairs. Ever since parade day last month, he'd been remembering to keep quiet around Mrs. Schmidt. As he crept down, he thought of heading to the river. It was a perfect October day and he aimed to spend as much time at his spot as he could before the weather turned wintery. He also wanted to see if River Boy had returned the bottles. River Boy had probably worked out that it was Emil who left the bottles and he just knew River Boy would return them. Like saying thank you for a favor.

But when Emil reached his bicycle, he remembered

it had a flat tire. When he grabbed it from the basement last week, a pin stuck straight out. He had tossed the pin and never told his family about the flat.

Emil kicked the sad-looking tire. Without his bike, he couldn't go far. Mama wouldn't want him going, but the Bund was the only place close enough to walk. It was on her growing list of sites she thought were too dangerous. Emil didn't even like the Jewish youth group, since everyone just talked about politics and table tennis, but he couldn't think of anywhere else. Maybe he could find somebody who would shoot marbles. Mama didn't have to know.

Emil walked a few blocks in the crisp October air. The cooler temperatures had forced a few leaves to the ground. Their bright colors contrasted the gray-brown sidewalk. Emil began a yellow-leaf game where he gave himself one point if he stepped on a yellow and took away a point if he didn't.

For a few blocks, there was so much space between the leaves, he barely broke even. But then he found a stretch of yellow-leafed trees. Emil's eyes widened at the golden carpet stretched before him. He jumped from one leaf to the next, racking up points. At the end, he found the next yellow-leafed tree was quite a hop away. He kept his eyes down and took a running leap. When he landed, he nearly crashed into a person walking in the opposite direction. Emil stumbled backward onto the leafless sidewalk. He was about to grumble about losing a point, but realized the person was wearing a Jungvolk shirt.

Emil's eyes darted to the boy's head. When Emil saw it was just River Boy, he was so relieved, he gave River Boy a whopping smile. Emil nodded and waved as he grinned, to show him how happy he was to see him. Emil started to wonder about the strange way River Boy glared at him, grinding his teeth, but then remembered Vati's glocken bottle.

He said as politely as he could, "If you are finished with the Glockengasse No. 4711 cologne bottle, I'd like to have it back, please. Oh, and my name is Emil Rosen. What's yours?"

River Boy stood so still, he looked like he stopped breathing. Emil reasoned he must be trying to recall where he placed the bottle, but then noticed how the boy's face changed from peach to pink.

"DO! NOT! SPEAK! TO! ME!" River Boy's words shot out like daggers. "EVER!"

He stomped off. As Emil watched him leave, he thought that maybe someone else would have seen an enraged boy in Hitler's uniform, but Emil just saw River Boy. It was like a thin, harsh coating covered the real person beneath. River Boy was not what Mama would call pleasant, but he had shared a special corner of the world with Emil and Emil was certain that no other boy wearing that uniform would.

And Emil still needed that glocken bottle, so as

River Boy turned the corner, Emil followed. Emil concentrated on controlling his movements. Toe-to-heel steps felt stealthier. Emil moved from tree to tree and flattened himself against walls. He followed River Boy around buildings and through crowds. Emil thought he hadn't been noticed, but when River Boy abruptly side-stepped into a slender alley, he wasn't sure. River Boy's pace hastened. Since there was nowhere to hide in the alley, Emil waited until River Boy's footsteps faded before he scooted through.

Emil poked his head out the other side. River Boy stood across the street with six other boys wearing uniforms. They surrounded what looked like a dead dog. The bluish-purple carcass was bloated so much, it looked ready to burst. One stiff, furry leg unnaturally stuck up into the air. A cloud of flies swarmed above. The boys held sleeves over their noses, as they bent over the animal.

Emil had never seen a dead dog, especially one this dead, and wanted a better look. The boys were so busy yammering over it, Emil figured they wouldn't notice if he crept closer. He crossed the street and gazed at the closest shop window, to pretend like he was window shopping. Emil found himself staring at ladies' shoes, which didn't help his act, but the boys weren't looking at anything but that carcass. He could hear them perfectly.

"Why does it stink?" a boy with a high-pitched voice asked.

"Organic substances are breaking down." Emil recognized River Boy's voice. "It smells putrid because decomposition releases gasses."

Emil stifled a yawn. He should have been glad River Boy never spoke at the river. He could have died of boredom.

"Decomposition is disgusting," another said. "There are a thousand flies!"

"It happened days ago," High-Pitched Voice said. "Why hasn't it been cleaned up?"

"It's in front of a Jewish store, idiot," a boy with a scratchy voice said.

Emil looked toward the far left of the window display so he could use side-vision to watch them. He scanned the group and realized they were the same six boys from parade day. Scratchy Voice was the boy with a big head of platinum blond hair and High-Pitched Voice was the boy who slouched and needed a haircut. Emil also remembered the shortest, freckle-faced boy with sharp eyes. And the gangly boy, who kept his mouth open too much and hiccupped. They all glanced at the tallest boy when they spoke. It was Leader Boy Johannes, the boy who nearly punched Emil on parade day.

"Günter was there when it died," Big Head said.

Emil's heart beat faster when he heard Günter's name.

"It was foul," Big Head continued. "Ask Johannes. He was there too."

They looked at the tall boy.

"It ran up to Günter like it knew him," Johannes said. "It started barking at his pockets, running in circles."

"He must have liked our uniforms," High-Pitched Voice said.

"You really are an idiot," Big Head said and punched High-Pitched Voice's arm.

River Boy tilted his head and leaned closer to the animal. His eyebrow began to tremble.

"The dog wouldn't let up," Johannes continued. "The filthy thing kept yapping and all of the sudden, if threw up on Günter's boot."

The boys squealed like pigs at feeding.

"Good God!" High-Pitched Voice screamed.

"I told you it was foul!" Big Head said.

"So what did Günter do?" High-Pitched Voice asked.

"He screamed, 'Learn your place!' at the dog," Johannes said. "It jumped backward in the street . . ." Johannes paused and looked around. "At the exact time a taxi drove by."

"Typical Günter!" Gangly-Hiccup Boy screamed between hiccups and made fart noises with his mouth.

"So typical! You should have seen him," Johannes said. "His mouth twisted in that way when he gets angry."

River Boy was silent as the other six flopped and shrieked.

"The best part was how Günter cleaned his boot," Johannes said. "He scraped it on the curb for ten minutes mumbling about inferior creatures dirtying his fine boots."

High-Pitched Voice stepped to the street. He exaggerated grating his shoe up and down, wailing in an ear-piercing pitch about boots. All the boys howled. All but River Boy.

"The funny thing was the dog had that one leg pointed right up at Günter the whole time he worked on his boot," Johannes said. "Like it was having the last laugh."

"His only white leg," the shortest, freckle-faced boy said.

River Boy gasped. "Brutus!" He clutched the side of the building.

The laughing stopped. Each boy faced River Boy.

Freckle Face stepped toward River Boy. "What's wrong Friedrich? Can't handle the decomposition process?" He picked up a stick and thrust it forward. "Poke it, Friedrich," he ordered. "Let's see about those broken-down organic substances."

"Burst it! Burst it!" they all chanted.

The boy's words looked like they cut into River Boy, reducing him into something Emil had never seen. River Boy stepped back and turned his face toward the stone wall.

"Friedrich's weak!" Big Head screamed.

"Maybe Günter should take a boot to him," Freckle Face said.

The boys edged away from the dog and formed a triangle in front of River Boy, just as they had done to Emil on parade day.

"Take the stick, Friedrich," Johannes said at the triangle head. His voice sounded milder when he spoke to Friedrich than when he had bullied Emil. "Poke it."

When River Boy didn't answer, Johannes said, "Maybe he ate something spoiled," to the others behind him. Like on parade day, the others waited for Johannes's cue, but not like on parade day, Johannes seemed to be stalling. Emil could see how this would unfold. River Boy would be unconscious in a minute, either from fainting or from being punched.

But this wasn't Emil's problem. He could turn from the old-lady shoes and run away. They wouldn't notice him. He tried to take a step, but Mama's kielbasa lunch churned in his stomach. His legs wouldn't cooperate. Emil looked back at the triangle creeping closer to River Boy. He felt a strange sensation and wasn't sure what it was.

"Last chance," Johannes said, wrapping River Boy's fingers around the stick.

Those two words hit Emil with the weight of a million marbles. Emil had plenty of squandered last chances and plenty of regrets. Now that a last chance belonged to someone else, it was obvious that River Boy couldn't let it slip away. Something hot surged through him. His body became limber and his mind sharp. It wasn't courage or anger or a talent for trouble. It was a certainty. A certainty that River Boy didn't deserve what he was about to get. He wasn't like the others. Emil knew what he needed to do. For the first time in his life, he would rescue someone other than himself.

He studied the group and in a flash, calculated a plan involving the route home, his clothes, and Mama's Kielbasa lunch. He took a deep breath and sauntered up to the dead dog.

The boys didn't turn from River Boy. Emil made a guttural sound like Uncle Leo when he drank too much milk. The boys still didn't turn toward him. Emil folded his arms and belched, loud and long. One by one, the boys peeled their eyes away from River Boy.

River Boy straightened. His eyes skipped between Johannes and Emil.

"It's that crazy Jew with the marbles," Freckle Face said.

"This is Jungvolk business," Big Head said. "No Jews allowed."

A few boys turned back to River Boy and Emil realized he had to act fast. He needed to give River Boy a sign. If River Boy didn't understand Emil's plan, the rescue wouldn't work. Emil shouted the only signal he could think of, "4711 should throw a punch after a vomit!"

The boys stared in silence.

"4711 should throw a punch after a vomit!" Emil repeated.

"There's something not right with him," Big Head said.

But Emil noticed River Boy's eyes focus and thought he saw a flash of understanding cross his face. Now was his chance.

Emil heaved down to his stomach and grabbed everything he could. He aimed and with the loudest barfing noise he could muster, Emil spewed. As precise as a sharp shooter, he covered his clothes, creating a putrid coat of invincibility. He knew they wouldn't touch him coated in vomit. Emil smiled. Part One of his plan worked perfectly.

Now's your chance to look tough, River Boy, thought Emil. *Let me have it so they won't let you have it.*

Silence.

Emil's signal didn't work. River Boy had to play his part or none of it would work. The boys would just go back bullying River Boy.

"4711!" Emil screamed.

The Jungvolk boys watched Emil with open mouths, as if their minds were trying to make sense of what their eyes saw.

Emil would try it once more, but this had to be the last time. He knew the vomit shield couldn't last forever.

Emil screamed directly at River Boy, "4711 should strike!"

Something clicked in River Boy. He rubbed his

uniform sleeve and stepped toward Emil. He seethed out, "Do . . . Not . . . Speak."

"4711," Emil peeped.

"Do not speak!" he bellowed. "Do not speak to us! Ever! Or I will kill you!"

River Boy lunged at Emil with swinging fists, but just as Emil had planned, he was far enough away. Emil bolted down the street as River Boy ranted on, screaming all sorts of curses Emil had never heard before. He sounded believable. So much so, Emil picked up his pace.

Emil glanced back before he slid in the alley for home. No one chased him. The others watched River Boy trudge back and forth, punching the air and kicking up dust. Emil saw Johannes nod and knew River Boy would be fine. Part Two of his plan was a success.

Only Part Three was left: making it home. The boys didn't touch him, but the police would. As Mama always said: "A person can't just walk around in such a state." Fortunately, Emil knew every side alley in Hannover. He kept his head way down as he ducked and sidestepped, never staying on one street for more than a few seconds. No one cried for the police.

As he tiptoed up his stairs, he felt big. His perfect rescue plan worked. Home was at his fingertips. Emil swung open his apartment door, like he'd been gone for years. He could imagine what a sight he must be coated in vomit and grinning like the Cheshire Cat.

Sarah was the first to spot him. She shrieked and then fell over laughing.

"Too much kielbasa," Emil called and wondered why she laughed so hard. Sarah had never been amused by Emil's body fluids.

"What is it?" Mama dashed from the kitchen toward the door to see.

"Emil!" she cried when she saw him and then started to roar as well.

This was not the reaction he expected. He had a speech all prepared about how he wasn't sick and just ate too much kielbasa, but now he wasn't sure what to say.

Sarah said through hoots and snorts, "Of course he looks like this when he gets the most important news of his life."

"What news?" Emil asked.

"It's happened, Liebchen!" Mama said.

"What has?" Emil asked.

"We Rosens have been in Germany for hundreds of years," Vati said. "Now it's time to honor another country with our presence."

"What are you talking about?" Emil asked.

"Our papers came," Sarah cried. "We can leave!"

"You mean the visas came?" Emil asked. "We're going to America like Herbert?" Emil's face flushed. Shame flooded him from the jealousy he felt toward his cousin earlier.

"Not the U.S." Mama turned toward Vati. "Oy! The boy doesn't speak a word of Spanish!"

"We'll get him lessons," Vati said. "We're not leaving until December 1st."

"Piano and Spanish lessons!" Mama said, dancing in a circle.

Emil couldn't believe Mama was talking about piano lessons at a time like this. "WHERE ARE WE GOING?" he shouted.

"TO PARAGUAY!" Sarah shouted back.

Emil wished he weren't covered in vomit so he could hug everyone in his family. He twirled at the door trying not to get vomit on the frame. Everyone glowed back at him. Everyone, except Uncle Leo. His uncle's eyes were dull, as he slumped in his chair. He smiled at Emil, but it was an *I'm-happy-for-you* smile, not a *happy-for-us* smile.

Emil stopped. "What's the matter, Uncle Leo?"

"I'll meet you there," his uncle said.

"You're not coming?" How could Emil leave Uncle Leo?

"It will all work out," Uncle Leo said, but his eyes told Emil something different.

Emil wanted to run to his Uncle, but couldn't. He stayed put in the doorway, chained by the vomit, feeling as helpless as his uncle looked.

17. Friedrich's Nudge

The world had seemed about 20 percent out of place all day. Friedrich's eyebrow first trembled this morning when he arrived at school. Everyone was going on about the anniversary of the Führer's Beer Hall Putsch. He never understood why the Führer wanted to celebrate the time he tried to overthrow the old government, failed, and went to jail, but it was a big celebration every year and his school seemed even more frenzied than usual. That was just the first thing askew.

After school, he raced home and found Papa sorting through stacks of papers from his old electric company. It was curious because Papa was never home on weekday afternoons and also because his electric business shut down years ago. Friedrich lied about not being hungry and shut himself in his room. He shined his model trains, hoping the world would sort itself out.

When he could no longer ignore his growling stomach, Friedrich came out for an afternoon snack. It was 15:40 and Jungvolk service hours started at 16:30. He wished he could stay home. He didn't want any more of the 20 percent. But that wasn't an option.

Friedrich entered the kitchen and stopped short.

The vase that was filled with dried poppies had been moved from the windowsill to the counter. It had never been out of place. The vase had even remained on the sunny sill while Mother hung what was left of the poppies upside down to dry out. It stood empty on the sill for a week before the dried stems reappeared. Friedrich picked up the vase and carried it back to its proper place at the window. He scooted it back and forth to center it perfectly. The sound of porcelain scraping on wood echoed through the quiet apartment.

As he nudged the vase back and forth into a flawlessly centered position, Friedrich wondered why the world was so skewed today. He tried to find a pattern in the numeric date. Maybe that would explain it. It was the 9th day of November, 1938. *9.11.1938*. If he got rid of a *1* and rearranged, he had 19.1938, which could be reworked to 19+19=38. But that was too many steps and wasn't really a pattern, so he started over. Friedrich didn't hear Mother walk in.

"Friedrich!" she shrieked. "Move the vase!"

"Mother!" he yelled. He couldn't believe she was really wailing about an asymmetrically placed vase. Friedrich had more patience with her since Uncle Hilmar explained why she was the way she was, but this was too muddy-hell dramatic, even for her.

"They can't stay on the windowsill today!"

Papa ran in. "Ute, what is it?"

"Friedrich, move the vase back to the counter," she

hissed in a low voice, like she didn't want the neighbors to hear. "Now!"

Friedrich was glad Papa was there. He would calm her.

"Take them off!" Papa ordered. "Quickly!"

Friedrich stood motionless, unable to wrap his head around what Papa was saying.

Mother snatched the vase and situated it back on the counter.

"He didn't know, Ute," Papa said. "How could he?"

Mother faced Friedrich. "When the vase is in the window," she whispered, "Hilmar knows it is safe to come in." She paused between words as if she wanted to be sure Friedrich understood. "Today is the Beer Hall Putsch Anniversary."

Friedrich felt like he was catching a glimpse of the way she used to be.

"Hilmar has been involved in activities these past few weeks and we don't know if anyone has figured out he's behind them." She was clever and calm. Everything he always wanted in a Mother.

"If Hilmar sees the vase in the window, he knows he can enter safely. No exceptions." Mother watched Friedrich for a moment before she added, "It's an old system we've always used. Today is unpredictable. Do you understand?"

"Yes." Friedrich's voice crackled. He loved that she trusted him.

"It is not safe for your uncle today," Papa said. "Every policing person is out and about; my colleagues could stop over; we just don't know."

"Will he be alright?" Friedrich asked.

"He's smart and probably isn't in Hannover, but we must still be thoughtful," Papa said.

"And you." Mother swung toward Papa. "You can't stay here all day. How would it look if you did not make an appearance?"

"I make appearances. I always make them. We agreed it was necessary to go beyond what's required." Papa ran his fingers through his hair.

Mother grunted.

Papa put his hand on Friedrich's shoulder. "I leave before he even wakes." His eyes moistened. "All for the sake of appearances."

"You must so no one will question," Mother said.

"And I pay a price!"

"Hush!" snapped Mother.

"Besides, everyone has been at the beer halls for hours," Papa said. "They're too drunk to notice if I'm there."

"Everything is noticed," Mother said.

It was strange to hear Mother and Papa talk about this in front of him.

"They just see me as a photographer," Papa said. "A silly artist."

"As you say, in the spiderweb of facts, truths are

strangled." Mother's voice softened. "Thank God you
are a silly artist. Now go and drink and toast and sing
their songs." Friedrich always worried about how people saw him. He never considered that Papa had to do
it, too.

Mother turned her back toward them and whipped
out a scrub brush. Her arm thrust back and forth as she
scoured the windowsill where Friedrich had scooted the
vase. He had probably left a smudge.

"It's clean," Papa said gently.

"We all have our parts to play."

"Ute, they won't take me. They won't take Friedrich."
Friedrich never heard his parents talk about Mother's
problem.

"They took my brother." Mother scrubbed faster.

The brushes in her robe pockets shook as she scoured.
Friedrich wished she would stop, but knew she couldn't.
If she didn't clean, she thought her husband and son
would be taken from her. How absurd that all three of
them trudged on like performers playing roles they had
never wanted. Their situation was like an incredibly tangled ball of yarn and Friedrich couldn't begin to figure
how to unravel it.

Papa grabbed his hat. He turned to Friedrich and
said, "Don't be late for service hours," and disappeared
through the door.

Friedrich looked at the dried poppies he gave to
Mother months ago. The few petals left looked so brittle,

he imagined bits flaking off onto the sill below. He said, "Fresh flowers won't make a mess."

"I prefer the ones you gave me." Mother didn't look up from her cleaning. "Don't be late for service hours."

Friedrich ran out of the apartment and down the dark stairs. He swung open the front door. Thousands of colored leaves struck his senses. Some dangled from trees, but most blanketed the ground, bunching along curbs and covering the straight cobblestone lines on the sidewalk. The colors were rich enough to drip right from God's paint brush, but Friedrich was too annoyed at how untidy the streets looked to care.

Friedrich walked briskly until he rounded a corner and a group of young children blocked his path. He didn't bother hiding his scowl. A woman who Friedrich guessed was their mother scanned his uniform.

"Children!" She clapped twice. "Let this young man through!"

They scattered and as Friedrich passed, he realized the children played the same leaf-stepping game as Pudding when he had crashed into him. "Idiot," he muttered at the thought of a boy his age playing a child's game. Friedrich still didn't know how to think about Pudding. He had saved Friedrich from a beating, but Friedrich never asked for help, and especially that kind of help. Pudding said his name was Emil Rosen. Friedrich snorted. Emil Rosen may be clever, but he was still an idiot.

As Friedrich walked on, the sweet and sour stench of alcohol told him he was approaching a beer hall. A lively buzz filled his ears. Staggering men in uniforms spilled onto the sidewalk. Friedrich understood why Papa didn't want to join. They slapped each other's backs and waddled about like ducks. Some laughed and toasted. Some cursed and argued. As Friedrich worked through the maze of men, he held his breath so he wouldn't have to breathe in their stink.

"He's dead!" Friedrich heard a sloshy voice say. "Of course, the Jews conspired! It was an assassination."

Friedrich figured they must be talking about Ernst vom Rath, a secretary at the German Embassy in Paris who was shot a couple days ago by a Jewish teenager. That's all everyone had been talking about. The teenager was angry because his Polish parents had to leave Germany and go back to Poland. The secretary must have died today.

A second voice slurred, "Goebbels said it's against the Reich and against the Führer himself." They didn't seem to notice Friedrich weave between them.

"It's unacceptable," The first said. "They all planned it! The Jews should all pay."

As Friedrich crossed the street, the drunken murmur faded, but the words—*the Jews should all pay*—planted itself in his mind like a pile of dung.

Friedrich was certain it was wrong that teenager shot vom Rath. The teenager's parents were Polish, so they should go to Poland. It wasn't like they were German. Plus vom Rath didn't have anything to do with deporting them.

The teenager should be punished, but why should all the Jews pay? Friedrich couldn't believe they all planned it together. He was sure Albert had nothing to do with it. Or Pudding.

Friedrich felt a nudge to do something. But what? He was an ant under battling elephants. His eyebrow twitched. Too many thoughts quickly tangled into an untrackable mess. None led to a clear answer. He was thinking in circles.

Friedrich spotted the meeting place and stopped thinking about vom Rath. The last thing he needed was to walk in with a trembling eyebrow. Friedrich rubbed his uniform sleeve.

As he entered, he noticed Günter whispering to Johannes and Fritz. The boys had serious expressions as they nodded along. The three glanced at Werner and then Karl. Friedrich hurried into his preferred seat. Located in the center of the third row, it was perfectly situated. The seat was central enough that Günter would think he was engaged, but back far enough to keep an eye on everyone. He sat and glanced at the clock. One more minute. He used it to watch the lowering sun through the murky basement window. Somehow its splendor shone in past the grime.

Günter moved to the front and snapped, "Heil

Hitler." The boys parroted back the greeting and as soon as they finished, Günter held up a tin cup. Before Friedrich understood what was happening, Günter hurled it across the room. Everyone jumped at its clatter when it struck the wall.

"We have a problem." Günter looked from boy to boy. The only sound came from a bicycle's squeaky gear outside.

"No, I take that back." Günter raised both arms. "We have many problems!" he screamed, slicing his arms through the air.

He held up his red notebook. "We have a duty to serve the Führer and I have discovered this has NOT BEEN MET!" His voice stretched and tore at the words until they almost weren't words. A few boys sucked in their breath.

"At a time when the Reich has been attacked by the most degenerative people, I have been informed"—Günter paused and looked around the room—"that one of you patronizes a Jewish store!" Friedrich's heart pounded. How did Günter find out about that pencil? It was months ago!

"Karl!" Günter screamed, slamming his notebook down. Karl hunched over and then sat back up quickly. He looked from side to side. The color drained from his cheeks.

"Stand up!" Günter shouted. "Explain."

Karl's shirt wrinkles disappeared across his back

when he grabbed the chair in front of him. He stood slowly and wobbled before Günter.

"I, uh," Karl stammered. "I . . . It's just . . . it's far . . . the other fruit store is far."

"Unacceptable!" Günter's word roared through the room. "Change your lazy habits or you will be dismissed from the Jungvolk. Sit!" Karl fell into his seat.

Günter scanned the room.

"We are not finished," he said. "I have also been informed that one of you enjoys the company of communists."

Friedrich grimaced. Who would be friends with a red?

"Werner! Stand up!" Werner shot up and hiccupped.

"But, he's my neighbor," he spurt out, and left his mouth hanging open.

"Unacceptable!" Günter screamed. "I don't care if he's your brother, there will be no contact." Günter glowered at Werner. His limbs squirmed every which way.

"Sit and shut your mouth," Günter said.

Werner flopped down, nearly kicking over the empty chair next to him.

"I am still not finished," Günter said. "I have learned one of you has parents who doubt the Führer's ideas. Who disrespects Germany. Who undermines what we have rebuilt over these last few years."

Günter found out! Friedrich's chest tightened. His body felt the way it did when the reds chased him down the street last year. His stomach knotted and the air was too thin to fill his lungs. Günter raised an arm and pointed right at Friedrich.

It's all over! thought Friedrich. *They'll put Papa and Mother in jail, just like Uncle Hilmar!*

"Fritz!" Günter screamed. "Stand up."

A chair squeaked from behind. Friedrich heard himself gasp as air rushed back into his lungs. He turned. Fritz stood directly in back of him. The short boy held his chin high.

"I have been informed of this by Fritz himself and it will be escalated." Günter's voice softened. "It is a gross misfortune to have parents with such traitorous ideas, but it is an honor that Fritz demonstrates such dedication. Had he not, he would have been just as disloyal as his parents."

Friedrich's eyebrow trembled. Fritz betrayed his own parents and Günter called him loyal. Friedrich needed to stay far from Fritz.

"Take your seat, Fritz," Günter said. "In case I have not been clear, you are not to do business or fraternize with anyone who contradicts the true and pure ideas of the Führer. No more warnings. I will deal with future violations harshly." Friedrich wondered what *deal with harshly* meant.

"Let us now continue with business as usual," Günter said. He began listing competition rules, and winners and losers. As Günter droned on, Friedrich tried to remember a time when everything wasn't so complicated. He was certain the Jungvolk used to be fun; certain there had once been a time when he could pick his own friends, have opinions, and shop wherever he liked. Friedrich thought of the easy days when he played at the river with Papa. His favorite memory of smearing himself with mud popped in his head. Cleaning up had been so simple. He would just scoot to the river and the water would wash the mess away. It was as though the world followed its own order, always righting his wrongs. The comforting recollection reassured Friedrich. Perhaps this order had something to do with his purest truth. And better yet, perhaps the order would one day wash away Günter's messes.

Friedrich felt the setting sun angle on his arm. Rays snuck through the clouded window, illuminating the room with a powerful late afternoon light. Like under a spotlight, nothing could hide. Friedrich saw it all. Decades of mud caked between wooden floor panels. Dust particles rushing to nowhere. Dirt under his neighbor's nails.

Friedrich looked down at the skin tightening on his arm. Hundreds of raised bumps on his flesh prickled the way it did before a storm rolled in. His eyebrow trembled and that strange nudge to do something returned.

18. When Nightmares Leaked

"C!" Mrs. Müller shrieked. "Not D!" Emil smashed his finger on the correct piano key and tallied all the scoldings he had received from the chicken lady in the last half hour. Eight. Not bad. He had been trying to play well today and hoped Mama noticed. He wanted to make her happy.

Mama had been making huge Mama-fusses ever since cousin Herbert's parents moved to Poland. They had to go, even though they didn't want to. When Mama heard they had to camp at the border because Poland wouldn't let them in, she really got out of sorts. Then a Jewish kid shot an important German man. More fuss. The newspapers said all Jewish people planned it and strangers started eying Emil the way Mrs. Schmidt did. After that, Emil wasn't allowed to go back to school. Sarah snapped at anything. Uncle Leo got louder and Papa softer. And Mama ran around, interrupting whatever he was doing, to make fusses.

"Again!" chicken lady ordered. "This time C." Emil held his breath and tried to hit all the notes he was supposed to for Mama.

The phone rang and Mama rushed to answer. Emil played on, so he couldn't hear her words, but by the way her voice pitched high, he knew she was upset.

Mama swept back in and without waiting for a pause in the music, she said, "Excuse me, Mrs. Müller. I just received a call. Apparently, the anniversary celebrations are livelier than usual. I wouldn't want you stuck in the midst of them." Emil wondered why-the-pickles Mama was so concerned about celebrations. "It would be best to wrap up early."

Mama's words bobbed around Emil's head. *Wrap up early?* It was a gift better than gold.

Mrs. Müller puckered her lips. She didn't look like she received a gift.

"Of course, I will pay for the full lesson," Mama said.

Mrs. Müller unpuckered. "Very well." She packed music sheets and squawked out a farewell.

Emil couldn't stop his grin from spreading.

"I have another matter," Mama said, and motioned Mrs. Müller toward the bedroom. That was strange because as far as Emil could figure, Mrs. Müller had no reason to be anywhere but the living room.

"What luck!" he exclaimed, when the bedroom door shut. This was turning out to be a great day.

"Quiet!" Sarah said.

Sarah, Vati, and Uncle Leo looked toward the bedroom. Emil heard drawers opening and voices murmuring. Then the bedroom door swung open and chicken odor drifted out.

It took Emil a moment to understand Mrs. Müller looked happy, since he had never seen her look that way.

As she stepped out the apartment, she said, "You've made a wise decision, Mrs. Rosen," and the door clicked shut.

Mama turned toward them. Tears overflowed. She said, "My friend Käthe just rang. They are rioting about Herschel Grynzpan." Emil knew that was the name of the Jewish kid who shot the German man.

"What?" Sarah asked.

"Those drunk Brownshirts. They came out of the pub near Käthe's house and took to the streets. They're not celebrating, they are raging about vom Rath. He died today."

"What did they expect?" Uncle Leo said. "His parents were deported for no reason."

"The deportation is an outrage, but that's not my point," Mama said.

"Someone needed to take a stand," Sarah said.

"Yes, but was that the best way to do it?" Mama said. "And that's not the issue."

"Good God, our sister was deported and left at the border for days!" Uncle Leo said. "Deported to a country that wouldn't let her in. And Lina is a German! Thank God Herbert got out when he did."

A knot twisted up in Emil's stomach. Aunt Lina and Uncle Rudolf having to move didn't seem fair no matter how Emil thought about it. Uncle Rudolf's father came from Poland, but they had lived in Germany their whole lives. Why should they have to move? Herbert must be having all sorts of bad feelings being so far away, maybe like Herschel Grynzpan. Emil hung his head at the thought of him being jealous of Herbert weeks ago.

"I cannot discuss Lina in front of the children." Mama's hands were shaking. "Besides, I said that was not the point."

Vati put his arm around Mama's shoulder. "We received the letter from Lina. They made it into Poland. They will settle." Vati rubbed Mama's back. "And to address your point, Käthe is across town. We are safe here."

Mama separated from Vati and looked at him as if she knew something that he didn't. She opened the window a crack and peeked out from behind the drapes. Far-off voices and thumps fused together into something menacing. Every now and then, punchy shouts cut through the evenness. It reminded Emil of his old nightmare of a huge, furry monster knocking about in dark alleys, lurking closer and closer.

Mama cranked the window shut. "Käthe got off the phone"—she paused to take a breath—"to hide their money."

"How much did you give Mrs. Müller?" Sarah asked.

Emil's mind pieced together what happened in the bedroom. "You gave the chicken lady all our money?"

"Henriette," Vati said, shaking his head.

"I didn't give her all our money." Mama put her hands on her hips. "Lina and Rudolf had to leave with hardly any notice and weren't allowed to take much money. We could be next. I trust Mrs. Müller will hide it safely for us until we leave for Paraguay in three weeks."

No one spoke. Emil waited for someone to tell Mama that since they weren't Polish, that wouldn't happen. But Uncle Leo only said, "So, what do we do, Henriette?"

"We do nothing," Vati said. "We sit and read our newspaper and eat our supper and then we play a nice game of rummy."

"I suppose that's it for now, but I'd feel better if we dimmed the lights." Mama reached for the candles. "I don't want to draw attention." Vati didn't say anything, so Mama lit a few and carried one into the kitchen.

As the evening wore on, Emil listened to the noises outside. Mama's kitchen clinks and clacks were softer than usual. They ate a quiet, candlelit supper. The five of them played cards with long silences between moves.

Emil felt sleepy around an hour to midnight and was about to go to bed when the phone rang. Mama ran to it.

"Frieda dear! How . . ."

"Yes, we heard . . . Oh."

"Yes, of course. Go, dear. Thank you for calling."

Mama hung up and checked all the drapes.

"That was Frieda," Mama said. "She heard Brownshirts across the hall from her. They were screaming all sorts of awful things and then . . . and then she saw them take her neighbor, Mr. Greenbaum, outside."

Emil couldn't imagine why anyone would take an old man outside. But then he remembered the way the stationery store owner's gray hair flapped in the wind when a Brownshirt slapped him.

Mama yanked coats out of the closet. "When an eighty-year-old man is pulled out of his home, we need to take precautions." She waved her finger near Vati's nose. "I will not stand to have my forty-nine-year-old man pulled out from mine."

"And where do you think we are going?" Vati asked.

"To the basement," she said. "We can lock ourselves in the potato room." The potato room was just a storage room, but since potatoes took up so much space on the floor after the autumn delivery, his family called it the potato room.

"So if we get hungry, we can nibble on a potato?" Uncle Leo said.

"Henriette, we are not standing in a cold cellar all night!" Vati looked flustered, like when he misplaced his pocket watch. "The potato room is the ideal temperature for a potato, not for a person."

Emil wondered whether Mama was right

"Where else is there? Everyone is in and out of the attic hanging laundry and the coal room is covered in soot," she said as she stuffed money in her bra. "Maybe we won't go. I'm organizing supplies just in case."

"'Just in case' looks uncomfortable," Vati said, pointing to the spiky brooch Mama pinned under her dress. "You are getting carried away. Sit and let's play another hand." He picked up the deck and started shuffling.

As Emil watched Mama shove a silver soup ladle down her stockings, his stomach knotted. He couldn't tell if this was just Mama-fuss or something more. Emil looked at Sarah. She shrugged.

"Children," Mama said. "Vati is right. There's nothing to do for now, so get to bed."

"Okay," Emil said, and dashed toward his room, hoping to unknot his stomach. He flopped on his bed and tried to sleep. His body tossed and turned in an on/off slumber for hours.

When the telephone rang at some dark hour, he knew something was wrong. His head was heavy, but he managed to walk to his window and crank it open a sliver. The night was lively when it should have been sleeping. Sharp shouts, thumping boots, and shattering glass were just outside. Emil's nightmare had leaked into his real world. The monster had arrived.

Emil lumbered into the living room and was surprised to see everyone already there. The old grandfather clock told him it was three in the morning. He tried to blink the fog from his eyes.

Emil heard Mama on the phone, "Frieda, dear. Calm down and tell me what happened."

Mama gasped.

"Arrested!" Mama bit her lower lip.

Frieda's jittery vibrations flew out from the receiver.

"I must go, dear." Mama's voice shook. "Lock your doors."

Mama slammed down the phone. "Put on your coats! We are leaving now!"

"What's happened?" Uncle Leo asked.

"They've arrested Frieda's husband! She said they are arresting every Jewish man they see!" Emil looked at Vati, who looked at Uncle Leo, who looked at Mama.

"We have to help them!" Sarah said.

"We have to help your father and uncle!" Mama threw Vati's coat toward him. He let it hit his chest and fall to his feet.

"This. Is. Insanity," Vati whispered. The room fell quiet as Emil's parents stared at each other in a standoff.

Mama said in her calming way, "If I'm wrong, Josef, we'll just come right back upstairs."

No one spoke. Emil looked from Mama to Vati, wishing the grandfather clock's tick-tocks were loud enough to mask the monster outside.

Vati said, "I don't want to believe it," and touched his war scar. He picked up his jacket.

Mama began barking orders as if she'd been planning for weeks, "Emil, Sarah, double socks and two coats. Leo, take the bills in the kitchen tin and the jewelry under my mattress. Sarah, tear the lining in everyone's coat a little under the arm to make a secret compartment. Josef, put the silver inside the piano."

The flurry of people rushing around Emil was surreal. He watched his fingers fumble with his buttons and peel off an extra sock when his shoe wouldn't fit. He grabbed a handful of marbles and before he knew it, he saw his feet creeping down the long hall staircase, flight after flight, along with his family. Not one neighbor opened their door, not even Mrs. Schmidt. Maybe he was as quiet as one of those round, furry critters at the river, or maybe all the neighbors were asleep, or maybe they also heard the monster and were too scared to peek out.

They reached the bottom step. The basement was dark. The pint-sized window on a far wall gave no help. Emil heard Uncle Leo feel around behind him.

"Don't turn the light on," Mama whispered. "We've walked here a thousand times."

"You've walked here a thousand times," Uncle Leo said. "Not me."

"Just run your fingers along the wall and listen for how I walk," she said. "I will lead, then Sarah, then Emil, then Josef and then Leo. We'll be there in a minute."

"I should lead," whispered Vati.

"I know the way best," Mama whispered. "Let's go."

Mama didn't wait for Vati to answer. When Emil heard Sarah start after Mama, he shut his eyes and touched the wall.

"Ooff," Mama said, stumbling.

"Henriette!" Vati whisper-yelled.

"Shhhh!" Mama scolded. "I'm fine. Just watch out. There's something on the ground."

Emil took a few more steps and came to where Mama had tripped. It was just a few clumps of coal. Step over steady step they snuck on, like a family of five round, furry critters.

He stopped when Sarah stopped; he heard Mama open the door to the potato room. The ancient metal hinges screeched. They probably made that sound every time anyone opened the door, but he had never noticed before.

All five people crowded in and the door screeched closed. Emil discovered a new color, one that was blacker than black. He shifted from one foot to the other, unsure what to do with himself.

"Let's make ourselves comfortable," Mama whispered.

Emil had never been inside the potato room with the door closed and learned how quickly regular air turned into musty potato air. Emil couldn't keep from sneezing.

"Gesundheit," Mama whispered. "But please sneeze quietly."

"Oh!" Sarah said the same time that Uncle Leo said, "Watch it!"

And then "He almost knocked me over" at the same time as "She's all elbows!"

"Quiet!" Mama scolded. "Everyone spread out."

Between a thousand potatoes, ten storage boxes, and five cranky people, Emil didn't see how they could spread out. Emil felt another sneeze creep up and tried to let it out that dainty way Sarah did when she's around boys, but it shot out like a missile.

"Cover your mouth," Mama said. "We may not wash for a little while." He heard her brush off her coat.

"Ouch," Vati said. "Careful where you step, Leo."

"Well how can I sit?" Uncle Leo said. "Potatoes are everywhere."

"Quiet, Leo!" Mama whisper-yelled.

"I'd like to see how quiet you are when you get a potato in your tuckus," Uncle Leo said. "And Emil, stop squirming. You're knocking potatoes everywhere."

"Just pile them next to you," Sarah whispered.

"If we pile them high enough, we'll have potato thrones," Uncle Leo said.

Emil shot out another sneeze and Sarah said, "Come on, Emil."

"I can't help it," Emil said.

"This won't do," Uncle Leo said.

"This will have to do," Mama whispered.

Everyone quieted, which made Emil's stomach knot more than the arguing.

"Leo is right," Vati said. "It won't do. It's too crowded and we're too noisy."

Emil sneezed.

"We'll be heard in no time," Vati said.

"Emil," Vati said, "We must leave, so they'll be safe."

"What? Where?" Emil didn't want to leave Mama and he didn't want to face the monster outside.

"That fellow I worked with, Mr. Hofmann. He always said he felt terrible about the Jewish plight. He made it clear he wanted to do more. I've seen his old house. It's grand, with lots of nooks and a large attic."

Mama didn't say anything.

Vati went on, "If it's just me and Emil, it will be manageable for Mr. Hofmann. Plus I feel better with Leo here, Henriette."

"He doesn't know you are coming," Mama said. Emil could picture worry lines sinking into Mama's forehead.

"I'm certain he is home," Vati said.

"They'll grab you right off the street," Mama said.

"It's almost morning and I know how to blend in," Vati said. "Besides if I get bored enough here, I'll have to tell the story of my war scar again."

"Good God, not that," Uncle Leo said. "Henriette, their leaving is a good idea."

"I don't feel right about separating," Mama said.

"There's just not enough room for all five," Uncle Leo said. "And Emil can not seem to learn to sneeze quietly. They'll find us and take Josef."

Emil heard Mama move toward Vati and then heard sloppy kissing sounds. Emil stepped as far back as he could. After it went on as long as Emil could stand, he missile-sneezed in Mama's direction to make them stop. It worked.

"I will return when it's safe," Vati said. "It will probably blow over in a day."

Mama shuffled toward Emil and wrapped her coat-bundled arms around him. She whispered, "Stay out of trouble," just like she said every day.

Vati screeched open the door. The light from the

pint-sized window now gave Emil enough to see Mama smiling at him from a pile of potatoes.

"Take care of him," she said to Vati. "And yourself."

"Remember," Vati said. "Don't go back upstairs until we get you."

Vati screeched the potato room door closed. When they made it to the stairs, Vati turned to Emil and said, "So, my boy, what to do about us?" The faint starlight illuminated the lines around Vati's eyes.

Emil waited, but Vati said nothing else.

"Which way to Mr. Hofmann?" Emil asked.

Vati leaned in and whispered, "There is no Mr. Hofmann."

"What?" There was no plan, no safety, no grown up in charge. "Where will we go?"

"Shhh," Vati said. "We couldn't stay. Mrs. Schmidt could hear us on the third floor."

Emil didn't speak. He couldn't wrap his mind around Vati not having a plan.

"So. Do you know any place to go?" Vati asked.

Of course Emil didn't know any place to go. That wasn't supposed to be his job.

"Someplace no one would think to look?" Vati went on.

Emil was too angry to think. Vati always knew everything, so why not now?

"Someplace secret and private?"

"Secret and private?" Emil repeated. Well, Emil did know one place.

"Someplace to pass time?"

"I have a plan," Emil said, and almost didn't believe he just uttered those words. He thanked God that he had finally gotten around to fixing his bicycle tire last week, prayed it would hold, and said, "You'll follow me on Sarah's bike."

For the first time, Vati didn't know what to do and Emil did. As Vati followed him to the bicycles, Emil pulled in thoughts of how he was saving Vati and pushed out ones of the monster waiting for them outside.

19. A Spiderweb of Facts

The clock told Friedrich it was 7:05 in the morning. The sun hadn't yet risen, but someone was knocking on his front door. Friedrich figured the world must still be 20 percent off. When he had gone to bed, Papa still hadn't returned from celebrations. Strange noises made him toss and turn all night. And now this unnerving knock, which was quickly strengthening into a pound, started echoing through the morning stillness.

The sound of Mother's slippers swished down the hall. The front door lock clicked open and Friedrich cracked his bedroom door ajar to eavesdrop. The murmur of Mother's voice came first followed by the murmur of a second voice. Friedrich's eyebrow twitched. Something about that voice wasn't right. Friedrich prayed Papa wasn't in trouble. He slipped into the hall and edged a few steps closer. The voice spoke again and this time Friedrich heard it clear as river water. It was Günter.

"Excuse the early interruption, Mrs. Weber, but Friedrich is needed immediately."

Friedrich joined Mother. Günter looked important in his uniform compared to Mother in her bathrobe, but Mother held her chin high and asked, "In what regards?"

"In regards to the heinous shooting incident." Günter looked at Mother, ignoring Friedrich. "The youths are needed for demonstrations."

"Heinous indeed," Mother snapped. Friedrich figured she probably did find the shooting terrible, but for different reasons than Günter thought. She was careful with her words.

"Precisely." Friedrich thought he saw the sides of Günter's mouth spring up a tick to an almost-smile. "Demonstrations will show that these actions will not be tolerated."

"Have demonstrations gone on through the night?" Mother asked. "Mr. Weber is a member of the SS and has not returned." Friedrich didn't know if Mother mentioned this because she wanted to show off Papa's work or because she was worried. Maybe both.

"Yes, they have," Günter said in a gentler tone than Friedrich had ever heard. "My father is a member of the SA. He just arrived home and gave me the Führer's order to gather the boys. Mr. Weber must still be needed." Günter's father was a Brownshirt. Maybe that explained why Günter was the way he was.

"Utterly unacceptable," Mother said shaking her head.

"Utterly unacceptable," Günter parroted back and smiled. Friedrich knew she meant keeping Papa out all night was unacceptable, not the shooting.

"Rest assured, Mrs. Weber, the order police, Brownshirts,

the SS, the Gestapo, everyone has directives." Günter gazed at Mother as if he wished she were his mother.

"Friedrich and I discuss the Führer's wisdom," Mother said, lying. "I once heard the Führer say, 'In the spiderweb of facts, many a truth is strangled.'"

She must be talking in code. The Führer never said that, Papa did. Maybe she was trying to warn Friedrich. Surely Günter would muddy facts with confusing ideas. She was telling Friedrich to look for truth. His broken Mother looked strong trying to protect him.

Günter nodded slowly and said, "Jews are masters of lies." He fell for it.

Mother reached for Friedrich's coat and asked, "Friedrich, have you eaten breakfast?"

He didn't know what to say to let her know he understood the secret message, so he just said something he figured Günter would want to hear. "The demonstrations can't wait."

As Friedrich put on his shoes, Mother walked into the kitchen and stood next to the flower vase on the table. She pretended to reposition the vase, as if it wasn't already perfectly centered. He knew she was reminding him if it wasn't on the windowsill, it wasn't safe.

As soon as Friedrich stood, Günter said, "Good day, Mrs. Weber," and slipped through the door. Friedrich hustled to keep up with him as they descended the stairs. He watched Günter's red notebook in his back pocket jerk up and down with each step. Friedrich was glad he watched, because as quick as a photo snap, Günter stopped short. Friedrich caught himself just before he collided into his back.

Günter faced Friedrich and said, "Your mother is a good German." Then he spun back and resumed his pace. Friedrich forgot to walk. Günter's compliment twirled in his mind.

"Come," Günter shouted.

Friedrich followed Günter outside. The dark street smelled woody and burnt. The sharp air stung his throat. Johannes and nine other Jungvolk boys stood next to a man wearing an SA uniform. He looked just like Günter, only much older and meaner. Friedrich could see the man's unkempt hair and bloodshot eyes even in the predawn light. He looked like he had been awake all night. Friedrich breathed in the scent of alcohol and stringent cologne and remembered it from the time he heard a man strike Günter in the stairwell. This had to be Günter's father.

They approached the group and Günter said to his father, "I have the ones I want."

"Take those little farts and obey the orders," the man snarled. "I've been serving the Führer while you've had your head on a pillow."

Friedrich shifted his weight away from the group.

"Yes sir," Günter said.

"I'll be doing the same as you, but I have orders to change clothes first," the man said as he smoothed the front of his uniform. Fresh cuts and scrapes zigzagged his hands.

"Change clothes?" Günter asked.

"Into civilian clothes!" his father snapped. "This is an outraged public reaction to the shooting. It can't look like it's all coming from the police." Friedrich didn't understand, but nodded.

The scowling man stepped close to Günter's face. "Do not disappoint," he said, and trudged off.

Günter turned toward the boys like nothing unusual had just happened and said, "The time has come to show those murdering Jews." He pulled a few rocks out of his pocket. "We will show them killing one of us is utterly unacceptable." Günter glanced at Friedrich when he used Mother's phrase.

A pack of older boys wearing Hitler Youth uniforms ran down the street screaming and waving sticks. Everyone turned to watch except Günter.

"I thought we were supposed to demonstrate?" Werner asked, eyeing them.

"Spontaneous demonstrations," Günter said, stretching out the word *spontaneous*. Friedrich wondered how they were spontaneous if Günter told them to do it.

"I can't wait until we get to wear that uniform," Johannes said, nodding at the older boys.

"Hitler Youth are a source of pride," Günter said. "Now, the Führer wants us to take care of this business with the Jews." He handed rocks to a couple of boys.

"It is necessary for German prosperity. Today we finally make progress against those bullies." Günter wove a thick, sticky spiderweb of facts.

Glass shattered from afar. Friedrich turned toward it. That wasn't the sound of demonstrating.

"Friedrich!" Günter shouted.

Friedrich whipped back around. Blood rushed to his face.

"Everyone will be paired to achieve efficiency," Günter said. "You are paired with Johannes." Günter faced the others. "Karl with Ernst, Walter with Heinz, and Hans with Rolf."

"How do we . . . ," Werner started. "What exactly are we supposed to do to demonstrate?"

"Am I not clear enough for you?" Günter asked. "You are to wreck Jewish businesses, ransack their homes, and harass them for destroying Germany." Johannes and Fritz nodded, but Friedrich's mouth nearly fell open like Werner's. How was this helping Germany? His mind raced for a way out, but couldn't find one. Friedrich wished he could turn into a rock.

"Are you sure we should . . . ," Werner started again. "Are you sure this is what the Führer wants?"

"Jews have been declared non-German," Günter screamed. "This directive is from the top. Do you have a problem?"

"No, of course not," Werner whispered.

"The Führer gave us jobs and food," Johannes said. "He was right about that and he's right about the Jews, the reds, and everyone else who doesn't support him."

Günter nodded.

"What about me?" Fritz asked. "I need a partner."

"Fritz, Werner, I have important work for you," Günter said. "You are to keep track of a few particularly bothersome Jews. Goldstein on Oberstrasse, Levin on Schaufelder Strasse and Rosen on Königswarter Strasse. If you find them home, notify the police or me."

Rosen on Königswarter Strasse, Friedrich thought. That could be Pudding, but Friedrich didn't have time to think about him. He had his own problems.

"The point in history we have been waiting for has arrived," Günter said. "Go. Your spontaneous demonstrations will not be hampered."

"We're ready to serve our country!" Johannes called out.

"We're not children today!" Ernst said.

"The Jews won't bully us anymore!" Fritz shouted.

Friedrich watched Günter walk off and realized the 20 percent crazy was gone. The world was 100 percent crazy. Friedrich was still himself, but everything else had turned upside down.

The group of boys dispersed until only Friedrich and Johannes remained.

"This is it, Friedrich!" Johannes said, jumping about

and knocking Friedrich in the arm. "We're part of something important. We can make a difference." Johannes walked ahead. "Come on!"

Friedrich followed, unsure where they were going or what he should be doing. He rolled Günter's instructions around his brain, but the words were indigestible. Maybe Uncle Hilmar's Would–Could–Should technique would help make sense of it. Would Friedrich have the guts to do it? Maybe. Could he physically break things? Yes. Should he do it? No. Muddy hell, no.

"We'll show them they can't get away with it!" Johannes called back, running ahead, picking up rocks along the way.

The technique told him no, but it didn't matter. Günter said it was a directive from the top. Friedrich had to obey. He saw no way out. He wished he could feel what Johannes felt. Then at least everything would make sense.

Friedrich heard himself say, "Murder is wrong!" His voice came out high and squeaky. He thought of the day Brutus died to feel angrier.

Johannes glanced at him.

Friedrich tried to scream, "Jews are clever and scheming," but it came out like a question.

Johannes stopped. As if he could read Friedrich's mind, he said, "Don't you remember how much money Jews had and how little food you had?"

The spiderweb grew. Of course, he remembered.

Albert's family didn't, but plenty of other Jewish families did.

"It's their own fault," Johannes said. The faint pastels of daybreak illuminated his face. Friedrich had never seen Johannes look more serious.

Johannes stared into Friedrich. He finally said, "Let's just start with some reds," and handed Friedrich a rock.

There it was. A way out. Günter didn't say not to go after reds. Reds threw rocks at him, so it wasn't wrong to throw them back. He would give Günter what he wanted and give the reds what they deserved. He curled his fingers around the stone and almost smiled.

20. Falling Off a Cliff

"We'll pretend like it's any regular, old morning," Vati said as they emerged from the basement. Emil tried, but it was hard to ignore that it was more night than morning and that the monster lurked around every corner. "Slow and steady," Vati said, mounting Sarah's bike. Emil started pedaling and Vati followed. The river never seemed farther than it did today.

They made it a couple blocks without seeing anyone, but when they turned the corner, they heard yelling. Emil and Vati ducked into a side alley.

"Into the truck! Quick!" an angry voice screamed.

The alley ground was so gummy, it nearly snatched Emil's shoe. The angry voice barked off a list of names. Emil watched from the shadows as men in black uniforms ran in and out of apartments, selecting people like groceries from a shopping list. Men wearing nightclothes and boys just a little older than Emil were gathered in front of a truck.

"Are they sending them to Poland?" Emil asked.

"I hope not," Vati whispered. "Seventeen thousand Polish Jews were stuck at the border. I don't think there's room in no-man's-land for more."

"We're German Jews so they can't send us there," Emil said.

Vati looked at Emil and wrinkled his forehead like Mama did when she worried. He said, "I don't know."

Emil watched from the alley as the truck filled and then drove away. After the street was quiet awhile, Vati said, "The coast is clear," and they started out again.

They made it a few more blocks, but had to duck into another alley when they heard glass shatter. From the darkness, Emil could see that someone had thrown a rock at a store window. People swarmed in and out through the broken window. Teenagers hurried in first, grabbing as much as they could hold. Then a couple men came with sacks.

"Where are the police?" Emil asked.

"Jewish people own the store," Vati whispered.

The police must have been too busy putting people in trucks. Emil looked away until it was quiet. It felt like an hour.

"Let's go," Vati said.

They made it only one block before they had to slide into another tight alley. A man with a long beard cried in the street as a Brownshirt tore pages, one by one, out of a book. One page caught the wind and drifted through Emil's slender passageway. It landed on his foot. He picked it up and tried to read the Hebrew letters in the dim light. He knew it was the Torah. Emil didn't know why anyone would want to rip apart something so sacred.

"They are tearing our flesh away," Vati whispered. Emil glanced at him and thought the moon must be playing twisted games with its shadows. Gentle Vati looked ready to charge. Emil couldn't stand the idea of those Brownshirts turning on his father, so he gently rolled the page and tucked it in Vati's pocket. Then Emil slipped his hand into Vati's. Vati blinked and the shadows shifted.

The Brownshirts must have gotten bored ripping pages. They shoved the man into their truck and drove away. Emil and Vati rode on. They traveled more ground and made it all the way to the part of town Mama called undesirable, but had to sidestep into another alley when they heard a woman scream. The stench was horrible. Ankle-high garbage spread as far as Emil could see.

Emil almost cried out when a cat, or what he hoped was a cat, swiped past his legs.

"The strays are worse in Venice," Vati said.

Emil wiped his pants where the cat creature had slinked past him. He tried to settle in next to Vati and peeked toward the screams. A Brownshirt shook an old man so hard, his body flopped like a broken doll. A woman in her nightgown shrieked behind them.

The Brownshirt screamed over and over, "Give us the keys to the store!" and the woman shouted, "Let my husband be!"

The old man refused and after a while, the Brownshirt said, "Enough." He let the man's arms go. Emil almost believed it was over, but then the Brownshirt reached out and slapped the woman, spun around, and slapped the man.

Emil couldn't watch anymore. Looking away would somehow give the Brownshirt permission, but he couldn't stand it. He shut his eyes, cupped his hands over his ears, hummed the C note, and wished for a Fairy Godmother to lift him up out of the garbage. He stayed that way for some time until daylight glowed from behind his lids.

Emil opened his eyes and peered at the horizon, past the awful scene. It was his first sunrise. Maybe its beauty would take away the ugly. He hoped it would be like the ones in fairy tales. Mama said she loved how untouched morning dew glistened. Sarah said daybreaks were as close to real magic as it got. And Vati told him how watching a sunrise made him feel like he owned the whole city. But as Emil watched the sun slide into place, the gray sky gave no brilliant colors. Garbage jabbed his ankles. Stray cats scampered like rats. And screams made Emil feel like Hannover was anything but his.

Emil looked at the old man and woman who were now sitting on the ground outside the store.

"The Brownshirt is busy in the store," Vati said. "We should ride."

Emil bit his lower lip. It was light but the monster wasn't gone.

"Just ride like it's a regular old morning," Vati reminded him. "Like you're going to school and me to work." Emil supposed that's what his morning would have been like if he weren't Jewish.

"Let's go," Vati said and hopped on a bicycle. "Those guys are too busy thieving to notice us. Which way?"

Emil took off and Vati followed. He held his head high, pretending to ride to school as if it were any regular day. As if he weren't Jewish.

The streets filled with morning. He rode right past men and boys in uniforms, grownups going about their business, and children riding their bikes to school. They rode on, slow and steady, until the roads turned country.

Emil didn't bother asking Vati what time it was when they approached the river path. Emil hopped off his bike and looked around. No one. He pushed aside the shrubs to the entrance with one hand and guided his bike through with the other. The branches snapped back in place after Vati entered. They had done it. They snuck past the monster.

"Walk behind me so you don't trip." Emil said as he led Vati about twenty meters up the path. "Tuck the bikes under these bushes, so people can't spot them from the road."

"Where are we?" Vati stood on his tiptoes to peer over the bush.

"We're . . ." Emil started to say, but stopped when he heard cracking, like breaking bones. Emil whipped around. Vati was on the ground, tangled in a web of dead branches.

"Vati!" Emil ran to loosen his leg. The branches snapped and splintered as he grabbed at them, making that awful cracking noise. When Vati started cursing in

Italian, Emil knew he was fine. Emil still didn't know what those words meant, but Vati said them so much, Mama had given up saying, "Not in front of the children." Vati stood, brushed off his slacks, and mumbled, "So this is where you make yourself such a mess."

"We're almost there," Emil said, eyeing the tangle of autumn branches scattered along the path. It really has been awhile since he'd been here.

They followed the path up the hill and over until Emil sensed Vati had stopped walking.

"It's beautiful." Vati stared out. Awe swelled in his eyes, not sadness. Emil wondered if he had looked like that the first time he found his spot.

Emil led Vati to a dry spot and sat. Dirt never felt more comfortable. Emil stretched his aching legs. He wondered when he'd see Mama again and froze an image of her in his mind.

Emil should have felt relieved, but he had a terrible, sinking feeling, as if he were hanging off a cliff, grabbing at the sides. But the more he tried to hang on, the more the soil would crumble, and the more he'd fall. He remembered feeling this way when Opa got sick. Once Opa's sickness started, it was too big to stop. Everyday Opa got worse and everyday Emil felt like he slipped more. Now the world was getting sicker and he was falling again. Something big had started and Emil wasn't sure if it could be stopped.

Emil turned on his side and shut his eyes. The river was quieter than the last time he was here. Fewer squawks and chirps. Only crackling November leaves and rushing water. If he weren't so cold, the sounds could have lulled him to sleep.

Vati must have noticed Emil shivering because he said, "Tuck your hands under your armpits."

Emil tried, but since he wore two coats, his arms bulked awkwardly over his chest when he crossed them. Vati wrapped his own arm over Emil.

"We should be thankful the weather is milder than usual," Vati said.

Emil supposed he should be thankful, but he wasn't. He should also be thankful for knowing Hannover's streets so well and for fixing his bike tire last week, but he wasn't.

"Sleep," Vati said, stroking Emil's forehead with his thick hand. Emil wanted nothing more. It was an awful day and he was desperate to escape it.

Emil closed his eyes and imagined he was five years old, safe in bed. Opa tucked the blankets tightly under his sides, snug and warm. The smell of baking filled his home. Vati shuffled around in the other room, packing for a business trip the next morning. Sarah giggled as she settled in her own bed.

Emil relaxed under Vati's arm and sleep finally came. But he didn't dream of Opa or of Mama's baking. He dreamt of hanging helplessly over a cliff. He couldn't stop himself from falling, little by little, as the earth gave way.

21. Friedrich's Rotten Bones Were Trembling

"Come on! I know where some reds live," Johannes yelled, rushing ahead. "They own a shoe store." Friedrich dashed after him.

The streets pulsed with a feverish energy that made boys and men howl. Everyone they passed hurried on, with wild faces and fists thrust in the air. They looked like frenzied leaves caught by a gust of wind, swirling up together, higher and higher.

"It's a father and three sons," Johannes called back. "They all believe in that communist garbage."

The city blurred into streaks as Friedrich raced after Johannes. The haze reminded him of when he was ten years old and the reds chased him with rocks. One good pitch and they could have killed him. He still gagged at the thought of how slimy his hair felt when they spat on him.

Friedrich became angry thinking about it. There was no reason for it. He never bothered them. He was just a boy. Muddy hell, reds! He picked up his pace and felt himself being pulled up in the same swirling wind as everyone around him.

They turned east and came to a large store window with the word SHOES neatly stenciled in the center.

"They own this store." Johannes handed him a rock. It felt cool in Friedrich's sweaty palm.

"Throw it!" Johannes coaxed, shifting his weight from foot to foot, clenching his fists.

Friedrich rubbed his uniform sleeve between his fingers. Those reds were so cruel, Friedrich wanted to show them, punish them. Sweat beaded along his forehead. He stretched his arm back. They deserved it.

Friedrich felt as if someone had injected him with hot, red energy. He screamed, "Damn you, reds!" and hurled the rock at the letter H. After never having any kind of power, control, dominance over anything in his twelve years of life, throwing that rock gave him a taste. And it was incredible. The rock hit the H. Friedrich expected it to just make a hole, but the entire window shattered into billions of pieces. Friedrich's arms shot up to shield himself from flying shards. The glass collapsed into a wave of sparkling daggers. It crashed to the ground and spread out like a blanket of razor-sharp teeth.

The shattered window stripped a layer of him, revealing a brutal rawness raging underneath. Repulsion crept up from inside. Friedrich held his breath so he wouldn't retch. He hated what he had done. He loved what he had done. He hated that it felt good. The air turned thick with shame. He wanted to roll on that jagged blanket and feel his destruction destroy him. But even more, he wanted to feel powerful again. Adrenaline surged through him.

The world blurred. Johannes jumped and flapped his arms, his mouth twisted into shapes. Shame dug deeper. Friedrich no longer felt like Friedrich.

"Come on! There are more reds!" Johannes sounded as if he was underwater.

Friedrich had one thought: *Those reds hurt me for fun.* And then another rock was in his hand. He ran, thinking that thought. Johannes sprinted behind him.

Friedrich stopped in the middle of the street and spun in circles, searching for any sign of communists. The world swirled around him. Johannes pointed at a store window and cried, "There!" As Friedrich heaved the rock, he was again filled with that intense feeling of power. He was right and they were wrong. But as the rock broke through the glass, shame tumbled down on him again. He loathed himself. He wanted more. He wanted to destroy everything.

Johannes contorted his limbs, cheering, rejoicing. Friedrich heard underwater shouting and wasn't sure if it came from Johannes. A new thought slammed in his head: *My family went hungry when a bunch of Jews weren't.* And then a new rock appeared in his hand. He didn't want the rock or the thought. He ran. He only saw the street in front of him. Everything else disappeared.

Haze. Running. Panting. Shame. Shouting. Balcony doors opened from above. A white-haired man saluted Friedrich. Was it a dream? Friedrich's anger was real. His throat burned like he'd been screaming, but Friedrich didn't remember shouting anything.

Johannes' lips moved. Friedrich heard nothing. Johannes pointed. Another throw, another crash, another ugly thought: *It's not fair I can't have my uncle.* Another rock. Friedrich tried to swallow. Pain engulfed the back of his mouth.

Running. Higher and faster. City streaks. Heart pounding. Broken windows. Teenagers leapt out with full arms. Clothes, fruit, pots, shoes. Grownups climbed through windows like monkeys. Mess everywhere.

Friedrich threw the rock. He turned away before it crashed. With each throw, he became hollower, like someone scooped out his insides, stealing his mind and leaving his body. Callous and rough, like a shell. Soon there would be nothing left.

Another ugly thought: *I never spend time with Papa.* Another rock.

Running. Underwater screams. Flames. Burning building. Rotten air. Gritty sky.

Colors poured outside through stained glass from a blaze inside. Beautiful colors. Friedrich hated beautiful. Everything should be ugly like him.

He flung a rock at them. Through a six-pointed star. The colors vanished.

Another thought: *I am worthless. Any life is better than mine.* Another rock.

Running. Blurring. Music.

School children sung outside. Teachers conducted in front. Row after row of little people. Neat blond braids. Mouths opened. A teacher nodded toward Friedrich.

Running. Lungs bursting. Scorching throat. A woman's screams.

A man limped into the back of a truck. A woman pulled a Brownshirt uniform. It stretched from his arm. A slap like a cracking branch. More screams. Another cracking branch. No more screams.

Running. Street after street. Johannes pointed to a window. Friedrich looked. An enraged boy stared back at him. The boy held a rock. His teeth bared, forehead furrowed. A black wildness in his eyes that should have no place in a boy. Friedrich hunched to attack. So did the boy. Friedrich stepped back. The boy did too. It was his reflection, but it wasn't him. Friedrich threw the rock at the hateful boy.

Hot pain sunk a claw into his shoulder. Friedrich clutched the throbbing spot, panting hard. Johannes bent over, gasping, smiling. The arm had thrown too many rocks.

Friedrich started walking, gulping air, gripping his shoulder. Many ugly thoughts came: *It's not fair everyone had it better than me. It's not fair Mother was ruined. It's not fair people thought I was strange. It's not fair Albert was gone.*

Albert! He stopped. Friedrich saw Albert go. He should be safe across an ocean by now. But what if Albert had returned? Friedrich had to check.

Johannes spoke words and nudged a rock at Friedrich's hand. Friedrich turned away and ran. Johannes jogged behind.

Albert's building wasn't far. Turn east, three blocks, turn north, and two blocks more.

An old lady stood by herself on the sidewalk. She held out her hand as they sprinted past. Friedrich looked in her eyes. They were what Günter called a Hitler sky, bright and blue. She opened her fingers to reveal caramel candies. Friedrich hadn't tasted caramel for a long time.

"Would you like candy, boys?" she asked.

Friedrich didn't stop, but Johannes paused.

"To thank you," the woman said. Friedrich ran past, leaving Johannes in the upside-down world. The world where grownups saluted children for breaking their city. Where old ladies with clear eyes gave candy to wicked boys.

As he ran, he thought of the great river current washing away the mess he made, righting all his wrongs. If only the river could flood the streets and clean his mess this time. Something about that idea tugged at Friedrich, but he didn't have time to think it through. Albert's building was in the distance. As Friedrich jogged, he ran past his own building. No vase was in the window.

Friedrich crafted a quick plan. He would pretend to take Albert to the police, but then sneak him to the river. He could bring food and water and warm clothes. That would give him time to figure something else out.

Friedrich drew near to Albert's apartment window on the ground floor. He peered in. There were no drapes, no furniture, no colors, no people. Just an empty apartment. Albert really was gone. Albert was safe. Friedrich pressed his hand over his heart and closed his eyes.

Someone screamed, "Tell us where the men are hiding!"

Friedrich spun around. The stink of alcohol and sweat wafted toward him. A jumble of men, some in uniforms and some not, swaggered back and forth in front of about twenty people across the street. Friedrich could tell the men in regular clothes were Brownshirts by the way they walked. Some of the people in the lineup were crying. Women in long skirts, wide-eyed children, and old men with beards held each other. There were no teen boys or men Papa's age.

"Tell us!" screamed a man in plain clothing. "They won't get away with destroying our country anymore!" Friedrich heard that voice before. The man's eyes were bloodshot and Friedrich thought he smelled awful cologne. Günter's father. Friedrich's eyebrow trembled.

"I know how to make them talk!" one Brownshirt said. He didn't look much older than Günter. He twirled scissors around his finger and dragged an old man from the line. He grabbed the man's gray beard. The man's head jerked down and some of the women in line shrieked. Then the Brownshirt pumped the scissors across the beard too close to the chin. Blood trickled onto the man's white shirt. The Brownshirts laughed. One of them took a photo.

It was like the demons that lurked in the niches, the most foul and monstrous ones that should be triple-shackled, broke free last night and danced in Hannover's sun. Friedrich felt as if he were in a dream. A dreadful, evil dream.

Friedrich leaned on Albert's building and watched like everyone else. No one called for the police; the demons *were* the police. The rules of yesterday were gone. It was all so senseless, he couldn't bear it. His head throbbed. He needed order.

His mind raced with the day. His spiderweb of facts was so snarled, so unwieldy, he couldn't keep track of it. Every fact seemed as true and as false as the next.

But there had to be truth. Maybe he wasn't looking at it the right way. The big picture didn't make sense, but maybe if he stripped it down, some of the small facts would. He breathed in, desperate to harness something true.

Friedrich analyzed and soon everything began sorting itself. First, he knew this old man didn't ruin Germany. Just as Albert and Pudding hadn't ruined it. Maybe it was true some of them had more money than him, but that didn't wreck his country.

Second was the river. The thought that tugged at him earlier came together. The river couldn't clean his mess because the river couldn't budge. He was always the one who had to move the mess to it. He righted his own wrongs, not the river.

And third was Pudding. Since Germany's problems weren't Pudding's fault, and since messes didn't get fixed unless Friedrich did something, Friedrich should help him. Friedrich's eyebrow stopped trembling.

Besides, Pudding had saved Friedrich from a beating, so Friedrich owed him. Friedrich was certain helping Pudding was the right thing to do. He didn't even need the Would–Could–Should technique.

The young Brownshirt waved the severed beard at the line of people. He pointed at another hunched, old man with a long beard. "You are next unless you tell us where the men are hiding!"

The old man shuffled up to Günter's father. "Please!" he pleaded. "Stop this madness! We are Germans. Protect us and treat us as citizens like you always have."

The Brownshirts snorted.

"You want me to protect?" Günter's father said. "Okay, I will protect you." Everyone quieted, but by the mocking way he said it, Friedrich knew he wouldn't.

"You may run away and no one is permitted to touch you . . ." Günter's father said, waving a finger at his men. "But only until I count to ten." All the Brownshirts laughed, as the younger one snapped his scissors in the air.

"One!"

Friedrich watched the old man try to hobble away.

"Two!"

Thoughts thrashed around in Friedrich's head. If Albert hadn't left Germany, Günter could have been watching his house instead of Pudding's.

"Three!"

The old man took six steps for every one Günter's father took.

"Four!"

Pudding was clever and probably found a hiding place.

"Five!" Günter's father yelled. "Remember, men! He is protected until I reach ten! Six!"

Where could Pudding be? There were tens of thousands of hiding spots between all the basements, attics, and closets in Hannover.

"Seven!"

The old man stopped.

"Eight!"

The image of the first time he saw Pudding at the river burst in Friedrich's head.

"Nine!"

The old man turned back to Günter's father and held his chin high. Friedrich saw something that reminded him of the flagbearer. The old man stopped running, but he wasn't giving up.

"Ten!"

Friedrich ran. He couldn't help the old man, but maybe he still had time to help Pudding.

22. After Emil's Night of Broken Glass

Emil usually woke up slow and gentle. He loved a good long stretch in his bed as he glided from a soft-shimmery-dream world to a bright-happy-morning world. But today his hands were half frozen and a crotchety bird honked down from a branch above. Emil tried to make sense of things as he woke. Once he realized there was no breakfast and a hundred twigs were poking into him, he jolted straight up into a gray-rotten-awake world.

"You've been sleeping for hours," Vati said.

Fog cleared from his head. He remembered boys looting stores, old men slapped, and the monster that tried to crush him. Emil had never woke into a real nightmare instead of out of one. His chest tightened at the thought of Mama in that rotting basement. Half-bare trees and gray sky surrounded him. He did not want to be here.

A breeze, not strong enough to fly a kite, bit at his ears. After spending the whole night outside, the chill was unescapable. It was just November, but an odd, heavy cold had set it. The kind that, once you breathed in enough, caught you and wouldn't let go. Emil crossed his arms and put his half-frozen hands under his armpits.

"How long do we have to stay?" Emil asked, rocking back and forth.

"Until it's safe." Vati clicked open his golden pocket watch that his Vati gave him when he married Mama.

"Can I hold it?" Emil's his fingers itched to touch the shiny disc. The flawless tick, the silky way it snapped open and closed, and the fancy etching made it the most perfect watch he'd ever seen.

"Not until the day you get married." Vati smirked and snapped it shut.

"Maybe I won't get married." No girl had ever liked Emil and he couldn't imagine how any would.

"Then it's an incentive." Vati opened and shut the watch just out of Emil's reach. "And just think how fun it will be to torture your children the way I torture you." Vati winked and stuffed the watch back in his pocket.

"The Nazis have to be tired after last night," Emil said. "Maybe we can go home later."

"I don't know." Vati's smile faded. He propped himself with one arm as he lay on his side, gazing out. There were no poppies. Emil wished he could have shown him how they bloomed and fluttered in the summertime.

The long silence made Emil stand. Since he was stuck at the river, he may as well have fun. The space between his pants and legs filled with cold air quick enough to make him want to sit right back down, but he walked over to his favorite flat rock. He squatted and pulled out his marbles.

"Want to play?" he asked Vati. "I'll give you my best shooter."

"My fingers are a little numb."

Emil wiggled his fingers and realized they were a little numb as well. He collected his marbles, grabbed a good long poking stick, and sat cross-legged. The rock's chill crept through his pants. He poked and nudged a few yellow leaves that got mixed in among reds. He tried to lift and stack them one on top of the other with his stick, but they kept blowing off.

"Pickl—" he started to say, but stopped because he didn't want to think about how much he wanted a pickle. He pushed the yellows together and thought of the leaf-to-leaf stepping game he had played the day he saved River Boy. It was just last month, but seemed so long ago.

After a good long time of poking around with his stick, Emil lay on his back and watched the gray sky. There were enough dark grays and light grays to find clouds in the shape of a key, a miniature toilet and a stretching cat. For a moment, the sun poked through behind a large oak tree.

It was long past lunchtime. Emil's stomach growled. But there was no sense in mentioning they had no food. He tried remembering everything he ate the past week. Since he had eaten so much, maybe it would help him feel fuller. Seven foods came to mind: Challah, schnitzel, goulash, potato kugel, chicken soup, plum cake, and radish salad. To pass time, he ranked them from best to worst. Six of them tied for first. Radish salad came in second. But Emil wished he had a big bowl of radish salad now.

He must have been ranking the foods out loud because Vati said, "Mama can always put a meal together, even if foods are harder to get nowadays."

All the thinking about food made Emil thirsty, so he squatted next to the river and plunged a cupped hand into the frigid water. His hand felt as if he made twenty snowballs without mittens. He raised a scoopful to his lips.

"Don't," Vati warned.

"I've drunk it before and I was mostly fine."

"Mostly?" Vati asked. "Try to hold out longer."

He ignored Vati and stuck his tongue into the water. But as soon as he did, he remembered there wasn't a toilet nearby. He glanced at the dried leaves that crumbled at the touch. Diarrhea would not be fun. Emil dropped the water.

He faced the wind and realized the cold was making his nose drip. Since Mama couldn't clean his clothes later, he didn't want mucus smeared on his sleeve. Emil sniffed and snorted up what he could. His throat burned.

This was no pocket-sized mishap. This wasn't even a backpack-sized mishap. This was real, terrible trouble and he hated it. He hated that his fingers couldn't move the way they were supposed to and he hated how the wind beat on his ears. He hated the dizziness and his stiff limbs. And worst of all, he hated not knowing when it would end. Coming here was not a good idea.

"Why don't I tell you how the Austrian mountains glisten like crystals," Vati said.

"Okay." Emil took a long breath. He liked Vati's stories about snowy mountains. But before Vati could start, Emil heard a stick snap. And then another. Footsteps!

Vati grabbed Emil's arm. More sticks snapped at a hasty pace. Emil pulled Vati behind the same evergreens he had hid behind when he first saw River Boy. The snaps grew louder.

Emil peeked through a bare spot in the bush. A figure appeared. Emil could only see it from the neck down and glimpsed a brown shirt. Vati put his finger in front of his lips. It could all have been a wild dream had it not been for the very real warmth of Vati's hand squeezing his own.

The figure stopped walking. Emil held his breath.

Then the figure said, "Emil Rosen," and Emil felt like his heart cracked. Now, it was all real, too real. Someone was here to arrest him!

"I know you are here," the figure said.

There was nowhere to go. The river circled behind him and Emil reckoned the figure could run faster than him, since everyone he knew was faster than him. Vati pulled Emil close.

Then the figured called, "4711, come out!"

It was River Boy! Emil popped up like a jack-in-the-box from behind the bush.

"No Emil!" Vati screamed. He snatched up a branch and pushed Emil behind him.

"It's okay, I know him," Emil said.

"Who is this?" Vati asked. He waved the branch like a sword.

River Boy's eyebrow shook. The poor light made him look older. Emil hoped he hadn't been wrong about him after all.

"They are coming to your house," River Boy said.

"How do you know?" Vati asked. "Did they find my family?"

"I don't know," River Boy said. "I heard my leader order a boy to watch your house."

Vati looked out at the field. Lines etched deep into his forehead.

"This is my father," Emil said.

River Boy extended his arm straight as a wood plank and marched toward Vati, "My name is Friedrich."

His name is Friedrich, thought Emil as he watched them shake hands. Emil tried to think of him as Friedrich, but couldn't. He was River Boy.

"Josef Rosen." Vati dropped the branch to shake hands. "What's happening out there?"

River Boy opened his mouth and shut it, as if he couldn't find the right words.

"They are targeting Jewish homes and businesses," he said. His eyes fluttered down when he added, "Also communists." Emil would have used different words to describe the monster.

"Is it settling down?" Vati asked.

"It's getting worse."

"Are they arresting people?" Emil asked.

"Men," River Boy looked toward Vati. "They're usually letting women and children go as long as they get the men."

Vati swallowed hard and turned back toward the field. No one spoke.

River Boy unzipped his backpack and pulled out a bag of almonds and a canteen. "I figured his pockets would be filled with marbles," he said, nodding toward Emil.

Laughter burst out of Vati, but Emil's face flushed at the insult. Emil didn't think he was that childish. After all, he did get Vati to the river. But it was wonderful to watch Vati chuckle and slap his knee. Emil smiled and clinked the marbles in his pocket.

As soon as Vati stopped laughing, River Boy started talking, "Naturally, you must have certain camping necessities. The canteen has fresh water for hydration. Of course, you should boil river water before you drink it."

"Boil, eh?" Vati said and winked at Emil.

"Fortunately, the weather isn't as bad as it could be this time of year. But it's still cool and it may get windy at night."

Emil chomped down almonds. His head began to clear as his starving stomach tightened around the food.

"Do you have protection against frostbite?" River Boy asked.

Vati pointed to the clothes he was wearing.

"I see," River Boy said. "It will have to do, since bringing proper camping equipment would have attracted attention. What about injury? Do you have a first aid kit?"

Vati wrinkled his forehead and glanced sideways at Emil.

"Um, no," Emil said. "We didn't bring a first aid kit."

"That's what I thought." River Boy unzipped his backpack. "I imagine you had to move quickly."

"Uh-huh," Emil said.

River Boy pulled out a sack. "I've gathered survival essentials. Here are bandages, a small metal pan, matches, knife, compass, fishing hook and cord, and three pairs of socks."

Vati accepted the sack.

"And don't worry," River Boy added quickly. "I won't tell anyone where you are hiding. Now that I've helped you, I would get in trouble."

Emil wondered if Vati had been thinking that.

"Why are you helping us?" Vati asked.

Friedrich looked out at the river. He said nothing.

"Anyway, how can I thank you?" Vati's eyes watered. "How can I repay you?"

"You can just return the items for me to pick up here at the riv . . ." River Boy started, but Vati cut him off.

"Friedrich, thank you," Vati said, putting his hand on River Boy's shoulder. Emil was sure the prickly boy would shrivel from the touch, but he didn't. He let Vati's hand stay and said, "You are welcome."

River Boy looked at the sun. "I need to go," he said. "If I'm gone too long, my leader Günter will notice."

Emil sucked in his breath. He had forgotten about Günter Beck.

"I can check in on you tomorrow and let you know if it's safe to return." River Boy looked from Emil to Vati. "Don't return until I come back." Something in his voice made Emil think River Boy knew more than he was telling.

"Please, you've done so much, but I need to ask one more favor," Vati said. "My wife, her brother, and my daughter are hiding in the storage room on the east side of our basement. The corner building on Königswarter Strasse. Can you check on them? Let them know we're okay? Maybe bring them some survival essentials too?"

River Boy's eyebrow trembled. He looked at the ground and mumbled to himself as if Emil and Vati weren't there, "I would have the guts. I could get there before Günter notices. I should do it." He looked up and said, "Yes, I will."

Emil locked his hands together. If he didn't, they would spring up and wrap themselves around River Boy in a hug he was sure River Boy did not want. River Boy turned to go, but Emil couldn't let him leave without giving him something.

"Wait!" Emil called. "Here." Emil reached in his

pocket and scooped out as many marbles as he could hold. His favorite, the one with crimson swirls that Opa had given him, was in the heap.

River Boy eyed them as if Emil held a handful of worms.

"Just . . . ," Emil said. "Thank you."

River Boy took the marbles and Emil watched him disappear beyond the path.

"A friend?" Vati asked.

"I gave him your 4711 bottle."

Vati laughed and said, "Fair trade," as he held up the sack of survival essentials.

Vati walked back to where they had slept. "Let's rest," he said. "We go home tomorrow."

"River B . . ." Emil said. "Um, Friedrich said we shouldn't go home until he comes back."

"Friedrich also said they were letting women and children go as long as they had the men." The lines returned to Vati's forehead. "By hiding here, I'm keeping your mother and sister in danger."

"Vati!"

"My mind is set. I can't stand the idea of them living in that dank basement."

"We don't know what they'll do to you!" Emil felt desperate. "Remember last night!"

"Don't worry, I won't make trouble with them and they won't bother me," he said. "It won't be so bad. Perhaps they'll let me go because I have a visa for Paraguay."

Vati always thought things weren't as bad as they really were, but maybe he was right about the visa. Emil put his arm around his father's shoulder. There was nothing to argue. Vati said his mind was set. Emil watched the sun sink in the colorless sky. He huddled close, bracing for the night's cold and tomorrow's journey home.

23. Because He Didn't Want to Be a Boy Who Threw Rocks

Friedrich stood at his bed packing a blanket and bandages into a sack for Pudding's mother. Yesterday he never would have believed he'd smash more store windows than he cared to count and destroy the stained glass of an old temple. Now he was ready to lug a sack of supplies to the very people he was supposed to capture. There was no time to think it through. No time to change directions. He felt like a boat set on its course, doing everything he could not to capsize.

He wondered if Mother would know what to do. Maybe she had helped hide people and knew some tricks. Friedrich took a step back from his bed, to head toward the kitchen for food, and collided into Mother standing in the middle of his room.

"How long have you been there?" His heart pounded as if she had caught him throwing rocks.

"Shhh. Papa is sleeping," she said, ignoring his question.

"Do we have dried food or nuts?" He pressed his thumbnail into his forefinger to try to calm his racing heart.

"Don't do this," she said, as if she knew what he planned.

Everything in the room darkened. The idea of Mother supporting him burnt up as fast as an old flyer in a flame. He was alone, as usual.

"I made a promise," he said. "Besides, you help."

"Not like this," she said. "It's too dangerous. If you get caught, they'll take you." The web of blue lines along her temples bulged.

"How is feeding a stray dog too dangerous?" he lied.

Mother stared at Friedrich long enough to make him squirm and then dashed out.

"You think I am bad," she called from the kitchen over the sound of drawers opening and shutting. She came back in with a tear streaming down her cheek, holding a small bag of nuts and three apples. She laid it on his bed. "But I protect you." Then she rushed out without looking at him and the bristly sound of scrub brushes started to echo through the lonely house.

Friedrich finished packing. The sack looked just right at 70 percent full, not overstuffed to attract attention. He swung it over his shoulder, forgetting how sore it was. Electric pain pierced in, as if someone just thrust a needle in his joint. He deserved it after throwing so many rocks.

After it faded, Friedrich carefully adjusted the sack on his other shoulder and tiptoed out his apartment without saying goodbye. After he pushed through the front door, he set off toward the Rosen's building. The address Mr. Rosen gave him was the same as the one he heard Günter give Fritz. Friedrich moved quickly. He wanted it done.

The late afternoon sun put him in the shade on the west side of the street. An intense brightness spread across crammed apartment houses on the east. It was God's spotlight. The eerie, orange light made the houses with large windows look like people with large eyes. They reminded Friedrich of wide-eyed children asking forgiveness in church. On the sidewalk in front, boys in uniforms swung sticks. Each howled louder than the next. They didn't seem to care about God's spotlight or asking forgiveness. It reminded him of how he felt about the reds and, suddenly, all the rage he still had fiercely troubled him. Friedrich sped past the boys and was glad that perverse wind that had swept him up and made him throw rocks earlier wasn't catching him now.

Friedrich approached Pudding's apartment house. He stopped across the street and looked around. No Brownshirts or Jungvolks were in sight, but he still waited for a group of ladies in big hats to turn the corner before he sped across the street and slid in the front door.

It was so quiet in the foyer, Friedrich could have believed no one was home in the whole building. He found the stairs and slowly crept down. Sweat beaded along his forehead. What if someone caught him? What if Pudding's uncle tried to hurt him? He was wearing his Jungvolk uniform after all. Mother's words—*too dangerous*—ricocheted in his head and down to his legs. They made his feet stop. She was right. It was too dangerous.

He turned 180 degrees and put a foot on the step above. But as soon as he did, his eyebrow twitched. Helping Pudding's family was dangerous, but he had to do it. These people could have been Albert's family. It was right no matter how he looked at it. He took a breath and turned back toward the basement.

With each step down, the stench of mildew grew thicker. Pungent and musty, like old potatoes, decaying wood, and coal boiled together. But as sharp as it smelled, it reminded him of happy days exploring basements with Albert. If he believed in what other people called omens, this would be a good one.

The daylight that filtered down from the first floor dwindled, but he didn't dare turn on a light. At the bottom of the stairs, he placed his right hand on the wall and started east. The thick darkness made Friedrich feel like any creepy-crawly could sneak up and sink its teeth in him. At the end of the wall, he stopped to search for a clue where to go.

Faint illumination snuck in through the basement window, giving enough to see outlines after his eyes adjusted. Friedrich studied the storage rooms along the east side. All but one was locked. He approached it, figuring if anybody in Pudding's family was like Pudding, Friedrich would hear them. He heard a hushed whisper and put his ear to the door. Friedrich couldn't make out words, but heard a woman's hum. It had to be them.

He wasn't sure what to do, but wanted it to be over, so he tapped the thick, crumbling door with his nails and whispered, "Mr. Rosen sent me."

The humming stopped.

"Mr. Rosen and Pud . . . Emil Rosen sent me to check on you."

Friedrich heard voices murmuring and then a man say clearly, "Don't believe him."

"Look," Friedrich said. He reached in his pocket and pulled the door open just enough to inject his arm into the room. "He gave me his marbles."

Friedrich felt the tickle of breath on his palm. Then hands tightened around his wrist. Friedrich was pulled inside.

Friedrich heard a man say, "Sarah! Are you crazy?" and saw the outline of a man's body jump back.

"They're Emil's marbles," a girl said.

"It's too dark to tell," a large silhouette with a woman's voice said.

"They are his," the girl said. "I can tell."

"Maybe he stole them," the man said.

The man's figure crept closer, like he was trying to get a better look at Friedrich.

"My God!" the man said. "He's Jungvolk!"

The woman pulled the girl behind her.

"Shh!" Friedrich said. The man was doing a terrible job at keeping quiet.

"They've come for us!" the man whined.

"I said Mr. Rosen sent me to check on you," Friedrich said, and then held his breath. The air smelled stuffier by the second.

"If there's one, they'll be more," the man wailed.

"Look," Friedrich said, matching the man's sharpness. He shook the bag. "I've brought food and supplies."

"How do we know it's not poisoned?" the man asked.

The question stole the last bit of Friedrich's patience. He tossed the nuts toward the man's feet. "Eat them or the muddy-hell mice will!" He turned toward the woman. "I could get into a lot of trouble for helping you."

"Then why are you?" the woman asked.

Friedrich thought, *Because Pudding helped me, because it could have been Albert hiding, because Uncle Hilmar would think it right, because the whole world was now as cruel as Günter, because I still believed in yesterday's laws, because it's my purest truth, and because I didn't want to be a boy who threw rocks*, but he said, "Because Mr. Rosen asked me to."

The woman stepped forward. "How are my husband and son?"

"Henriette!" the man cried.

"Enough, Leo," the woman whispered.

"Secure," Friedrich said. "They are hiding on a riverbank. I brought them a pan and . . ."

"A riverbank! Outside?" the woman interrupted. "I thought they were with Mr. Hofmann."

"I don't know Mr. Hofmann," Friedrich continued.

CRUSHING THE RED FLOWERS

"Anyway, I brought them bandages, snacks, and survival essentials. Here are some for you." Friedrich pointed toward the sack.

"Thank you," the woman said. "Is it safe to return?"

"What's going on out there?" the girl asked.

"Did you bring gloves?" the man asked as he opened the sack.

"How did you find my father and brother at a river?" the girl asked.

Friedrich wondered why they all talked at the same time. He chose to answer the most important question. "No, it's not safe. I'll let Mr. Rosen know when it is."

"This has been going on too long," the man said. "The Brownshirts have a propensity for violence. And you Jungvolk . . ."

"They've been brainwashed," the girl interrupted. "They think they're doing right."

"That's because they're rewarded for it," the woman said the second the girl finished.

"I have to go," Friedrich whispered. The job was done and Friedrich didn't want to spend time debating.

"Thank you," the woman said. She grabbed Friedrich and pulled him toward her. She somehow embraced him, pinched his check, smoothed down his hair, and straightened his collar at the same time. It was the most awkward hug he had ever experienced. He wiggled out, but a small part of him wished he had a mother who gave hugs like that.

Friedrich couldn't risk being caught in that basement, so he said, "Goodbye," and slid through the door.

He heard the girl ask, "Are you a friend of Emil's?" as
the man asked, "Can you bring something hot?" as the
woman said, "So skinny! He needs a nice stew." Then
the door closed.

Friedrich exhaled. From that moment on, if anyone
caught him in the building, he could say he was following Günter's instructions to check on the Rosen's.

He raced up the stairs toward light. But halfway up,
his feet tangled. He threw out his hands to catch himself on the step and felt something sharp slice through
his palm. Pain rippled through him. The world swayed,
forcing him to sit. Tears squeezed out. He bit his lower
lip to keep from screaming.

After some time of steady breathing, he raised his
throbbing hand and walked the rest of the way up. A
cool trickle of blood flowed down his arm. Outside
in the street, a bright red puddle pooled in his palm.
The color of poppies. He remembered how the petals
had smelled when he tried to crush them. He inhaled,
half expecting to catch a whiff of summer. The shot of
fresh air cleared his head. He pulled out a handkerchief,
wrapped his wound and headed toward home.

The world had calmed from earlier. Garbage and glass
lay abandoned on the ground. Fewer people sprinted here
and there. Longer periods of quiet stretched between distant cries. He pictured packs of wolves resting after hunts.

Two blocks in, he spotted a circle of boys in Jungvolk uniforms, waving around candlesticks and vases. Friedrich walked on, numb and dazed. He was nearly next to them before he realized they were his own Jungvolk group. It was too late to slip away before they spotted him. He joined the circle.

Werner smiled wildly as he clutched a crystal bowl. "Better get some while it lasts!"

"What else?" Günter asked, nodding.

"I'm giving this to my Mother," Karl said, stroking a fur wrap. "They had so many and my mother doesn't even have one."

"Look how these shine!" Ernst said, flashing two silver candleholders. He faced Friedrich. "Why didn't you get anything?"

"Friedrich has been busy," Günter said. "I heard what he's been up to."

Friedrich froze. How did he know? The boys edged in. Friedrich shut his eyes. He was too weak to fight.

Karl pointed down and shouted, "What happened?" They all started at his bandaged hand. Blood had seeped through the handkerchief.

"Look at how he stands!" Günter boomed. Friedrich was ready to pass out.

"Johannes told me everything," Günter said. "Not only has Friedrich served the Führer with loyalty and passion, he has bravely endured injury."

Friedrich could barely feel the pats on his back.

"See that it is properly treated," Günter said, nodding toward Friedrich, and then turned back to the group. "Now, back to business. I want status reports. Fritz and Werner?"

"We went to all the addresses," said Fritz. "Only the Rosens weren't arrested. We saw Brownshirts in their apartment and . . ."

"That's where I got the bowl!" Werner interrupted.

Fritz thrust his elbow in Werner's ribs. "And they told us they were missing."

"Unacceptable!" Günter hollered. Günter slammed his fist into his palm.

Friedrich wobbled.

"Fritz, I want three status checks a day on those Rosens." Günter had the same wild look in his eye that Friedrich had seen all day. "When they return, I will deal with them myself."

24. The Return

Emil clasped the banister with both hands to keep from trembling. The hallway stairs were the same ones he had climbed every day of his life, so he couldn't believe how different they felt. Vati had started up first. Then Mama, Sarah, Uncle Leo, and now Emil.

"How wonderfully warm," Vati said. "What a pleasure to unbutton my jacket." The peaks and valleys in his voice made Vati sound like he was singing.

"How can you stand the brightness?" Uncle Leo asked. Emil noticed how Uncle Leo, Sarah, and Mama had been squinting since they left the potato room.

"The light is perfect," Vati said.

"I don't even know what day it is," Uncle Leo said.

"Friday!" Vati sang out. "We're home in time to light Shabbat candles."

Emil tiptoed past Mrs. Schmidt's door. It opened just enough for Emil to see the white of an eye. He held his breath, expecting Mrs. Schmidt to fly out screaming words like "objectionable" and "inappropriate," but the door snapped shut. Something wasn't right.

Mama must have sensed it too because she said, "Josef, maybe you should have waited until that boy came back."

"Whatever is meant to be, will be. But my girls will not spend another second in that basement!" Vati bent to kiss Mama on the step below. Everyone stopped behind like stalled train cars.

Emil finally called out, "I'm hungry," to make the kissing stop.

They all resumed climbing the last few steps to their fifth-floor apartment. But when each person reached the landing in front of their door, they stopped. When Emil caught up, he saw why. Their door was open. The wood along the edges near the knob was scraped apart. Someone had forced their way in.

"Let's get it over with," Mama said. She reached for Vati's hand.

Vati pushed open the door and they stepped in to an apartment that Emil almost didn't recognize. It looked like a giant had juggled their furniture and dropped it every which way. Their thick curtains had been ripped off, leaving the windows bare. All the sparkly crystal and painted vases were gone. What should have been inside drawers was littered around the floor. Mama's red velvet cuddle chair was now a pile of sticks and fabric. And at the center of everything, a swastika the size of a tree trunk was carved into the shiny black piano top.

No one spoke. Emil glanced at Mama. She didn't wipe the tears that ran down her cheeks. Vati held one of her shaking hands and Sarah reached for the other. Emil waited for Mama to give some hint that everything would be alright, but she didn't. He wished that Vati would say something, or Sarah would stomp around, or even Uncle Leo would complain.

Finally, Mama said, "That!" pointing to the swastika on the piano, "will not keep you from practicing, Emil Rosen!" She plucked a large, round lacy doily from the ground and covered the swastika.

Vati and Sarah smiled. Something lifted, making it seem like maybe it would be alright after all. Mama was still Mama and Emil was still Emil, even if that meant there really was nothing that could get him out of practicing piano.

Uncle Leo walked to the lamp and twisted the knob. After four clicks, he hollered, "They stole the lightbulbs!"

"They are just things," Vati said.

"They are our things," Uncle Leo said.

"Where's the silver and crystal?" Sarah asked. "They took everything!"

"Don't panic," Mama said and slipped into her bedroom. "I hid some things in just-in-case spots."

Emil smiled.

She called from her bedroom, "I'm sure they didn't check every shirt pocket." Then she scurried into Sarah's room and said, "Or in between the pages of every book." She cradled a few small packages as she raced into Emil's room. "Or for things taped under every dresser drawer," Mama said.

As she walked toward the kitchen, she winked and

said, "Or inside the flour bin." Her arms were stuffed with bills and jewelry.

Vati kissed his hand and blew it toward her.

"You are full of tricks, Mama," Sarah said.

"Just in case," Mama said.

Uncle Leo smiled.

"And remember Mrs. Müller," Mama said, as she came back into the living room. "She's keeping the bulk of our money safe until we leave for Paraguay, but this will hold us over."

She smiled as warm as the July sun. Emil soaked it in. For those few seconds, Emil really believed everything would be alright.

Mama heard it first. Like someone flicked a switch, her expression darkened. She grabbed hold of the piano top, flung it open, and poured everything she held on top of the strings. The moment she closed it was the moment Emil heard it too. A stampede raged up the stairs. The monster was coming.

Emil faced the door just as two figures wearing green police uniforms burst through.

One said, "Josef Rosen?"

But Emil still heard the stampede in the staircase and understood what it was. There was nothing like the angry clomp of SS boots.

Vati stepped forward, but before he answered, two more people charged in. Two snarling men in black SS uniforms waved around guns. One pointed a weapon right at him. It happened too so fast to think. His heart felt as if it jumped to the moon. Then a fifth person entered and Emil knew that everything would not be alright. Günter Beck stood in the middle of his living room.

The older of the two SS men pointed a gun at Vati's war scar and shouted, "You!"

"And you!" the younger man hollered, lunging toward Uncle Leo. "Come with us!"

Vati held up his hands. "Yes, yes, of course." His pitch was high.

"Now!" the older SS man screamed. "Or I will give you a new scar!"

"I got this one fighting for our country in the Great War," Vati said.

The older SS man stopped. "Fighting for our country, eh?" he said. The man stared at Vati for a long moment. He then raised a hand and struck Vati right on his war scar.

Mama screamed. Sarah grabbed onto her arm.

"Germany is not your country!" the man shouted.

Blood trickled on Vati's collar.

"Let's continue with business," the policeman wearing a green uniform said. "We still have more. Josef Rosen, we are here to arrest you and Leo Grünburg."

"On what grounds?" asked Mama.

They all faced her. She looked small standing among the tall green and black figures.

"On the grounds that you own more than five thousand Reichsmarks and on the grounds that you have not left Germany."

The old SS man pushed his gun into Vati's back, making him stumble toward the door.

"Wait! We are leaving in just weeks!" Mama said and pulled papers from her pocket. "Here are our visas."

They were the most important documents in the world and looked so flimsy in Mama's shaking hand. Only a few papers separated his family from a new, safe life.

"We'll see about that," sneered an SS man.

The green uniformed policeman grabbed the papers. What if he tore them? Emil felt like he would throw up.

"We leave December 1st," Mama said.

"Everything is in order." Vati pulled a handkerchief from his pocket and his pocket watch tumbled out. It swayed as he dabbed blood from his cheek.

"Everything is not in order," the policeman said. "I see no visa for Leo Grünburg." The policeman shoved the papers back at Mama and pointed at Uncle Leo. "You both come with us. If your story is verified, Josef Rosen, perhaps you'll be released."

"No!" Emil heard himself scream.

One of the SS men stormed toward Uncle Leo and grabbed his arm.

Günter narrowed his eyes. "One can't be certain about anything with Jews."

The policeman turned to Vati. "Make no mistake," he said. "If we find you here December 2nd, we'll come for you."

"But there is still the matter of the next three weeks," Günter said, moving toward Emil. "Jews are tricky. Perhaps check-ins should be conducted."

Günter moved toward Sarah. "Daily check-ins," he said, almost nose to nose with her. She clenched her jaw and didn't look away.

Günter glared at Mama. "And that puts undue strain on our resources." He walked to Vati. "So to compensate for the extra work you cause us, we will collect a payment."

The older SS man said, "Get on with it. We have more houses."

Günter wrapped his fingers around Vati's dangling pocket watch. The watch Emil was not allowed to touch. The watch that was supposed to be his one day.

Günter yanked and Emil heard Vati's shirt seam tear.

"This," Günter said, holding it up, "is today's payment." The golden disc spun on its chain.

Günter walked toward the door, but before he left, he said, "I will be back tomorrow for a check-in and I expect fair payment for my services."

Five people in uniforms, Vati, Uncle Leo, and the pocket watch moved toward the door.

"I will be released in no time!" Vati called back to Mama.

"Take care of yourself, Henriette!" Uncle Leo cried, "Take care of the children!"

Emil closed his eyes and heard the door slam shut. The house was so still, he wondered if he had imagined it. Maybe none of it happened. He opened his eyes and looked toward Uncle Leo's favorite chair. It was on its side, with newspapers strewn all around.

Tears gushed out. Emil was falling, falling off a cliff. He dropped to the floor and heard terrible howls. Moments passed before he understood the shrieks that sounded like an injured animal came from him.

Emil felt Mama on the floor with him, holding him, rocking him, murmuring, "Shhhhh."

"I'm sorry!" Emil cried. Sobs shook his body. "You saw it coming. No one believed you."

"No, Emil," Mama said in a far-off way, "This, I did not see coming."

Mama released him and walked to Uncle Leo's favorite chair. She turned it upright, collected the scattered newspapers, and folded them as if it was any regular, old day. Then she sat and folded her hands. There was an expression on her face Emil had never seen. It reminded him of Ari on parade day. And reminded him of how he felt the day Opa had died.

25. Watching the Plague Spread

Friedrich sped up past the Chilean Embassy on the way to Jungvolk service hours. Rain poured down on people waiting in a line that wrapped itself around the corner. The storm drenched them, turning them as gray as the late November sky. They looked away when they spotted his uniform.

Yesterday Friedrich read a newspaper article about how Jews were standing in long lines and clogging up sidewalks at South American embassies. It said they probably wouldn't get visas even if they waited all day. Friedrich was glad the rain came down so hard. He didn't want to hear what the gray people said.

He hurried two more blocks, eager to escape the biting downpour, until he saw the backs of Johannes and Fritz under the meeting-place canopy. Rain muffled their voices until Friedrich was in front of the building. They didn't see him approach.

"He's so strange," Fritz said.

"Strange yes," Johannes said, "but you should have seen him on Kristallnacht. He was fiercer than anyone."

They were talking about him. He pretended he hadn't heard and said, "Hello," as he slid past.

Friedrich brushed the wetness off and took his seat

in the center of the third row. So much had changed since he had thrown those rocks. He lost part of himself that day and gained a new part. Last month, he would have fretted over what Fritz said, but not today. He never thought he could smash windows or scream through the streets. And he never thought he could help hide Jews, but he did. Now he knew what he was capable of. He was Friedrich. They thought he was strange. So be it.

The boys edged closer to their seats, which meant Günter would start the meeting any minute. Friedrich reached in his pocket and ran his fingertip along a model train. Since the day the world had gone mad, he always carried one of Uncle Hilmar's trains and Pudding's marbles with him. The train because it made Uncle Hilmar feel closer and the marbles because they reminded him that he could be more than a boy who threw rocks. The next time Hannover turned upside down, he prayed the train and marbles would ground him.

Günter placed a pair of candlesticks at the front of the room. Sunlight was sparse, but the candlesticks still sparkled. They were probably what Günter called his daily check-in payment. The Saturday after everything happened, Günter called a Jungvolk meeting and announced all hiding Jews had been caught. A golden pocket watch and a silver cake server were passed around. They were fair payments, he had boasted, for his time.

Günter stood to start service hours. Within seconds, every boy settled in his seat.

Günter started with the standard greeting and ceremony and then said, "I'd like to share highlights of the Führer's speech specifically directed at German youth." He cleared his throat.

> Our nation is shaped by your image.
> Because you are our ideal of loyalty, we also want to be loyal.
> We want you to be obedient, courageous, never collapse.
> In you Germany will live hard, not soft.

The speech stirred something in Friedrich. He wanted to eat the words up and feel all the honor they promised. But for the first time since the day he threw rocks, his eyebrow twitched. Friedrich glanced at the boys around him and wondered how it was so easy for them to just fit in.

"And so to move on with business, for today's check-in payment, I received these." Günter motioned toward the candlesticks. "The Jews have been fined one billion Reichsmarks for all the damages they caused on Kristallnacht, and as you can see, we're doing our share to help."

Günter hoisted the candlesticks. The boys cheered and cackled. Germany charging Jews for Kristallnacht damages seemed as unfair as France charging Germany for Great War damages, but Friedrich wasn't about to share that idea.

"I wonder what tomorrow's payment will be," Günter said.

Oh, just let them go, Friedrich thought.

Fritz spun back from the seat in front.

Did I say that aloud? Friedrich sucked in his breath.

"Is there a problem, Fritz?" Günter asked.

"I heard Friedrich say to let them go," Fritz said.

What a weasel!

Günter furrowed his forehead. "Friedrich?"

Everyone stared at Friedrich. His mind raced for something to say.

"It's just that . . . ," he started, sewing thoughts together. "They'll be someone else's problem soon, not Germany's, so they need to go."

That didn't make sense, so he kept talking.

"Like you said, the check-ins are extra work."

Günter said nothing. Friedrich wasn't sure if Günter was trying to understand or getting ready to turn the boys loose on him.

Friedrich spurt out, "I just want the Jews out already so I never have to think about them again!" That last sentence sounded good enough, so he stopped speaking.

"Oh, I assure you they will be gone," Günter said. "Take the Rosens. If they don't leave for Paraguay, Josef Rosen will be arrested. So either way, we are rid of them."

Günter pointed toward Fritz's raised hand.

"But if they leave for Paraguay, they won't be punished," Fritz said.

"Explain," Günter said.

"Josef Rosen got out of jail only after one day and soon he'll leave for Paraguay. He won't be arrested again, so the Rosens are not really being punished."

"True," Günter said, clenching his jaw. "Unless . . ."

Friedrich's skin prickled. Watching a grin spread over Günter's face was like watching the plague spread.

"Unless they miss their boat," Günter said.

"Miss their boat?" Fritz asked.

Günter said, "On December 1st, they plan to take a taxi at 10:00 to catch an 11:00 train to take them to their boat in Hamburg. Perhaps a late taxi would have them miss their boat. And then Josef Rosen will be arrested."

Friedrich envisioned it unfolding. Günter would block the taxi. Some pedestrians would stare and some would hurry past. Pudding would miss the boat and Mr. Rosen would be arrested.

Friedrich felt nauseous. He wanted to warn them, but he couldn't go to their house. Günter checked in every day and who knew when Fritz kept watch. It was dangerous. Friedrich calculated. He would be 100 percent safe if he didn't help and 80 percent safe if he did. 80 percent was too risky.

One of Papa's sayings popped into his head: "The strongest bonds are with people who are there for you when no one else is." Except for Albert and his own family, no one had ever helped Friedrich. Except Pudding. And he had helped him twice. Once when he gave him bottles for his project and a second time when he saved him from ending up like Otto that day he found Brutus. Friedrich already helped Pudding in a big way, but only once. He still owed him one more to make it even.

Friedrich felt like two giants were pulling him apart. His hand shot up to cover his trembling eyebrow. If he didn't help, it may never stop twitching. He ticked through the Would–Could–Should technique. Yes, he would have the guts to warn them and yes, he should help. But no, he didn't think he could get past Günter.

The 80 percent had to increase. Friedrich closed his eyes. He spun the wheels of the train in his pocket and pushed his mind to run through possibilities. Round and round they twirled until he had the beginning of something. Friedrich couldn't warn Pudding before, but maybe he could help the day they left.

He worked out the details. It was a good plan, not great. It would keep him safe, but wasn't as likely to work. There was a 95 percent chance he wouldn't get caught and a 60 percent chance the Rosens would make it to the train station on time. Friedrich opened his eyes and glared at Günter. Those were the best odds, so they muddy hell would have to do.

26. The Day Had Come

Mama had been flying around their apartment since 5:00 o'clock in the morning, packing and unpacking four gigantic suitcases. Now as Emil hauled one down the stairs, he didn't care that it thumped like an elephant in front of Mrs. Schmidt's door because today was the day he was going to Paraguay. It was an adventure more thrilling than any Vati had told him. He was leaving for an exotic land with colorful animals and new foods and warmer winters and not even Mrs. Schmidt could squash it.

Mama led the way down the stairs, followed by Sarah, then Emil and Vati in the rear. They each tugged a suitcase behind. Their formation reminded Emil of a line of baby ducks trailing after Mama duck.

Thump! echoed in the hall, as Emil dragged his suitcase down to the step below.

"This is a wonderful move, but get used to being poor," Mama called from the front. "The cabin boys better not expect a tip."

Thump! came from someone else's suitcase.

This was the third time she mentioned the cabin boys' tip. She has been really worried about money. Each of them was only allowed to take a little bit of their money to Paraguay. The rest had stayed in Germany.

"Lots of people are poor in Paraguay," Sarah said.

"That Mrs. Müller should be ashamed!" Mama said.

Thump!

No one had heard from Mrs. Müller after Mama asked her to hide their money. Emil wasn't surprised.

"Anyone who smells like chicken shouldn't be trusted," Emil said. If that wasn't a real saying, it should be.

"Let it go," Vati called from behind. "We have no recourse."

Mama waved her hand at him like she was shooing away a fly.

Thump!

"You know there aren't many Jews in Paraguay," Sarah said.

"There aren't many Nazis either," Vati said.

Thump!

"We'll make a nice home while we're in Paraguay," Mama said. "And then hopefully we'll find our way to Argentina. There's a nice Jewish community there."

"Better opportunities," Vati said.

Thump!

"Remember," Mama said, stopping on a landing to wave a finger. "No talking politics on the ship! I don't want to get this far only to be turned out!"

Uncle Leo was the one who couldn't stop talking politics. Emil stopped himself from telling Mama she didn't have to worry since Uncle Leo wouldn't be with them. His uncle hadn't returned since the day he was arrested. The police had released plenty of arrested men, so no one wanted to think about why not Uncle Leo.

"I'll try, Mama," Emil said.

Thump! Thump! Thump!

"And don't worry Emil," Sarah called. "I'm sure we'll find a piano."

"Priority number one!" Mama called.

Pickles! Emil had a better chance of playing a game of marbles with Adolf Hitler than getting out of piano lessons.

"Maybe Sarah should start playing again too," Emil said. "You said change was good."

Sarah swung back. She looked ready to throw him out a window.

"Hmph, you have a point," Mama said. "New land, new lessons!"

Sarah glared up at Emil as she thumped down another step. Emil smiled and waved.

"And Emil," Mama said. "The train ride to Hamburg is a few hours. Find a way to entertain yourself quietly."

Sometimes, Mama must forget he was twelve. How could she think two hours on a train would be a problem after he had been penned up inside for the last three weeks? Right after Uncle Leo was arrested, all Jewish people had to give up their driver's licenses and weren't allowed in movie theaters anymore. After school had expelled Emil, Mama stopped letting him out altogether.

It was so boring, he thought he would go crazy, just like his third cousin Herman. Herman had been quarantined with, as Mama said, "an ailment you didn't want." After a month in isolation, he started catching and painting houseflies. Blues, yellows, and reds whirled around like an unraveling rainbow. After the last three weeks, it didn't sound like such a bad idea. Emil snorted. Two hours on a train! That would pass in a blink.

Four Rosens and four suitcases crammed into the front foyer.

"The passports!" Vati exclaimed, patting his pockets.

"I told you I have them," Mama said. She reached her hand into the side of her bra and pulled up four passports. A bright red *J* for Jewish exposed itself. Pretty soon, Emil would have a new passport that looked like everyone else's, with no letter *J*.

"And I have the visas and everything else," Mama said. She pushed the outside door open for the last time. "Let's go!"

Sunlight flooded the dark hall and Emil suddenly thought of all the furniture they were leaving behind. Emil squinted as he walked outside. Saying goodbye to his apartment would be the hardest part, so he was saving that for last, right before he stepped into the taxi. For the past few weeks, Emil had been trying to focus on what he would gain in Paraguay instead of the life he was losing in Hannover. He didn't like thinking about his family being forced to abandon the apartment they had called home for generations. Or the city they loved. The bakeries, the markets, the energy. None of it would be as good as in Hannover. He was leaving everything and everyone for a land that spoke a language he couldn't understand.

Emil took a few steps on the sidewalk and waited for his eyes to adjust to brightness. But once he saw clearly, he found four figures watching him from the curb. They wore uniforms. Günter Beck and three other boys stood in front of the parked taxi. Vati pulled Sarah behind him.

Mama gritted her teeth. "I have your final payment," she said as she slipped her hand into her coat pocket and pulled out a butterfly brooch covered with jewels.

"Here," she said, and thrust it toward Günter. Emil remembered her wearing it to fancy dinners long ago. It was one of her favorites.

Günter snatched it and said, "But today requires an additional payment."

Emil's stomach churned. This wasn't supposed to happen.

"It is my most exquisite brooch." Mama's voice cracked and Emil could tell she didn't have anything left to give.

"Since you've caused so much trouble, I must claim your passports," Günter said.

"Now see here!" Vati stepped between Mama and Günter. "We have given you everything you've asked for, even though it was not required by law. That is an extraordinary brooch worth a great deal. Our train leaves in . . ." Vati fumbled in the pocket where his watch used to be. "We are leaving now!"

"I'll take the brooch and your passports, and then you may enter the taxi," Günter said.

Mama wrung her hands.

"No," Vati said and stepped closer to Günter. "We need our passports to board the ship."

"Very well." Günter signaled the driver and the taxi sped away.

"That was our taxi!" Sarah screamed.

"This is an outrage!" Vati said.

Mama sat down on her suitcase. Her face turned pale.

"We'll call another," Sarah said.

"Then I'll send that one away, too," Günter snapped.

Mama hunched over. She looked like she had when Uncle Leo didn't return after he was arrested. Sarah ran to her. She spoke softly and rubbed Mama's back.

Emil couldn't believe this was happening. He didn't know if missing their boat would mess up the visas, or if they would arrest Vati, or how long it would take to get new boat tickets, or if they even had money for new boat tickets. Günter could really ruin their lives.

Günter looked as calm as if he were waiting to buy bread. He walked to Sarah's suitcase and sat on it.

"This is ridiculous!" Vati said and stamped a foot. "We are leaving!"

"Go ahead up and call another taxi," Günter said.

"I'll stay with your family." Vati didn't move.

Vati frantically looked up and down the street. Maybe there was another taxi. Maybe one would stop. Maybe Vati could talk his way in. Minute after minute passed and none came. Emil gazed up at his apartment. Instead of saying good-bye, he was praying he wouldn't have to sleep in it tonight. Mama put her face in her hands. Pedestrians sped past, darting their eyes away. Emil's heart ached. He couldn't stand seeing Mama this way.

Vati walked to Mama. "Don't worry," he whispered. "I know what to do." Vati glanced up and down the street and Emil could tell he was just pretending to have a plan, like when he pretended to go to Mr. Hofmann's house.

Tears flooded Emil's eyes. The world blurred. He turned from Günter, so he wouldn't see him cry. Emil blinked fast to push aside the tears. The other side of the street refocused and that's when Emil saw him.

It was River Boy, tucked into an entrance across the street. He pointed to something Emil couldn't see around the corner. Günter and his boys didn't seem to notice. Emil shrugged in his direction and River Boy ducked out of sight. After a moment, he reappeared, looking angry. He put his finger straight over his lips, pointed around the corner, and then used both hands like he was steering a car.

There must be a taxi around the corner waiting for

them! Emil choked back a smile. They could still make it. He just needed to get his family around the corner without Günter.

Emil gave a faint nod to River Boy. River Boy nodded back and walked toward the boys. He stopped next to Günter and crossed his arms over his chest. His face twisted into one of them. River Boy sneered, "No boat for them."

Mama glanced up when he spoke. She must have recognized him. She looked back down and shook her head. Vati glared at him. Sarah looked back and forth between River Boy and Emil. Emil had to act quickly before someone said something to wreck the plan.

"I know!" Emil said, sprinting toward Mama. "We can catch the trolley! Come on!"

Günter took a step toward them, but River Boy said, "Let them go. The trolley stops at every block. It's Thursday, midmorning. It will take an hour. They'll never make it." That part was true. The route to the station wove endlessly through the city.

The shortest, freckle-faced boy said, "Too bad you didn't think of that earlier."

"Hope you can manage luggage on the trolley," another boy said.

"We won't make it," Mama murmured.

"It would be a pity not to try," Günter said and gave a wicked laugh.

"Come on, Mama!" Emil said. "Please try!"

Emil heard River Boy say to Günter, "Let's get your

father. He can arrest the man when they get back."

At that, Mama stood up.

"Well, I'm going!" Emil said. There was no way his family would let him go off alone, so if he ran around the corner, he knew they would follow.

"Emil!" Mama screamed. "Don't you go anywhere!"

There was no time to think. Emil grabbed his suitcase and dashed in the direction of where River Boy had pointed.

"Emil Abraham Rosen!" Vati shouted.

Emil looked back. Just as he thought, his family had grabbed their suitcases and ran behind to catch up.

A boy said, "I can't wait to see their faces when they get back." The rest hooted.

Emil turned the corner and saw the most wonderful sight he could imagine: a parked taxi. He ran to it without greeting the driver and shoved his bag in the trunk. Vati, Mama, and Sarah hustled toward him. No one said a word. Mama sat in front and Sarah jumped in the back. Emil and Vati packed the rest of the luggage and rushed inside. Mama had never been so quick, Sarah had never been so quiet, and car doors had never shut so softly.

Emil unrolled the window and heard someone scream, "Wait! That's not the way to the trolley!" It ricocheted around the car like a rubber bullet.

Vati told the driver, "Train station, please hurry."

As the car started to move, Emil reached for his

marbles in his pocket and tossed a handful out the window. He turned to peer back through the rear windshield. The car had only moved twenty meters when Emil saw five figures charge from around the corner.

They chased after the car, screaming, "Stop!" Emil coughed and hacked, as he rolled up the window, so the driver wouldn't hear.

"Sir," Emil said loudly, "our train leaves at 11:00."

The boys were close enough to catch them. Emil held his breath. If the car stopped at all in the next minute, it would be over. He turned back to see how far the boys were. Emil held back a gasp when he saw that they were nearly on top of them. But just then, two figures slid as if they were on ice. It was where Emil had thrown the marbles. Günter and River Boy tumbled to the ground. The other three stopped running.

Emil could have believed River Boy had a microphone by the way "Muddy hell!" ripped through Hannover. The driver glanced back at the scene, but didn't seem to think much of a pile of boys in the middle of the street. The figures got smaller as the car drove. Their heads were smaller than marbles by the time the driver turned the corner and sped away.

"Thank you," Vati said to the driver. "We"—he stopped when Mama shot him a look.

"The train station, right?" the driver asked. He looked younger than Vati, but his voice was gruff, like a man Opa's age who had worked outside all his life.

"That's right," Vati said.

"I usually wait at an entrance, but that boy said you'd come," the driver said.

Emil wondered if his family figured it was River Boy.

"He seemed like a fine boy plus he gave me this for my wait." The driver held up a glistening model train in one hand as he clutched the steering wheel with the other. It was a beautiful piece of work. The driver spun a wheel with his thumb. Emil couldn't believe River Boy gave away something so nice and he swore he would find a way to pay him back.

"She's a beauty! My boy will love it," the driver said. "Never had money for something like this."

Everything seemed to be falling into place. Still, something bothered Emil. He turned backward to look through the rear window. No sign of Günter. When he looked forward, he caught the driver's eye in a mirror staring at him. It looked bright under his gray hat. The driver glanced at Mama and then Vati.

"Why'd he want me to wait along the side, not by the entrance?" he asked.

"Fewer cars, so easier loading," Mama said, without blinking.

"Where's your train heading?" The driver asked, watching Mama more than the road.

"To the country," Mama said. "Who doesn't need fresh air in this city."

The driver snorted and said, "Well that's the truth!"

The driver spun the train wheel again and went back to watching the road. No one said a word after that. Sarah sank back. The lines on Mama's forehead faded. Vati smiled at Emil.

But Emil couldn't smile back. Something still nagged at him. Perhaps it was because he never said good-bye to his home. Or perhaps Emil had forgotten something. He looked out the window and watched a bicyclist weave in and out of pedestrians on the sidewalk. Then he remembered. A pile of bikes leaned against his building. He'd never seen them before. They must have belonged to the boys. Günter could still make it to the station.

27. Muddy Hell Luck

Five boys crammed onto three bikes and charged toward the train station. Friedrich's brain jostled around his skull as he whipped through the Hannover streets. Johannes stood, pedaling furiously, while Friedrich clung to the seat with both hands, struggling to hang on. No one spoke. When Günter threatened, he was frightening, but when Günter said nothing, he was terrifying. Friedrich had never seen Günter angrier. He no longer worried that Pudding would miss his train, he worried that Günter would kill him.

Günter had a sizable lead in front of Johannes. Ernst fell further behind with Fritz on the handlebars. Johannes screamed back to pedal faster. Friedrich needed a plan. They were just minutes from the station and Friedrich didn't know what to do. He lashed at himself. After all that preparation, he couldn't believe he had forgotten to account for the bikes. The boys used them often enough, so it was a stupid mistake.

The boys swerved into the station and Friedrich still didn't know how to fix things. Günter jumped off and threw his bike against the wall. The others toppled their bikes close by.

Johannes checked the time. "10:54!"

Six minutes. That was enough for Günter to catch them.

"Which way?" Fritz yelled.

Friedrich heard himself say, "Follow me," before he realized what he was doing. "They won't make it up to Hamburg!"

UP! thought Friedrich. *That was it!* Their train was heading up . . . north. He could lead Günter to a train heading south to throw them off. It may give the Rosens just enough time. Thank the stars he won that award last year for remodeling a train car. He knew the station inside and out.

"This way!" Friedrich dashed ahead. The others followed. He calculated as he ran. There was only about a five percent chance someone would figure him out.

He steered them through the side door to avoid the track number board and raced toward a staircase that led to a southbound platform. He prayed the station still used the same tracks for north and south.

A station clock read 10:56. They were running too fast. When they got to the southbound platform, Günter could figure it out, turn around, and make it to the northbound track. Friedrich had to slow them down. He reached in his pocket and felt for the marbles Pudding had given him.

Friedrich stopped short and shouted, "Look!" As the boys crashed into his back, he dropped a marble.

"They were here!" Friedrich said, pointing toward the ground.

"What?" Günter screamed, baring his teeth.

"There!" Friedrich said, shaking his arm.

"What?" Fritz said.

"A marble!" Friedrich picked it up. "They were here!"

Seventeen seconds successfully stalled and no one seemed to suspect him.

"And there!" Friedrich pointed to nothing in the far corner.

The boys crept closer to the corner, following Friedrich like sheep, until Günter roared, "Come on!"

They pushed past Friedrich up the stairs. The moment they were out of sight, he dropped a handful of marbles. If they figured out they were at the wrong platform, they would have to come down the same way. Pudding's trick worked once, so maybe it would work again.

Friedrich raced up to the platform, behind the others. At the top, there was no train and no people. The boys spun around, searching for any clue where to go. Friedrich could see crowds around a parked train on a northbound platform across the tracks. The clock read 10:57. Günter could still make it to the northbound side.

"Quiet!" Fritz said and put a hand to his ear.

A voice crackled city names and track numbers over the loud speaker. As they listened, Günter glared at Friedrich in a way that made his legs wobble. Günter probably didn't figure out he had sabotaged him, but that scowl told Friedrich that Günter blamed him for setting them on the wrong course, even if by accident.

"Track two!" Fritz screamed.

"Come on!" Friedrich yelled and charged ahead of them all. He wanted the Rosens to make it, but he had to save himself. The only way was to make it look like he wanted to catch them more than anyone. Friedrich raced back down the stairs a half step ahead of Günter. The others were right behind.

When he reached the bottom, his feet swung up from under him. He threw his hand out to break his fall. His palm and hip slammed on the grimy floor. Pain radiated through his wrist. He had forgotten about the marbles.

"Damn him!" Friedrich screamed without thinking. He gripped his throbbing wrist and rolled onto his back over the muck.

"That's right!" Günter said in a way that told Friedrich he may have been forgiven. Günter stepped over Friedrich and the others trailed in his shadow. In a second, they were gone. Pudding wouldn't make it.

He clutched the wall, slowly pulling himself up. An old lady wrinkled her nose as she made her way past. There was no point running. Günter was too far ahead. Friedrich cradled his wrist, weaving between people across the slick main lobby. The clock read 10:59. One minute. Günter would surely get them. All because of a single minute.

Friedrich scurried up the stairs to track two. Step by step, he braced himself for what he would find. Pudding beaten, strewn suitcases, Mrs. Rosen sobbing and that bloodthirsty look on Günter's face. Friedrich took a last step to make it to the top and held his breath.

The scene was not what he expected. A handful of people lingered on the platform, facing north, watching a train chug away. It picked up speed. The stillness swelled as the train distanced itself. Günter and the others glared at the blackened sky. The clock read 11:00. The train must have taken off at the beginning of the minute, not the end. One minute.

"What muddy-hell luck," Friedrich said aloud.

Günter swung around. He looked ready to throw him on the tracks. He rushed toward Friedrich shouting, "Muddy-hell luck is right!" Friedrich spread his legs apart and bent his knees for balance in case Günter really tried to toss him.

But when Günter reached Friedrich, he stopped. Günter's mouth opened and shut. He finally said, "I know you wanted the fat one, but there are plenty more." It took Friedrich a moment to understand Günter was trying to reassure him.

"We'll get them." Günter shook his red notebook. Friedrich could picture name after name scratched in.

Günter walked past and disappeared through the doors. Friedrich watched the others follow. No one looked back at him, not even Fritz. Friedrich felt a smile spread across his face. He had gotten away with it. Despite the incredible risks. He followed his purest truth. He did it. Friedrich filled his lungs with as much air as they would hold. He felt like a whole person.

Friedrich looked back toward the direction the train had gone and put his hand in his pocket. It felt lighter without his uncle's train. One lonely marble remained, wedged deep in a corner fold. He picked it free and pulled it out. Crimson swirls wove through its body. It reminded him of red poppy petals fluttering in the wind and for some odd reason, it felt lucky. He never believed that a thing could bring luck, but after what he had just seen, this time he could.

As he started for outside, Friedrich thought about Günter's promise to "get them." Those words meant days like these would happen again. A new normal. He'd have to figure out new rules. Friedrich closed his eyes. It was just beginning and he was already exhausted.

But he was almost thirteen and would be leaving the Jungvolk for the Hitler Youth in a year. They went on lots of hiking trips. Maybe his Hitler Youth leader would be more like his old Jungvolk leader. Maybe he'd meet a new boy who loved to camp. Maybe if he just hung on for one more year, it would be better.

Friedrich walked out into the bright sun and looked down at the marble. A cold wind lashed at his ears. He gazed in the direction from where it blew and squeezed the marble tight. He didn't know what the next season would bring and wished Günter wouldn't be a part of it. But Friedrich did not have a choice. He had to trudge on. All he could do was try to keep up and pray for a little luck.

28. A Hero and a Lot of Luck

The world looked different through the train window. The passenger car propped Emil up high as it whizzed past brown-and-tan countryside. He ran his finger along the window, smearing an *E* into a thin layer of soot. It made him feel strong. Emil wondered how the world would look from a gigantic ship deck or from a sandy riverbank in Paraguay.

Mama had been right to fret about him not having anything to do during the train ride. He could barely sit still thinking about Paraguay. He wondered how many children would be in his new class and if Paraguay had fairy tales and if Mama's dumplings would taste the same.

Emil glanced at his family. Vati sat to his right and Mama and Sarah faced him in the seats across. Vati read a newspaper. Mama's purse sagged on her lap like a fat housecat. She clutched the handle with one hand and held open a German-Spanish dictionary with the other. His parents lounged in their seats, untroubled. Emil was certain they didn't know Günter Beck had chased them right up to when the train left. Sarah gazed out the window. Emil wondered if she had seen Günter jump out on the platform too. He'd ask later when Mama wasn't around.

A sweet apple smell wafted in from the dining car. It reminded him of spending afternoons at Mama's friends' houses when he was little. They had often served apple strudel, with flaky, buttery crusts. He wondered if Mama would eat strudel with new friends in Paraguay.

Mama reached in her purse and pulled out four wrapped sandwiches.

"Just-in-case sandwiches?" Vati bent across the aisle to kiss her.

Emil bit off a bite as big as his mouth could hold. The sandwiches weren't really sandwiches, just bread slices with a smear of something salty, but they were delicious. He wondered what the food would be like on the boat. Maybe there would be lots and lots of butter.

Sarah didn't touch her sandwich. It remained, tightly wrapped, on her lap.

"I'll take yours if you don't want it." Emil wiped his fingers on his pants.

"Eat, Sarah!" Mama ordered. "And use a napkin, Emil!" She smacked the back of Emil's hand.

Sarah stared out the window. She whispered, "Günter will get away with it," as if she hadn't meant to say it aloud.

Mama stopped eating.

Sarah turned toward them. "He took our beautiful things, treated us like criminals, tried to ruin our lives. And he'll never have to answer for any of it."

"Sometimes people don't see crime as crime until

much later," Mama said. Emil wondered when much later would be.

"And sometimes people don't see a hero as a hero until much later," Vati said, nodding toward Emil, "like your friend."

River Boy wasn't his friend, but he was his hero. Emil focused hard on the words *thank you, thank you, thank you*, and telepathically sent them to River Boy. Maybe when much later happened Emil could tell him in person.

"We're losing everything, Mama!" Sarah snapped. "Our home, our friends, everything we had worked hard to build . . ."

"We have not lost each other," Mama interrupted.

"We can rebuild," Vati said.

Sarah's eyes filled with tears and she sank back in her seat. "There are just too many bad people in this world."

"No, Liebchen," Mama said, "Most people aren't bad."

When Sarah didn't say anything, Mama went on, "A few are bad, really bad, no matter what chances or kindnesses they are given. And a few are really good no matter what hardships they face. But most people, like you and me, are somewhere in between, but closer to good than bad. Now eat."

"Günter is someone who's really bad." Sarah shook her head. "I just don't know how we made it."

"I guess it took a hero and a lot of luck," Mama said softly.

A shiver ran down Emil's spine as he thought of how easily they could have not made it. It was all like a game of cards, just coming down to a couple good moves and luck. He prayed he'd never need a hero and a lot of luck in Paraguay.

Emil looked out the window at blurred fields flashing past. They were bare and brown. Not like summertime when red poppies danced against emerald greens. Emil sighed. None of it would be his anymore, but it was okay because he was going the right way. That was a certainty. He wondered if Paraguay had poppies that he could give Mama if he forgot about the time.

"Well," Mama said, smiling. "I have good news." She plucked a crisp letter out of her purse and Emil wondered how Mama kept things organized in there.

"I received news from Uncle Leo yesterday," she said.

"It came yesterday?" Sarah said. "Then you should have told us yesterday!"

"I did not want to share it until I felt settled and now, I feel settled." She shot Sarah one of those looks she gave Emil when he got himself in a mishap. "May I continue?"

Sarah grunted.

"Uncle Leo was released and will make his way to the Holland border."

"That's great news!" Emil said.

"No, that's not great news," Sarah said. "I heard what happens at the border."

"This is different," Vati said. "We have a cousin who . . ."

Sarah interrupted, "My friend Rachel's brother went two weeks ago. He thought he could talk his way in, but no one got in, not even people with the right papers. He saw a teenager try to run through . . ." Tears escaped down Sarah's checks. Her voice strained higher. "The guards dragged him back, kicking and screaming, and beat him."

Emil couldn't remember the last time Sarah cried.

"Schatzi," Mama said, wrapping an arm around her. Vati handed Sarah a handkerchief. Emil said, "I won't eat your sandwich." Sarah put her head on Mama's shoulder.

"Sarah, the people with the right papers eventually did get in, didn't they?" Mama asked.

Sarah shrugged.

"They did," Mama whispered. "And Uncle Leo has the right papers."

"Listen," Vati said, taking her hand across the aisle. "Mama's cousin Kurt lives in Amsterdam, do you remember?"

Sarah nodded.

"Kurt agreed to sponsor Leo," Vati said.

"We've been working on this for a long time now," Mama said, stroking Sarah's hand.

"He will get to Holland," Vati said.

A man in a gray hat cracked open a window a few seats ahead. Their compartment filled with cool air and loud rumbling. Emil stuck his face in the wind. He wanted to feel it blow across his cheeks. The tips of his nose and ears chilled. He gulped it in. It tasted like fresh, new air no one had ever breathed. He wondered if the air in Paraguay tasted like this.

The conductor flung open the cabin door and called, "Hamburg, twenty-five minutes!"

Vati folded up his newspaper and Emil felt his heart beat faster. Paraguay was really happening. Emil wondered if his new piano teacher would smell like chicken, and how he would feel when he became a Bar Mitzvah next year, and whether there would be another twelve-year-old boy who played marbles. He glanced out the window. A large, bare tree bowed its branches in the wind, as if it waved farewell. Emil waved back.

He squinted toward the soft hills outside to try to see Holland. Some hills were close and some were in the distance. As he looked further out, each hill became fainter than the one before. It reminded him of how memories worked, with near ones as clear as water and the oldest ones so faded he could barely make out their outline. Maybe there were even hills beyond the last, but were so faint, he couldn't see them at all. Emil hoped that would never happen to his memories of Opa. He ran a few favorites through his head. Maybe memories only faded when no one thought about them. He ran through a few more, including visiting Opa's graveyard last summer.

Emil wished it hadn't been so dangerous these past

weeks. Then Mama would have let him visit Opa's grave to say good-bye. He would have brought Opa the best rock in all of Hannover. Then he would have picked up fallen stones for everyone else in the cemetery one last time. Emil wondered if there were fallen stones that needed picking up in Paraguay. He planned to find out. Opa would like that.

Author's Note

On October 28, 1938, thousands of Jews of Polish nationality living in Germany were arrested and deported. On November 7, Herschel Grynszpan, the seventeen-year-old son of expelled Polish Jews, shot Ernst vom Rath, third secretary in the German Embassy in Paris. Vom Rath died two days later. This triggered the pogrom commonly known as Kristallnacht or Night of Broken Glass.

• • •

It's been stated that a writer better be certain of their intentions before taking on a project about the Holocaust. The era remains one of the most emotionally charged periods in history with as many viewpoints and truths as people involved.

I had three aims in writing *Crushing the Red Flowers*. First, I wanted to capture meaningful portions of my family's history. The novel is fiction, but its story pulls from true experiences. I was born in Germany and moved to Philadelphia at the age of three. Since my father was German and my mother a German Jew, I grew up with a multilayered understanding of the challenges that Jewish and non-Jewish residents of Germany faced during WWII. The stories I heard from both sides of my family were filled with love and devotion, as well as pain and loss.

Second, I wanted to challenge assumptions about this complex era. To properly study the war years, it is necessary to understand the political and cultural mentalities of the prewar years. 1938 gives us a unique platform to not only examine how life in Germany was before, but to also glimpse signs of what would come after. Unfortunately, I've sometimes found this critical year overlooked by middle and high school educators.

My third aim was to help young people become more self-aware of their morality and decision-making in our modern day. In 1938, official youth organizations of the Nazi party, such as the Hitlerjugend (Hitler Youth), for boys aged fourteen to eighteen, and the Deutsches Jungvolk (German Youth), for boys aged ten to fourteen, actively contributed to the destruction during Kristallnacht. I've heard some people assert that those children were brainwashed and were themselves victims of the Nazi regime. I've also heard some condemn the youth of that generation for not opposing the positions put forth by the Nazi government. It's difficult to fully appreciate the circumstances of the children who lived in Germany at a time when parents, teachers, and leaders encouraged young people to discriminate against those deemed non-Aryan.

A telling assessment would be to look at responses

to modern-day predicaments. We continue to grapple with attitudes and political directives that parallel 1930s Germany well into a new century. My hopes are that *Crushing the Red Flowers* will further the understanding of the political, social, and economic factors that led to WWII, and that this novel will give young people courage to question and stand up for what they believe is right.

• • •

The red poppy flower emerged as a well-recognized symbol of WWI. In *Crushing the Red Flowers*, I stretched this symbolism to represent the German culture that emerged after WWI and lasted through the rise of the Third Reich. Crushing these flowers symbolizes the end of the distinct political, social, and economic culture that was present in Germany between the world wars. Additionally, the poppy also symbolizes childhood innocence throughout the novel.

The characters in Emil's life explore the optimist/pessimist dichotomy present in the German Jewish community before Kristallnacht, the complexities of emigration, early twentieth-century German Jewish prosperity, patriotic loyalty, and newly clouded German Jewish identity.

The characters in Friedrich's life highlight the debate about how much Germans actively supported, went along with, or challenged Adolf Hitler. Many of the characters have pro-Hitler mindsets and were affected by Germany's earlier economic struggle that enabled Hitler's rise to power. And a few characters—Friedrich, Mother, Papa, and Uncle Hilmar—delve into the nuanced experience of German resistance to Nazism. The anti-Hitler German conscience is most clearly symbolized by Friedrich's eyebrow twitch.

• • •

This is a work of fiction. Names, characters, businesses, places, events, locales, and incidents are either used in a fictitious manner or the products of the author's imagination.

It should be noted that writing fiction is by nature subjective; writers of history attempt to portray events genuinely, but some degree of bias is inevitable. To minimize misrepresentation, I conducted extensive research, interviewed multiple family members who lived through the era, worked closely with Myrna Goldenberg, Professor Emerita of Holocaust History at Montgomery College, was counseled by Dr. Patricia Heberer-Rice, Director of the Office of the Senior Historian at the United States Holocaust Memorial Museum, and received guidance from Dr. Joshua Kavaloski, Director for the Center for Holocaust/Genocide Study at Drew University.

Acknowledgments

Crushing the Red Flowers was born from my own family stories. The launching point of my research came from extensive interviews with family members who lived through this era: Herbert Ert, Lore Ert, and Werner Dannhofer. This book wouldn't have been possible without their enthusiastic support. I am beyond thankful for their encouragement and cherish the opportunity we had to work together.

I'm grateful to my great-grandfather, Samson Reichstein, a concentration camp survivor, who even after losing his beloved wife Käthe in 1942, had the courage to document his experiences of the Holocaust in a personal memoir. His written accounts were vital in weaving together our family's oral traditions.

My deepest appreciation to Myrna Goldenberg, Professor Emerita of Holocaust History at Montgomery College, for painstakingly combing through the manuscript for historical accuracy; to Dr. Patricia Heberer-Rice, Director of the Office of the Senior Historian at the United States Holocaust Memorial Museum, for ongoing counseling; and to Dr. Joshua Kavaloski, Director for the Center for Holocaust/Genocide Study at Drew University, for clarification of a few specific questions.

A colossal thank you to my sister, Jessica Myers, for her invaluable help with translation and editing.

My gratitude to Ruth Dannhofer, Eileen Ert, Edith Rosenbaum Maddeloni, Hans-Jürgen Voigt, and Jan Voigt for keeping our family stories alive.

I'd like to credit Linda Kaplan Thaler for guiding the book into the light and thank her for her steadfast enthusiasm.

A heartfelt thank you to Robert and Elizabeth at Ig Publishing for believing in my novel and guiding me through the publishing process.

I am indebted to my critique partners for hammering my novel into shape and for being there when I needed to vent: Jennifer Ali, Linda Bozzo, Viji Chary, Connie Colon, Ann Malaspina, Genevieve Petrillo, and Michele Prestininzi.

A special thank you to Carolyn P. Yoder for a constructive and encouraging critique. I was fortunate to receive her uplifting words at a time when I really needed them.

I am extremely grateful to my husband Jeff and three children, Samuel, Madeline and Gabrielle, and my wonderful extended family. Had I not had their unfaltering faith and support, this book would not exist.

And final thanks to the inventor of highly caffeinated tea and to the entire children's literature community, which despite coming from an insanely competitive industry, remains amazingly helpful and warm.

Discussion Guide

Part One

- Why might you think chapter one is titled "Pawns"?
- In chapter one, Friedrich felt "like a shell. Hollow inside, jagged outside." What does this mean? Have you ever felt like this?
- Emil's uncle suggested taking down the mezuzah that hung outside their apartment so that the family would be more inconspicuous. What does this say about how Jews were viewed in Hannover in 1938?
- Otto's beating was the first time Friedrich had seen violence within the Jungvolk. Discuss Friedrich's reaction.
- Why does Emil's mama believe the family should leave Germany? Emil's father disagrees with her. Why?
- In chapter four, Emil feels like he can't change anything in the world. Have you felt that way?
- What is the new Jungvolk competition for the summer and why is Friedrich optimistic?
- Why is the spot by the river so important to Emil? And why is it so important to Friedrich?
- Why does the incident at the Klein Stationary Shop remind Emil of his marble game with *the boys*?
- Emil wonders why no one helps Mr. Klein. Why might this be the case? After witnessing the incident, Emil feels the world was "different, twisted." Explain this in your

own words.

- In chapter seven, why was Friedrich not permitted to shop in a Jewish store?
- Explain Uncle Hilmar's Would-Could-Should technique.
- Why does Mama give Mrs. Schmidt her favorite piano brooch?
- Discuss how life for German Jews had changed in 1938
- Why didn't the Rosens leave Germany earlier?
- Friedrich and Albert used to be best friends. How do you think both boys feel about not being able to be best friends anymore?
- How does Friedrich's mother's belief that "Impression are important" affect Friedrich? List at least two examples from chapters 1-9 as evidence to support your answer.

Part Two

- While in the graveyard, Emil sets out to replace the stones that had fallen off tombstones. He says, "the stones had a specific place in the world and it didn't seem right they were pushed out." How are these stones similar to the experiences of Emil's family?
- Both Emil and Friedrich spend time in their special spot by the river. Describe what each boy does there. How do they react to each other?
- Friedrich's Uncle Hilmar believes that Friedrich should have a choice to belong or not to belong to the Jungvolk. If Friedrich had a choice, what do you think he would choose?

- Why was Friedrich concerned about Günter finding out about his Uncle Hilmar?
- What qualities does Günter find important in Jungvolk boys?
- Why did Günter have a problem with Ari being chosen to be the flagbearer in the children's parade?
- Many spectators watched the incident with Ari at the parade and didn't intervene. Why do you think that? Would you have intervened?
- The last sentence of chapter fourteen reads: "Instead, his eyebrow flapped like it was starting a fire." Broadly, the Fire symbolizes the fabric of society unraveling, but on a smaller scale, it symbolizes Friedrich's contribution to the deteriorating situation. He doesn't agree with Günter's actions, but by going along with it, he makes it worse. Did you ever go along with something you didn't think was right?
- Friedrich lived in a time when many adults, parents and teachers encouraged young people to discriminate based on race. How do you think you would have behaved?
- Why, according to Uncle Hilmar, does Friedrich's mother clean all of the time?
- Uncle Hilmar asks Friedrich what his "purest truth" is. What is a purest truth? Do you have a purest truth? If so, what is it?
- At the end of chapter fifteen, Friedrich feels as if he has lost "his friend, his uncle, his country, and himself" all in one day. Explain why he feels he has lost each of these?
- In chapter sixteen, Emil's Mama asks, "We are all still civilized, aren't we?" What is the historic significance of

this question given it is October 1938?

- What happened to Brutus, the dog?
- Have you ever had a certainty that you knew was right like Emil in chapter sixteen?
- The Rosens receive wonderful news at the end of Part Two. What is it?
- Why couldn't Uncle Leo attain a VISA to go to Paraguay with the rest of Emil's family?

Part Three

- What is the purpose of the vase of dried poppies in Friedrich's window?
- In chapter seventeen, Friedrich's mother says, "we all have our parts to play." What does she mean by this? What part does Friedrich's father play? His mother? Friedrich?
- Explain what happened to Ernst vom Rath. What is your opinion? Was it a necessary act of resistance? Should the Jewish teenager who shot him be punished? Should all Jewish people pay?
- Conduct Internet research and explain the Pogrom we call Kristallnacht.
- What prompts the Rosen family to hide in the potato room? Explain how Mama and Vati each feels about hiding, based on their words and actions in chapter eighteen.
- Why do Vati and Emil leave the potato room? Do you think they made a good decision?
- What is meant by "in the spider web of facts, many a truth is strangled"? Why do you think Friedrich's mother

says this to Günter?

- Explain Friedrich's internal conflict during the Pogrom we call Kristallnacht. What causes him to throw so many rocks? And what prompts him to help Emil?
- How does Friedrich help Vati and Emil at the river?
- Why do Vati and Emil return to the apartment before Friedrich tells them its safe? Do you think this was the right decision?
- In an early chapter, Friedrich felt reassured that the way of the world was right when he watched the river correct a mess. How did his belief change by chapter twenty-one?
- Discuss some of the ways the Nazi government took power away from Emil's family. Was there any way to fight the mandates?
- At the end of chapter twenty-four, Emil says of his mother, "there was an expression on her face…It reminded him of Ari on parade day." What does this mean?
- In chapter twenty-five, Friedrich said he, "lost part of himself…and gained a new part." Explain what this means.
- How does Friedrich help the Rosens and get them to the train station in time?
- Imagine that it is two years after the events of *Crushing the Red Flowers*. What is Friedrich's life like? What is Emil's life like? How have things changed?

After You Read…
- Friedrich's eyebrow twitch symbolizes the German

pre-war conscious. Discuss the times it twitched in the novel.

- Why do you think so many Germans embrace Nazi ideology in the novel?
- Have you ever heard conflicting facts, maybe two points of view to the same story? How can you find the truth?
- What can we learn from this past, so that we don't repeat it in the future?

Guide content © Copyright 2019 by Marcie Colleen (www.thisismarciecolleen.com).

A full Common Core aligned Teacher's Guide is available for free download at JenniferVK.com/books

Selected Resources

Bard, Mitchell G. *48 Hours of Kristallnacht: Night of Destruction/Dawn of the Holocaust: An Oral History*. Guilford: Lyons Press, 2008.

Campbell Bartoletti, Susan. *Hitler Youth*. New York: Scholastic Inc., 2005.

Center for Jewish History: Digital Library and Archive Collections. www.cjh.org.

Conot, Robert E. *Justice At Nuremberg*. New York: Harper & Row, 1983.

The Double Headed Eagle: Hitler's Rise to Power 1918–1933. DVD. Directed by Lutz Becker. VPS Studios, 1973.

Imaginary Witness: Hollywood and the Holocaust. DVD. Directed by Daniel Anker. Anker Productions, Inc., 2004.

New York Public Library Picture Collection: German Interiors 1900's Collection; German Life Collection; German History Collection. 476 5th Avenue, Room 100, New York, NY.

Steinweis, Alan E. *Kristallnacht 1938*. Cambridge: Belknap Press, 2009.

The History Place. www.historyplace.com.

The Holocaust Explained. www.theholocuastexplained.org.

The Nancy & David Wolf Holocaust & Humanity Center. www.holocaustandhumanity.org.

Time Photos: Kristallnacht in Words and Photographs. http://content.time.com/time/photogallery/0,29307,1857458,00.html.

United States Holocaust Memorial Museum. www.ushmm.org.